HOT SEAT

THE HOT CANNOLIS, BOOK ONE

ELI EASTON

TARA LAIN

To Robert, Raleigh & Tara – my sources of inspiration
-Eli Easton

To Eli, who dreamed of two charming, complex guys with so much potential and shared the idea with me.
-Tara Lain

NOTE TO READERS

Back in distant 2021, Eli Easton wrote a novella about two young guys, a firefighter and a college student, who meet in the midst of a terrible fire and act heroically, while sharing a memorable kiss in a canoe. (This story, FIREMAN'S CARRY is available for free download from ProlificWorks.) But leaving these two adorable guys with only a kiss? No way! Unfair to romance readers. So she got together with coauthor Tara Lain and together they told the much bigger tale of Mike Canali and Shane Bower, their amazing families and the hard, inspiring, funny and heart-rending path they have to follow to share more than a secret kiss. That much bigger tale is HOT SEAT, book one in a new series, The Hot Cannolis. You'll quickly discover as you read that this story involves much more than one couple, so plunge into the wild world of the Canalis and throughout the year (at least) we'll bring you their struggles and laughter. We hope you love them as much as we do.

Get your copy of FIREMAN'S CARRY on Prolific Works:
bit.ly/YBBBGroupGiveaway

ONE

SHANE

"Heathcliff's a flaming asshole."

My head snapped up from where I'd been sneakily staring at my phone, and I had to swallow a snort of laughter. *Hissy strikes again.* No one in the Sacramento Seniors Story Society could ever predict what Mrs. Hester "Hissy" Archibald would say.

George, sitting across the circle from Hissy, punched the air. "I'm with you, Hissy. Did people back then find a dude like that heroic? What a crock."

"I'd have thought you could speak from personal experience, George. You're old enough." Randy, George's competitor in one-upmanship, punched George's arm and howled at his own joke.

It was a Friday in early October, and the cozy room in the Senior Center where we held our book club meetings was festooned for Halloween with orange-and-black crepe paper and tatty old cardboard cutouts of black cats and owls. I'd zoned out in the benign ambience, but I had to focus if I was going to regain any control of the group. I scrunched my straight-backed chair forward a little and said, "*Wuthering Heights* was influenced by romanticism and the Gothic novel tradition. It was pretty controversial in its time since it challenged Victorian mores and morals."

"Morals indeed. Heathcliff reminds me of Christian Grey. Childish drama queen."

I gaped at Anthea, our praise-the-Lord Baptist, who usually set the record in straitlaced. Had she really just referenced E.L. James's highly questionable erotic-fanfic-turned-blockbuster? Jesus take the wheel.

Hissy barked, "You've got it, Anthy. I can just imagine Heathcliff strapping Catherine up in his dungeon for fun." She thrust her arms in the air like she was hanging and drooped her head to the side, which looked pretty damned funny with her white hair streaked with blue and pink hanging around her face like a flag.

Lissa, one of the younger oldsters, looked up from her knitting. "Do you think Anastasia was secretly in love with her roommate? I mean she seemed to like her a lot more than she liked Christian."

And Bam! We were back to E.L. James. I opened my mouth—

George raised his dark eyebrows. "You think the heroine of *Fifty Shades of Grey* was actually a lez?" He laughed, and Randy joined in but looked confused.

Anthea delivered a withering glance. "Please, George, don't be crude. The word is lesbian." She pursed her lips. "I never kissed *my* roommate on the forehead when *I* was in college."

Hissy leaned forward in her chair. "Seriously, I don't get that book. You'd have thought Christian invented BDSM since Anastasia's apparently never heard of it, except he sure as Hades wasn't very good at it. I mean, what kind of dom plays like his sub is just some martyr who has to give in for his pleasure? What a flaming asshole!"

"Hey, Shane, how about we all read this dungeon book next time? Everyone keeps yammering about it. I need to catch up." That was Randy.

George yelled, "Yes! I want to read about lesbians. I think my sister is one."

Randy raised his hand. "I know one."

Anthea added. "I knew a bisexual once."

Lissa frowned. "Shane, can you tell us what enby means? And also precisely what gay men do in bed. How does that even work?"

Hissy leaned forward and gave Lissa a friendly pat on the arm. "Oh, I know all about that! I've got hundreds of gay romances if you want to read one. My favorite is when the *top* pushes the *bottom* against a wall and—"

I waved my arms. "Hello? Can we get back on track here?"

Lissa nodded at Hissy. "Perhaps we should read some of those books. They sound very informative."

George yelled, "I'm not reading about two dudes doing it."

I jumped up from my chair, stuck my fingers in my mouth, and whistled.

The piercing noise did the job. They stopped talking and looked at me.

Brushing my hair off my face, I gave them the Shane Bower fearsome gaze, which, considering I was dressed in tight pink jeans and a sparkly long-sleeved T-shirt that said *I was supposed to be a Fairy Princess. What the hell happened?*, might have been only moderately fearsome. "We've diverged somewhat from Emily Brontë, wouldn't you say? Detoured straight into the gutter. And not even a tasteful gutter, I might add." I raised my eyebrows expectantly and poised a finger under my chin.

I didn't really have any control over the group. Of course, that was patently obvious to any casual observer, but it was also fact. Yes, I'd been appointed the leader of the book club since my almost-degree in world literature gave me a modicum of expertise. Also, there was the fact that I'd blundered into the club by accident, attracted by a handwritten poster on a bulletin board at school, only to discover that the Sacramento Senior Center wasn't just where the book club met, but also defined its members. Instead of running in terror, I'd stayed. They were a frigging hoot. I figured they decided to reward the twenty-two-year-old gay guy by making me the tacit moderator. At the same time, it was a democracy. Actually, more like anarchy. Jesus, they made the French look governable.

Hissy shrugged. "I *was* talking about Brontë. Heathcliff's a flaming asshole. Maybe if he'd had a dungeon and dragged Catherine in there, instead of pining endlessly, he'd have had a better temperament."

And just like that, we'd come full circle. I sighed and plopped my butt on the chair. "So I guess we're over *Wuthering Heights*, guys?"

Lissa said in her quiet voice, "I haven't finished it yet and would like to give it a chance to reveal why it's considered such a classic."

Hissy waved a hand. "How about we discuss it for one more session and then move on to something more fun?"

"*Moby Dick*," George said.

Anthea harumphed. "The way today's session has gone, that would only hold Hissy's interest if it was about a man with a whale-sized you-know-what." She crossed her arms censoriously.

The whole group stared at her, but then Hissy went, "Ha."

George snorted.

Randy started to laugh, and the whole crew joined in. Finally, Anthea laughed too.

The session dissolved into discussions of other possible books ranging from *Pride and Prejudice* to something just north of *Debbie Does Dallas*. With nothing decided, everyone fell on the refreshment table like marauding hordes. I recalled my grandmother eating *peckishly*—her word. Not this lot. I sneaked back to gazing at my phone.

Still nothing. Shit.

"You look like my son, Tommy, when the mailman failed to deliver his new bicycle."

I glanced up into the compassionate gray eyes of Hissy Archibald. While I loved all the members of the book club, she'd become a real friend, even outside the group. "Sorry. I didn't mean to get distracted."

"Is it a man, dear?"

"One hell of a man." I forced a smile.

"You two had a moment last night, but he didn't call today?" She smiled with the wisdom of a nearly ninety-year-old who'd been there and done that.

I sighed at my own idiocy. "More like we had a moment a month ago and he's never called since."

She grimaced. "Ooh. Not much excuse can be made for him, I gather."

I wrinkled my nose. "Well, he's a firefighter, and we met in the middle of a fire, so he might have had a few other things to do."

"Oh! Was that when you made that insane drive to save your grandfather?"

"Yeah." I'd told Hissy that's where I was because I'd been scheduled to have coffee with her, but I hadn't really given anyone, even Hissy, details about that horrible, terrible, wonderful day that I'd defied the authorities to try to get my stubborn-as-Attila-the-Hun grandfather out of his apartment in Crest Lake as the town burned down around him. That's when I'd met Mike Canali and spend some horrific moments directing people out of the path of a fire and some fabulous moments snuggled in the bottom of a canoe while flames roared past us.

"Firefighters are sexy AF." Hissy fanned her hand in front of her face. "He asked for your number?"

"Sure did," I said despondently. He'd made a point of asking for it. And then… zero. Zilch. Ghosted.

"Well, you'd think in thirty days he could have found time to call. Why ask for it, then leave you hanging out to dry?"

"Exactly! Right?" I sighed again. "The thing is, I don't think he's out to his fire crew. Or family. So—" I shrugged.

"Ouch. Always a bad sign." She slid an arm around me and hugged. "You deserve an out and proud gay man who knows the depths of your fabulousness."

Tears stung my eyes, and I blinked. "Thank you, Hissy." I sniffed. "I'd never make it without friends like you." That was so true. It didn't take a Freudian psychologist to know that my friendships with older people were a way to replace the parents that had kicked me out, anathema as I was to their Seventh Day Adventist principles. Funny how people picked and chose their anathemas.

Lissa slid up behind me and put a warm hand on my back. In a group that averaged over seventy-five, Lissa was a junior of about seventy. "Hey, sweetheart, are you okay?"

Hissy nodded for me. "Just a little romantic disappointment."

Lissa's face lit up. "You know what? I have this adorable nephew who's gay. I'll bet you guys would hit it off."

I smiled and shook my head. "Thank you, Lissa, but I'm not looking for a boyfriend. Since my pops came to live with me, I haven't had much time for a social life. There was just a guy I met who I sort of hoped would call, and he didn't. That's all."

Lissa looked at Hissy. "We should get his grandfather over here and introduce him to a nice lady, so Shane has time to date my nephew." She blinked her lashes like she might think the nice lady she had in mind was her.

This was definitely getting out of control. "Uh, he just got out of a wheelchair for a broken hip, so he's not getting around too much yet, but maybe sometime in the future."

I'd invited my grandfather to the book club, but he'd told me he'd rather get a colonoscopy than read *Wuthering Heights.*

Hissy said, "His grandfather was in that horrible Dixie fire. Shane saved him."

"What?" Lissa's mouth dropped open.

I waved a hand. "No, no, no. Enough, dears. My grandfather is fine. They even say his apartment building survived the fire, but we can't get back in for another few weeks. Then it's going to be a ton of work trying to get his belongings smoke-free."

And would he even want to stay in Crest Lake since most of the town had burned down?

Hissy gave me a look. "Well, tell him if he wants to meet some hot chicks, you know a good book club he can join." That made us all laugh.

I said, "By the way, Lissa, you asked about enby. The term is sometimes used as a short-form way of saying nonbinary. Be aware, though, that some people don't like it, so it's usually best to say nonbinary people."

Lissa nodded with wide eyes.

I grinned. "As for your other question, that's a topic for another time and place." Hopefully, a time and place when I was far, far away, but I didn't add that.

Lissa kissed my cheek and then headed back to the refreshment table and off the topic of her nephew. It wasn't that I didn't need to look for a boyfriend. Hell, my single state was verging on legendary. But those moments in the canoe with Mike had touched some part of me deeper than I cared to admit, and my heart hadn't given up on having that feeling in my life. Stupid heart. As if an incredibly hot, gorgeous, macho firefighter would want to date me.

A half hour later, I swung into Get Perky, my coffee shop

of choice. As usual, people were lined up from the counter to the door, and most tables were full.

Roland, my BFF, was making drinks. He waved as I walked in and pointed to the checkout line, which was much shorter. Bless him, he was swamped, but he'd make my two drinks fast. I tried not to tap my foot. I had editing deadlines to meet. God, I'd be up until three. I loved the book club, and I'd never leave it, but some weeks, it was just one more thing.

Roland hurried over from his barista duties with my two personal cups decorated with unicorns, rang me up with his Roland discount, and leaned over to kiss the air next to my cheek. "Kiss. Kiss. How's you?"

"Good. Can't wait to tell you about the meeting later."

"Any calls?" He also knew about Mike or the lack thereof.

"No."

"Fuck him. Love you. Talk later."

I kissed at him, grabbed my drinks, and walked out the door onto the sidewalk. Fucking Mike was precisely what I had in mind. Well, after a long session of kissing. God, I remembered those lips. I sighed. *Get over it, dammit.*

But he'd *kissed* me. Mike Canali, firefighter, had held me in the canoe and kissed me passionately! And then he'd asked for my phone number and said he would call. I hadn't just imagined all that. Damn it.

God, I needed to stop thinking about this.

As per usual, I got a few stares as I walked the four blocks to my apartment. My fuzzy pink jacket matched my coffee cups and gaped open over my sparkly T-shirt that offset my rhinestone-studded sneakers. I might have bought my clothes from the thrift shop, but I didn't do inconspicuous.

At the apartment building, I had to set one cup on the top of the wall so I could use my key. I opened it, stuck my foot in the door, and stretched to grab my cup. It was a well-rehearsed ballet.

My apartment was on the first floor. This was fortunate, in

that we'd been able to wheel Pops's chair right into my front door. It was *un*fortunate in that the view from the windows was overlooking the headlights of cars or the backs of trash-cans. Pops liked to say ironically that it wasn't so bad since there weren't many windows. It was in every way a student apartment, although I'd worked to make it nice. I'd been lucky to find it.

I bumped the door with my foot, Pops's signal if he was nearby. Sure enough, the door opened. He was standing, if leaning just a little on the doorframe.

"I bring plasma." I held up the cup, but he didn't take it, since he still used a cane when he was walking. I toed off my sneakers at the door and strode across the smallish room to set the cups on the coffee table in front of the secondhand sofa that was also my secondhand bed since Pops had moved in. Then I turned back and accepted the gentle pat on the back Pops delivered. I looked at him standing with no help. "Wow. You chucked the cane."

He grinned, and it lit up his lined face. "Just for practice, but it feels good to be able to move around on my own two feet. About damn time."

Yep, that was Pops all over. Self-reliant to a fault. I smiled up into his face. Even in his seventies, he was a little taller than me and kept his bushy head of steel-gray hair.

He sat down gingerly in one of my old seventies-type chairs that I'd gotten at a recycle center. I dug them. Mid-century and all. Even though I'd only paid a few dollars for all my furniture and décor, people often thought it was expensive. Roland called it *the Shane touch*. It might have been a cliché that gay men were good at decorating, but, in my case, it was true, and I was grateful. We all deserved a bit more beauty in life. That was my motto.

Pops said, "Go get into your comfy clothes and then come talk to me." He gave me an enigmatic smile.

"Um. Okay." I hurried into the bedroom where I kept my

clothes even though I no longer slept in there. A fact which Pops hated but that really worked better. No way he could sleep on that couch with his recovering hip. Five minutes later, I was back, in sweats and sipping my vanilla tea. I slid onto the couch. "What's up?"

He handed me an envelope, and I frowned. Snail mail? Nothing good ever came via the postman.

"What's this?"

"You might find out if you open it."

The Cheshire Cat look on his face made me ask, "Did you already read it?"

"Is it open?" He spread his hands innocently.

"Maybe you steamed it and then glued it closed."

He planted a hand on his hip. "Shane, just read the damned letter."

I stared at the return address. *California State Firefighter's Association*. Just the word firefighter made my heart leap. Was it from Mike? I tried to slip my finger into the gap in the envelope and missed twice before I managed to open it thanks to my shaking hands.

Dear Mr. Bower –

The California State Firefighter's Association invites you and your guests to attend a special award ceremony honoring civilians and professionals who demonstrated exceptional valor during the recent Dixie fire. You will be recognized for your outstanding bravery. Please join us on Saturday, October 15 at 11 a.m. at the Oroville City Hall.

That was next weekend.

"So what is it?" Pops asked.

"Um. I'm invited to some kind of firefighters' ceremony." I handed him the letter, still not sure what to make of it.

"They *should* recognize what you did in that fire. You and Mike both. Good!"

"They'll probably just read off a list of names or something. I'm sure lots of people did stuff."

"Well, I guess we'll find out when we go."

Did I want to go? My brain did its *looking for Oz* thing where I got whirlwind thoughts flying in a gazillion directions with witches and cows sailing by.

If I go, I could see Mike. He'll be there, right?

But do I want to see Mike when he didn't even call me? Or could he have known that we'd see each other this weekend, and so he is waiting? Or maybe this has nothing to do with Mike, and he won't be there at all. Or maybe he was injured in a fire? Maybe that's why he never called? Or killed? Or—oh shit!

Pops said, "Take a deep breath."

I did as he said.

"Another."

I breathed.

In his scary Pops way, he said, "Mike did not get injured or killed, or we would have seen it in the papers. I have no idea if he'll be at this event, but we're going." He flashed me the mind-reading Bower grin. "Deal with it."

———

Deal with it.

Yes, well I'd dealt with it by having a semi-nervous breakdown in between school and work for a whole week. Now, reckoning was at hand. Oh yes, drama are us.

I stared in the dresser mirror. "Pops, I look like a banker!"

Pops stuck his head in the bedroom door and stared at me. "No banker ever had such a well-tailored suit."

I had to grin. Like any self-respecting gay man, even a starving student, I owned a suit, and it happened that my medium-tall, skinny frame looked good in off-the-rack. The suit was gray, slim-cut, and had been purchased on sale to go to a wedding the previous year.

Pops said, "Plus, few bankers wear pink ties or flowered scarves draped around their necks."

I struck a pose and quoted *The Birdcage*, "Well, one does want a hint of color."

Pops laughed, and my heart smiled. How did I get so lucky as to have a family member with whom the whole *Shane thing* was okay? More than okay. Pops loved me for who I was.

I pulled my fall of curly black hair off my neck and held it back in a tail. "Shall I tame the mane?"

"You're asking me for fashion advice? Ha! Whatever floats your boat, Squirt, but it's time to go."

My heart slammed, and I released the hair to let it wave around my face. I swallowed hard. "Actually… I'm seriously thinking I should stay home."

"Oh really?" He raised his bushy eyebrows and waggled his fingers in a *let's go* motion.

"This is probably an award ceremony for the firefighters who fought the Dixie fire. Maybe they'll mention me or something, but this is really about Mike. And I don't want to ruin his big day." I started pulling my scarf off. "He hasn't called me. I don't want to show up and embarrass him in front of his whole unit."

I remembered the way I'd felt after we were rescued at Crest Lake—all those macho, beefy firefighters hanging out at the trucks and me feeling like the weak, queer kid again in high school, afraid to approach the cool jocks. Let's face it: this wasn't my scene. I tossed my scarf on the bed.

"Shane!" Pops's voice cut through my mental flurry. "I don't care if you strip out of all your clothes. We're going to this ceremony."

I whirled on him, preparing to argue. But the set look on his face gave me pause. We stared at each other, willpower to willpower. Pops almost never tried to tell me what to do. He respected me as an adult. For some reason, this was important to him. And the truth was, some tiny, masochistic part of me *did* want to see Mike again, even from a distance.

If I kept my distance, that would be okay. Right?

"*Okay*. Fine." I picked up the scarf and tossed the end around my neck like a Musketeer's cape. "My ego probably needs a good trampling. Hope you enjoy the show."

I swept out the door, trusting Pops would follow.

TWO

MIKE

"Mikey! Baby bro. Look at you! You ready for your big day?" Donny slapped my arm—hard. I was used to my brothers' roughhousing, so I steeled myself for it, but Donny worked hard to be the most macho of all of us, and I felt the effects. The smile I gave him in the hotel room mirror was as weak as my knees. I focused on my reflection again and pulled down the cuffs on my black dress-uniform jacket.

"Yeah, sure. It's cool. I'm fine."

"*Fine*." Donny snorted. "Bro, you were on active duty with Cal Fire for, what, two weeks? And you earned the Medal of Valor. You should be high as a fucking kite on smugness right now. I sure as shit would be."

"This is me looking smug." I pointed to my face and gave him the smuggest expression I could manage. But when I looked back in the mirror, I saw a pale and nervous-looking stranger. This was the first time I'd worn the Cal Fire dress uniform, with its black double-breasted jacket, gold buttons, badge, and colorful Cal Fire patch on the sleeve. I wore it with the white dress shirt, black tie, and matching black trousers.

It did look pretty awesome, I had to admit.

And it really *was* fucking amazing to be getting this award. Growing up the son of a firefighter, with a bunch of older brothers, cousins, and uncles in Cal Fire, I'd spent a lot of years hero-worshipping with stars in my eyes. It was a dream come true to be honored myself. Of course, I was proud. Not even so much for my own sake as for my family's. Since we'd gotten word about the commendation, my dad had been practically glowing. He loved hearing the other fire-fighters say things like *Mike's a chip off the old block, huh?* And *You sure know how to raise 'em*. My mom had opened every conversation on every phone call she had—which was a lot, given our extended family and her love of gab—with *have you heard about Mike's Medal of Valor?* Even my siblings wouldn't let me hear the end of it, alternating between teasing me and an embarrassing amount of praise.

But I'd had two weeks to get used to the idea that I was getting the award. At the moment, all I could focus on was the fact that I was about to see Shane Bower at the ceremony in… I checked the time on my phone… the next half hour or so.

Holy shit.

My stomach was a wreck with a cocktail of nerves, excitement, and icy fear. I hadn't laid eyes on Shane since we parted ways at Crest Lake. I'd asked for his number and told him I'd call. I'd meant it when I asked. Like, a lot. I intended to call right away. But then I'd gotten back around all the guys in my station, and I'd come home to a huge gathering of Canalis. Practically everyone in my extended family had been at Ma and Pa's that day, keeping a vigil for me.

The Dixie fire had hit Crest Lake hard, and I'd been in serious trouble. The chief had sent me into town with a guy—Shane—to help him evacuate his grandfather. It should have been an easy in-and-out. Only it turned out to be anything but. We'd nearly died, and so had a lot of other people that we'd managed to help.

Hence the award we were getting today.

But afterward, being around my station and my family had been a dash of ice water on all the warm fuzzies I'd developed for Shane. I'd been so into him while we worked together. He was funny and smart and real. I admired his guts and how he'd put himself on the line that day to save others. We'd shared the best kiss of my life in the canoe where we sheltered from the fire. But.

But that had been temporary madness. In my real life, there was my family and my career as a firefighter, which was just getting started. When I finally came out to all of those people, it would be hard enough without bringing someone like Shane around. I still had the image in my mind of his hot-pink BITE ME hoodie and gold lamé tennies, of his dramatic hand gestures and too-pretty, almost-fragile features. I couldn't picture someone like Shane with my big macho Italian family. No. No way. It was just oil and water. Or maybe oil and a match to light it.

Now, I was about to see Shane again. And I'd have to do it in front of the entire Canali clan.

Donny grabbed my black dress cap from the bed and put it on my head with exaggerated care. He waggled his eyebrows. "You look good—even if you are my pain-in-the-ass little bro."

"Aw, that's so sweet," I said sarcastically.

"That's me. Mr. Feels. Now c'mon. We're gonna be late."

We left the hotel, and Donny drove the few blocks to the Oroville City Hall. When we pulled into the parking lot, it was crowded. There were lots of people I didn't know, along with some firefighters I did, and a whole sea of Canalis milling about, talking. I didn't see Shane. Relief and disap-pointment fought like two snakes in my belly. Jesus. What if he didn't come?

What if he did?

"Shit. We should go around back," Donny said, looking over the crowd.

"Fuck yeah," I agreed. Any given Canali could talk your ear off. Walking through a crowd of them all focused on me, and I'd be there until doomsday.

"Ah. No, it's cool." Donny pointed. People were streaming for the doors. I glanced at my phone. Oh, yeah. It was almost time. Ugh.

"C'mon, Mike. Bust tail! We're late." Donny threw his door open. I followed.

It was a whirlwind of smiles, nods, and half-sentences as Donny dragged me double-time across the parking lot to a side door. I'd been here before for commendation services, but I'd always been in the audience with the family. This was the first time I'd been the one in the ceremony.

Backstage, the atmosphere was surprisingly hushed and serious. But then, several awards were being given posthumously today. Whenever firemen showed special bravery, it was a given someone had gotten hurt. My heart grew heavy thinking about it.

Yeah, Shane and I had been lucky. It could so easily not have been a happy ending.

Donny guided me past clusters of firefighters all looking smart in their dress uniforms until we found Chief Reiger, my station's chief.

"Hey, Mike." Reiger held out his right hand, and I shook it while he clapped me on the shoulder with his left. "You ready for this?"

"Yes, sir, uh, I hope so." I blew out a shaky breath. "You sure they can't just mail me the thing?"

Donny snorted, and Reiger smiled. "Now where would be the fun in that? I bet your entire family is out front."

"Better believe it," Donny said proudly.

"Yeah. I know." I rolled my head around to ease the tension.

Donny squeezed my shoulder. "Bro, you already did the hard part—the fire. Nothin' to be scared about today. Be cool, and I'll see you after." He took off.

His tone was a bit judgy and teasing, but that was just our way. If you were gonna say something nice, you had to do it in a way that didn't make you sound like a wuss. Donny had been there for me today. If I'd had to drive myself, I probably wouldn't have shown up.

"Let's go, Mike." Reiger nodded at a line that was forming. Someone with a clipboard directed Reiger and me to the back of the line. And then, before I was ready, we were walking onto the stage.

The stage was small with gray curtains on both sides and above. A single row of padded folding chairs sat behind a microphone stand and small table with a draped basket. The chairs were nearly full by the time we walked out. Reiger took the next empty chair in line, and I sat beside him. Damn. It was like being in a fishbowl. The audience was right there, staring at us like we were bugs pinned to a board. A guy with a video camera was filming just in front of the stage. I looked out over a sea of faces, saw Ma, and smiled at her tightly, then glanced away. If I stared at my family, I'd lose it.

This is no big deal. Just breathe.

That's when I saw him. Shane.

He walked onto the stage, hesitantly, from the curtains on the other side. The moment I laid eyes on him, my heart stuttered in my chest, missing a few beats, like a bad engine. I couldn't help but stare. He looked so different from the day of the fire. That day, he'd been dressed like a college student, though a flamboyant one. Today, he had on a gray suit. It emphasized how slender he was, from his narrow shoulders, long arms and legs, to an impossibly trim waist. His curly dark hair had been tamed with water or product. His face was pale and blank. The only nod to the Shane I'd known that day was a baby-pink necktie, some sort of scarf he'd tucked under his lapels, and a hint of soft pink lip gloss. He looked amazing.

His gaze swept the stage and found me. He stopped in his tracks, a crease appearing between his brows. And wow. I'd forgotten how incredible his eyes were. They were large, blue, and insanely clear and bright. Memories flooded back to me. *You must have a picture of Dorian Gray in your attic.* I'd told him that because his eyes were unnaturally sparkling and pure, as if he'd never seen a day's trouble in his life. Those eyes could be the death of me.

"Shane!" Reiger half-stood and waved, then pointed to the empty seat next to me.

Oh shit. Shane was supposed to sit there.

Shane licked his lips. The frown on his brow smoothed out, and he looked at Reiger, not at me, as he crossed the stage and sat down gracefully, managing to avoid so much as a brush of his leg against mine.

"Nice to see you, Chief…." Shane hesitated. He had to look across me to see Chief Reiger, but he somehow managed to act like I wasn't there.

"It's Reiger." The chief held out his hand, and Shane shook it. "Nice to see you, too, son. And congratulations."

As Shane let go of Reiger's hand, he finally glanced at me. "Hi, Mike." His voice was cool. Then he looked straight ahead again.

Ouch. So that's how it was going to be. Sweat prickled on my back as a wave of shame went through me. He'd taken my not calling him to heart. That made me feel shitty in all kinds of ways. I should have at least checked up on him after all we'd been through together. And then there was how it felt to receive Shane's cold disinterest instead of the smiles and warmth I remembered. It sucked.

Welp. Play stupid games, win stupid prizes.

I deserved Shane's cold shoulder. I sat stiffly as they started the ceremony. We stood and put our hands over our hearts for the national anthem and then sat again as the Butte County Cal Fire Chief, Ralph Einnes, got up to speak. I glanced at Shane, but he stared straight ahead. It could've been my imagination, but I could swear he was sitting as far left on his chair as possible to avoid touching me.

I wanted to nudge his arm, get him to look at me, give him an apologetic smile. I wanted to explain that I'd *wanted* to see him, but I didn't know how to do Shane *a little bit*, or in secret —that he didn't understand my family. But we were in front of an entire audience, so I just sat there.

Still, I *felt* him. Being this close to Shane was a form of torture. My skin tingled, my belly fluttered, and my lap warmed. Even my mind grew muzzy.

Chemical attraction, man. It's definitely a thing. And obviously feeling this way about Shane hadn't been a fluke that day of the fire. If anything, it was worse now. It was like tasting a bite of something sugary again after not having it for months. Hordes of *yes, please* hormones flooded my body just from being close to him, like some teenager with his first crush. It was ridiculous.

"Fireman Mike Canali and Mr. Shane Bower, will you please come forward?" Einnes was looking at us and smiling.

Oh, shit. This was it. Shane gave me a nervous, wide-eyed glance and stood. I followed him the few steps to center stage. I had no idea what to do with my hands, so I put them behind me.

Everyone was staring and smiling. Goddamn.

"During the Crest Lake fire, these two young men went above and beyond to save the lives of sixty-two people," Einnes began, looking between us and a sheet of paper in his hand. It shook a little. I was glad to see even Chief Einnes was nervous.

"When a tree fell across the highway just outside of Crest

Lake, forty-nine vehicles were trapped behind it, with no escape route as the fire encroached on the road. Cal Fire fireman Mike Canali, only two weeks out of training, with the help of Shane Bower, a civilian, risked their own lives to redirect every one of those cars to Crest Lake State Park. Once there, people were able to get out onto the water in rental boats or by swimming. This no doubt saved their lives as the fire blasted through the entire area. For this act of heroism, and in recognition of their courage and calm under pressure, Cal Fire awards Mike Canali and Shane Bower with the Medal of Valor."

I looked at Shane, and he looked back, his eyes wide and filled with tears. I was a little choked up too. It was strange to hear Chief Einnes talk about what we'd done like that. It sounded like a movie. In reality, I'd flown by the seat of my pants that day, and everything I'd done had seemed like the only possible thing *to* do. I couldn't leave those people to die. But Shane had been right by my side the whole time, giving me the courage to push on.

He was the brave one. He had no training at all, but he refused to leave me on my own to try to do my job—insisted on sticking by my side to help, no matter how dangerous it got. He really was a good person. Looking at him, my chest grew so tight I thought I'd burst. We could be friends, at least. No one could take that much away from me.

"Mike." I looked at Chief Einnes, who came up to me holding the gold Medal of Valor on a ribbon. He put it over my head, then handed me a framed certificate from the table. He shook my hand. "Thank you for your bravery. Congratulations, Mike."

"Thank you, sir," I managed, my voice hollow in my ears.

When he put the medal over Shane's head, Shane's face was pink, and a tear escaped down his cheek, but he straightened his spine, shook hands with Einnes, and said, "Thank you, sir."

"Atta boy, Mikey!" someone in the audience shouted. It sounded like my brother Tony.

And suddenly everyone was clapping and cheering. I grinned at the audience and winked. I had no idea who I was winking at. The world in general, maybe. Shane and I floated back to our seats.

More awards were given out, but I hardly heard a word. I just sat there clutching my framed certificate and trying not to do anything stupid while I was on stage, like grab Shane and hug him. He, on the other hand, paid rapt attention to the proceedings.

Suddenly, it was over. Chief Einnes thanked everyone for coming, and there was a general round of applause complete with wolf whistles. I turned to face Shane, a smile on my face. But Shane wasn't there. He was already crossing the stage to the exit, his shoulders rounded forward in his suit, head down.

"Shane!" I started to go after him, but Chief Einnes stopped in front of me, nodding and smiling, so I had to shake hands with him again, and then the other firefighters on stage as I tried to make my way through. I exchanged congratulations with the other people who'd received commendations.

By the time I made it to the wings, Shane was nowhere to be seen. Rushing past people, I located an exit through a curtain and down a few steps to the front of the hall. The audience was leaving, but a lot of people, including a bunch of Canalis, were standing around talking.

I spotted Shane and his grandfather making their way down the side aisle and raced to catch up. My heart pounded. I had his number, but for some reason, it felt like if I didn't talk to him before he left, I never would.

"Shane, hold up!"

I reached the pair of them as Shane turned. He smiled a

little, but it didn't reach his eyes. "Oh, hi," he said, as if he'd just spotted a distant friend on the street or something.

"Uh… hey. Hi, Mr. Bower. I hope you're doing well, sir."

"Fine," Pops said, his eyes twinkling. "Congratulations, Mike. I see you have a big cheering section here today. And a vocal one."

"Yeah. The Canalis, and there are many of us, are all nuts. Shane, I wanted to talk to you before you left."

"Oh?" Shane folded his arms over his chest. "Funny since you haven't wanted to talk to me for the past month. But do go on."

"Thank you for recommending Shane for the medal." Pops nudged a hard elbow into Shane's side. "That was sure something. I bawled like a baby."

Shane gave off a little *oof*. "Yes. I mean… that was nice of you, Mike."

I blew out a sigh of frustration. "Well, hell. When they told me I'd get the Medal of Valor, of course I was gonna tell them you did just as much as me, and you deserved it just as much. Because you do." What kind of a creep did he take me for?

"You see?" Pops said, giving Shane another nudge. "He didn't have to do that."

Shane's Adam's apple bobbed as he swallowed hard. "You're right, Pops. Thanks, Mike."

"I'm gonna go sit down for a minute," Pops said.

"Pops—" Shane began.

"No, talk to Mike. I'll be right over here," Pops said sternly. He made his way into a row of benches. I remembered he had a bad hip, so it probably hurt him to stand. But he was also giving me time with Shane. *Thanks, Pops.*

Shane lifted his chin, arms still folded, but his gaze was softer. He hesitated, then said, "I had no idea they were giving us a medal today. The letter was a little vague. That was incredible. And I'm glad you're okay. I mean, with all the wildfires and everything."

He'd been worried about me? My heart melted a little. "Yeah, yeah, I'm fine. We're all fine. I've been working a lot. Shit, eight days in a row when we went up to help with the Monument fire." I took off my cap and ran a hand through my hair. I wasn't trying to use it as an excuse, but it was true.

Shane's arms relaxed, and he put one hand in a pants pocket. "Ah. Sounds busy."

"Yup. But nothing as hairy as what you and I went through, fortunately." I smiled.

"That's good." He looked at me expectantly, and his gaze held mine. He didn't appear cold anymore. He looked soft and… hopeful. Like maybe he felt a little bit of what I felt, being around him.

What did I say now? On stage, I'd thought we could at least be friends. But now, standing so close to him, looking into his eyes, I wanted him so much it hurt. I wanted to see him, be around him, have him smile at me again, laugh. I wanted to kiss him right there. I didn't know how it could work. Hell, I knew it *couldn't* work. It never would. But maybe… maybe I could see him now and then? If no one in my family knew about it? If I visited him in Sacramento, chances were good no one I knew would see us together.

That would be playing with fire, a voice in my head informed me.

Yes, yes it would be. Totally. And it would be far more dangerous than the fire I faced for a living. Because the more I saw of Shane, the more likely it was that I would hurt us both, badly. But I couldn't help but want it anyway, and damn the consequences.

"So." I cleared my throat. "Maybe we could… do dinner or something? Tomorrow? Next weekend? I—"

"Shane! Oh, Shane!"

To my horror, I saw my mother working her way through an empty row toward us, waving the end of her scarf in the air like a flag of surrender, her face glowing.

"Oh, shit," I muttered.

"Shane!" She reached us and opened her arms for a hug. Not from me, her son who had just received a Medal of Valor, but from Shane, a person she had never met.

Shane gave me a confused glance before leaning in for her hug. He patted her back awkwardly and glanced at me over her shoulder. I probably looked as horrified as I felt because the light went out of his eyes, and he frowned.

"I'm so excited to meet you!" Ma squealed as she let him go. "I've heard so much about you!"

She had? From who? Me? I might have mentioned Shane a few times, but only because Donny kept retelling the story of the fire, and Shane had been part of that story, obviously.

And yes, I might have mentioned how brave Shane had been. Because he had been. I hadn't been exaggerating. Or obsessing over him. At least, I hadn't let my family in on my obsessing.

"Oh, um, that's nice," Shane said.

Ma gave him an *oh, you!* look and lightly batted his arm. "Don't be modest! When the spotlight's on you, *shine*, my grandmother always used to say. You saved my son's life!"

Shane grimaced. "I'm pretty sure it was the other way around."

"Well, the two of you saved *each other* and a bunch of other people. So you deserve all the gratitude. You certainly have mine!" She beamed at him.

My mother, Lucille Canali, was in her late forties, but she was still fit despite having birthed seven of us. She kept our rowdy household clean and fed and running efficiently—no small feat given what eating machines we all were. Her black hair was dyed these days and worn in a floofy layered style that reached her shoulders. Her dress was as flowery as her personality, but she had on sensible brown shoes. As always, her face was animated, and her nature was to embrace people loudly and effusively—until you did something unforgiveable like leave your shoes in the middle of the living room floor. But even her scolding was full of love.

"Thank you, Mrs. Canali. That's so sweet of you to say." Shane had gone a little pink, and I could tell he was nervous talking to my mother. I didn't blame him. I was having a fucking cow.

"Ma, we were just trying to have a—" I began.

She ignored me, smoothing the front of Shane's jacket. "What a nice suit! You look very handsome, Shane. So dashing in that pink tie. I wish I could get my husband to wear a color like that."

"Um, Ma—" I tried again desperately.

"But you're so skinny! Look at you! I hear you're a college student. Is that right?"

She still had her hands on Shane's jacket. He nodded. "Yes, ma'am. Sacramento State."

"Well, I know all about college students and cheap food! You poor thing. I insist you come to our house tomorrow for dinner. Every Sunday, we have the whole family over. There's so much food! And we'd love a chance to get to know you better. Anyone who's a friend of Mike's is a friend of the family!"

Horror struck through me like an arrow. Oh fuck.

I had not seen this coming. Shane at my family's house for dinner, with the whole extended family there? My dad and brothers, including Gabe, who made no bones about his feeling regarding *homos*. It would be a fucking *disaster*.

"Ma. Please." I tugged at her elbow, trying to peel her away from Shane. Our whole family was gregarious and touchy-feely, so she was just being, well, my mother. But this was not going to happen this way.

She gave me a funny look, then turned. "Oh, my poor Mimmo! I'm so sorry. Of course you get a hug too!" She wrapped me in her arms. I wondered if she could feel my heart trying to pound its way out of my chest.

I looked at Shane and gave him a tight shake of my head along with a flat-hand gesture, both meant to convey *no* in the strongest possible terms.

Ma gave me a loud, smacking kiss on the cheek. "Mwah! So proud of you! Just a baby and already winning medals! What a *gioia*."

"Uh, thanks, Ma. But, oh, look! Uncle Mark and Aunt Lily are over there. Let's go say hi."

"In a minute." Ma stepped back from the hug, but she took my hand in hers, faced Shane again, and took his hand too, like we were both toddlers and she was getting ready to walk us to school. "You boys! I'm so proud of you both. So! You'll come to dinner on Sunday, Shane? Stay for the afternoon. We start eating around one, so any time after twelve would be good. We're in Resolute, just north of Yuba City. It's not that far to drive from Sacramento. Or maybe Mike could pick you up."

Jesus Christ. "Ma, Shane is not my friend!"

It just sort of exploded out of me. They both turned to look at me, smiles gone, faces shocked.

Fuck. Okay, that was rude. My face burned. "Sorry. I mean, we don't know each other that well. We only met during the Crest Lake fire. So…."

They both just blinked at me.

"So…" I continued desperately. "I'm just saying I'm sure Shane has other plans for Sunday. And he's under no obligation to meet up with a bunch of strangers. He's probably got studying. Or…." I looked at Shane for help. But he said nothing. His eyes had gone cold and shuttered again. I trailed off, feeling like I'd dug myself a hole—or a grave—and I had no idea how to get out of it.

Shane turned to my mother, a bright smile on his face. "Mrs. Canali, I would absolutely adore the opportunity to join you and your family for dinner. Thank you so much for being *so nice* and inviting me."

My mother clapped her hands together. "Perfect! Now you don't have to bring a thing. Believe me, when we get cooking, we make enough for an army. Let me give you our address."

She rattled off the digits, and Shane typed it into his phone with every appearance of calm, the two of them huddled together like besties. But me?

I had just entered the first level of Hell. And I had no idea what I'd done to deserve this.

THREE

SHANE

"Oh, baby, I know I've asked you to keep going through fire, flood, and a lack of oil changes, but today might be the day to fail." I patted the steering wheel of Mable, my trusty 2001 Toyota Prius. "Could you muster up a good backfire? Then I could legitimately call Mrs. Canali and tell her I'm having car trouble."

Mable sailed confidently along the narrow road that led off the freeway and up the mountains toward the town of Resolute, California. The only thing I could imagine this town resolved to do was continue to exist because it was so tiny it didn't make it onto most maps. Apparently, this was where the Canali family hung out.

I made another turn, and the density of pine trees increased but not much else. There was a drop-off view to the right of more mountains. "Come on, Mable, I could get stuck here and claim I had no cell service. They'd believe me."

Since leaving the Oroville City Hall yesterday, I'd driven myself nuts about my angry, visceral decision to accept Mrs. Canali's invitation to Sunday dinner. *Shane's not my friend,*

Mike had said. Indeed! Asshole. I'd been feeling almost friendly toward Mike when I found out he'd said nice things about me to his mom and family, but then he'd blurted out that assholic remark and I'd lost my cool. Also my sense of self-preservation because I was now driving toward the ultimate Den of Alphas—Mike, his brothers, his father, his uncles, his cousins, all firefighters and cops. Fuck, for all I knew, his aunt was probably the chief of police! And I was about to take my little gay ass into that roiling stew of testosterone. *Oh god. What have I done?*

My GPS on my phone said, *In 400 feet, turn right.*

Jeez, I'd suddenly emerged from California forest into a small town. Uhhh, in fact, it looked like the set for a movie that ought to star Luke McFarlane or Michael J. Fox, back in the day. One long main street oozed ridiculous quaintness and a lovely fall vibe. I passed a town plaza with trees in bright yellows and oranges, grass, and a statue. Controlling the nonexistent traffic was a single traffic signal and a couple of stop signs, one of which now caused me to pause. There to my right were—they had to be kidding—the Resolute General Store and Milly's Resolute Cafe, with not a Taco Bell or McDonald's in sight. Two gray-haired dudes sitting in front of the General Store stared at me, so I pressed the accelerator and slowly progressed through town.

When I got out of sight of pedestrian traffic and prying eyes—yikes, imagine living in a place where a new car in town was cause for notice—I pulled to the side of the street. Time for serious thought. I'd begged Pops to come with me, but he refused. He said he wasn't invited, and this was my own personal Waterloo. That gave me chills.

But at this moment, I was face to face with a decision I'd already made. One of my defense mechanisms, rather than camouflage like most intelligent animals, was anti-camouflage. Since it was pretty much impossible for me to look like anything but what I was—a flamboyant gay college student—

I tended to push it in people's faces. *Oh, you say you're not comfortable with guys wearing pink? How about spangles? A little latex? Fairies and unicorns?* It wasn't phony. I wasn't secretly longing to switch to gray sweats or Dockers and Henleys. I adored my outrageous clothing. But that morning, I'd decided if I was going into the belly of the beast, I'd do it with flags flying. Yes, I was dressed nicely for a family dinner, but my navy sport coat covered a pink, long-sleeved T-shirt, and my ultra-slim jeans topped my gold lamé tennies. Yes, I was pushing who I was in Mike's face, defiantly. But now, seeing Resolute, I knew I'd stand out if I was dressed in a paper bag. It required no special effort for these people to think I was queer in every possible way. *Nice move, Bower.*

I glanced at my phone. In five minutes, I'd be making apologies for being late on top of everything else. *Come on, Shane. You can't back out now.*

As I pulled away from the curb, the GPS said, *In one half mile, your destination is on the right.*

Oh joy.

The half mile turned out to be a bit of an understatement. It was a half mile to the turn off to the Canali house, which was about a half mile off the road. Damn, this was remote. When I finally got there, I'd used up every second of my five minutes.

Oh shit! A ton of cars were parked at various angles in front of the sprawling ranch-style house, most of it one story, with a two-story wing added on the back. I found a space between a Ford truck and another called a Ram. *Double joy.*

As I slid out of Mable, sparkly tennies catching the light, I heard, "Shane!" Followed by a squeal.

I looked up to see a missile of enthusiasm hurling toward me, black hair flying, which made me smile. Hell, it wasn't everyday one got a greeting like this. "Hi, Mrs. Canali."

She took my arms in her hands. "Please dear, call me Lucille or Mama. Everyone does." She looked me up and down. "Aren't you a fashion plate. So handsome." She slid her arm through mine and started walking me toward the house.

I held up a finger. "Wait. I left something in the car." I opened the back seat and extracted a large bouquet of flowers. I'd put them together with broke college boy ingenuity, buying them at the supermarket and then adding extra baby's breath and beautiful paper to make them look like they'd come from a high-end florist. I handed them to Lucille.

"For *me*? Oh my goodness. Aren't you the sweetest?"

"Lucille, are you out here?" The voice came from the front porch.

"Over here, Carlotta. Come quick and meet our special guest."

Another dark-haired woman, this one in a flowy skirt, a long gold sweater with dozens of chains and bracelets dangling over it, and an improbable scarf wrapped around her head, came rushing around the trucks. She stopped and pressed a hand to her chest. "Shane! It is Shane, isn't it? I saw you at Mike's Medal of Valor ceremony. You two boys are such an inspiration!"

"Thank you. But I just did what seemed to make sense at the time. We were lucky," I said, feeling like a fraud.

"Nonsense. I know you're just as brave as they say. Tell me, when were you born?" She regarded me thoughtfully.

"Uh, October."

She put a hand on my chest, her eyes keen. "That makes total sense. You're a powerful son of Venus, appearing gentle and gracious, when really you're made of solid steel."

"Carlotta, don't give Shane the wrong impression." Lucille heaved a long-suffering sigh and spoke to me. "We're a good *Catholic* family."

"I'm a good Catholic!" Carlotta said with a huff. "Doesn't mean I can't be open to astrology. *There's more in heaven and earth.* Right, Shane?"

"Ohh yeah. A lot more," I agreed, thinking of all the things these two Catholic ladies probably didn't know about.

Lucille held out her flowers with a smile. "Carlotta, look what Shane brought me. Personally, I think he can be a good influence on those rascals of ours." She sniffed the bouquet, then grinned. "By the way, dear, this is my sister Carlotta Scarlatti." Lucille slid one arm through mine. "Let's go in."

Carlotta took my other arm and playfully coaxed a strand of my curly hair off my forehead. "Such a lovely boy."

Locked between these two overwhelming women, I let myself be escorted through the open front door of the house.

Two immediate impressions. The place smelled like paradise and sounded like Hades. Wonderful scents flowed from the huge open kitchen, separated from the large living space by a giant island and a couple pillars. Two young women, one blond and one definitely a Canali from the look of the glossy dark hair and smooth olive complexion, scurried about with a couple of kids racing around them, jumping up to grab snacks from the large island.

To my right was a big living room with a fireplace and, above the fireplace, a massive TV from which blared officious football announcers. Why did they always sound like they were discussing something with the import of ending world hunger? In front of the TV gathered "the men." There was no other way to describe it. Every being with testosterone dominant assembled on two long couches and some chairs, every head turned toward the TV. In the middle of the cluster of males was a long wooden coffee table littered with snacks. Bowls of chips and large containers of dip occupied both ends. In the middle stood a plate of crudités with carrots, celery, and chopped cauliflower, largely untouched. Glasses of beer and soda stood half-empty among the pieces of chips that had fallen here and there. I almost laughed. It looked like a scene directed by Martin Scorsese or Francis Ford Coppola full of handsome Italian men, dark-hair shining, pressed together in tight, teasing camaraderie, an exclusive clan, intimidating in their overt masculinity. Unlike Martin or Francis's guys, the Canali men wore jeans, not suits, but probably in deference to Sunday, several of them had donned dress shirts with sleeves rolled up, like maybe they'd come from church.

Eight men gathered around the coffee table, but I could only focus on one. Mike sat on the left side of the couch wearing jeans and a white sweater. Oh man, did he look gorgeous in white. Almost as beautiful as he had in that dress uniform at the ceremony. Right. That would be the ceremony at which he essentially denied all knowledge of me to his mother. I wiped the incipient smile from my face.

For a second, I got to observe him in his natural habitat. Totally at home, riveted to the TV, shoving chips into his mouth and comfortable, pressed tightly against his family. Anybody who thought all gay men were like me, only had to look at Mike to get their mind changed. He was clearly of this tribe in every way. Well, except for one very important way, but I suspected I was the only one in the room who knew that.

Lucille looked past me at Carlotta. "Do you even believe this crew?"

Not one head moved until Mike must have felt the heat of my gaze because he slowly turned, saw me, and visibly blanched in the truest sense of that word. He looked like someone dipped him in hot water in preparation for cooking.

Lucille yelled, "Okay, Canalis, heads up."

Everyone quieted, and an older man who looked so much like a huskier Mike he had to be his father actually paused the game on the TV. Big step.

Lucille gave them an overly sweet smile. "This is our guest, Shane, who received the Medal of Valor along with Mike for saving sixty-two people's lives—including, I suspect, our own Mikey. You hoodlums mind your manners and make him feel welcome."

The man with the audio control looked around him as if checking to see if anyone else was going to take initiative, then stood. "Hey, Shane. Welcome." With some awkwardness, he scooted past three guys and strode across the room to me, hand extended. "I'm Angelo Canali, Mike's father. The whole family really appreciates everything you did to help Mikey that day."

"Thank you, sir. But it's really Mike who saved my life and that of my grandfather. I'm the one who's grateful."

I glanced at Mike, and he finally seemed to remember he could speak. "Nah. You did good, Shane. Uh, glad you could make it."

But the rest of the guys on the couch focused on Mike, hammering his back and comments like "Damned straight" and "You're a real Canali, man" were murmured. Right. Clearly, a *real Canali* didn't need any help from some fancy fairy boy.

"Can I get you a beer?" Mr. Canali's gaze strayed to my T-shirt, then back to my face with a puzzled smile. "Or whaddya want? A soda?"

I didn't really drink either one. "I'll take a sparkling water if you happen to have it. Or regular water is fine, thank you."

"Sure, sure."

Donny gave a little snort and nudged Mike with a smirk. Maybe sparkling water wasn't a thing in this household. Mike ignored him, staring fixedly at the frozen image on the TV.

Another guy with the Canali dark hair and a round jawline got up and smiled. "Hey, I'm Tony, Mike's big bro. Have a seat while Pa gets you a drink."

I smiled down at Lucille, who patted my shoulder, and at Carlotta, who did the same to my cheek, and stepped away from their sheltering embrace toward the much scarier group of Canalis. Tony dragged over a dining room chair and set it at an angle so it was part of the group. Still, no one made room on the couch, which felt a little less than welcoming. When I sat, Tony pointed toward the kitchen. "That babe in the kitchen is my wife Viv, and the two kids running around are our rugrats, Matteo—we call him Matt—and Lucy, short for Lucille."

Donny spoke up. "The other one's Tessa. She was the baby of the family—until Mikey came along. Sur-prise!"

He tried to give Mike a noogie, but Mike pulled away with a grouchy, "Knock it off."

Tony pointed around the couch. "These turkeys are Gabe and Donny, who you might know since he's also with Cal Fire like me, Pa and Mikey. Gabe's a cop. His girlfriend, Anita, is on duty today at the police station. Our other two brothers, Ace and Paul, aren't here. They're roadies for a band, so they're always traveling." His pointer finger moved. "That's our Uncle Ricky and cousin Tito." Each guy waved as Tony called his name, except for Tito, who gave me a tight smile and went back to staring at his hands. And, damn, Uncle Ricky was maybe late thirties and looked like a young Cary Grant. Holy shit these were some good genes. Then Tony pointed to a recliner where an elderly man was sleeping. "That's our granddad, Giuseppe. He's, uh, he sleeps a lot."

Mike had told me his grandfather had Alzheimer's and was a big favorite of his. I glanced at Mike, who was watching me with a blank expression, but he had a death grip on the arm of the couch.

Tony said, "Of course, you know Mike, the hero."

Angelo showed up with a glass of sparkling water and ice and handed it to me. "We had some bubbly water. Who knew? Help yourself to snacks." His host duties complete, he waved a hand at the TV and said to me, "Big game." Then he plopped into what looked like Dad's favorite chair and forcefully clicked the game back on. Every head turned to the TV with evident relief.

Donny clapped. "Yeah. Let's go!"

Tony slumped back in his chair next to Angelo and propped two socked feet up on the coffee table. And Mike... Mike went back to staring at the screen, but I doubted he saw it. He looked stiff as a board—and not in that oh-so-good way. Part of me wanted to yell *Ha! Serves you right.* My more compassionate nature, however, won out. Jeez, if I lived in this Temple to Testosterone that also happened to be a big, adoring, admiring family, would I have been brave enough to come out?

The thought made me feel a little sick. I shouldn't have come here. What the hell was I doing? Just because I was pissed off, I didn't have any right to make Mike uncomfortable in his own home. And now it was plain as day why he hadn't called. I didn't fit into this scene. And thus into Mike's life.

I sat in the dining room chair Tony had provided and carefully chose a carrot stick, dipping it in something that looked like onion soup mix and sour cream. It was good, even if my stomach was tight with anxiety.

As I munched, the brother closest to me—Gabe?—leaned over from the couch and said, "Brady's playing the Giants."

Angelo waved a loaded chip. "Hell, Gabe, you make it sound like Brady plays alone. All he does is throw that damned ball while everybody else protects his ass."

Gabe shrugged exaggeratedly as he weighed two teams in his hands. "New England. Tampa Bay. We all know the common denominator for winning, right?" He snorted. "I rest my case."

Tony pointed at me. "What about you, Shane? Brady, yes or no?" Tony was obviously the family welcomer, includer, but he expected me to have an answer.

Since my only exposure to the controversial Tom Brady

was my BFF, Roland, pointing out the *excellence of his ass for an old guy,* and I doubted they'd appreciate that observation, I plastered on a grin and held up my hands. "I plead the fifth."

Angelo barked a laugh. "Wise move in this company, Shane. A guy could get mugged."

I forced a smile, but that was way too close to home.

"Oooh!" Donny shouted, half jumping out of his seat as some play happened on screen.

"No way!" Gabe exclaimed.

"Fuck—I mean, dang, I missed it. Rewind?" Tony pleaded, sitting forward.

"Don't rewind, Pa!" Donny scoffed. "If we're gonna watch the game, then watch the game!"

"So tell me what happened?" Tony insisted.

Donny went on to describe some play—I couldn't follow it since I knew jack about football.

"Okay, okay, shush! I can't hear!" Angelo interrupted.

Meanwhile, Mike stayed glued to the TV screen. I ate another carrot, just to have something to do.

It went on like that for another fifteen minutes. Since I had nothing intelligent to say about football in the few times one of the guys made a comment to me, they stopped trying, and I went invisible. Mike wouldn't look at me. My stomach got more fluttery. Even the crudités weren't working as a distraction.

Was it possible to be bored to tears and simultaneously ready to jump out of my skin?

Yes. Yes, it was.

Man, did they keep the temperature turned up in this house, or what? And I wasn't sweating because all the Canali men were smokin' hot either. *Hot Cannolis*, Mike said that was their nickname in the department. Oh yes, accurate. But I was so far out of my depth in this room, I wasn't even able to appreciate the view.

Just as I was wondering how long I'd have to endure this

torture of a football game before I could leave, a crash in the kitchen made every head turn. Carlotta planted her hands on her hips. "Anthony Giuseppe Canali, come get your son."

Tony laughed and headed for the ruckus. Seeing an escape route, I hopped up, too, and hurried into the kitchen. It was a big space, and despite its modern open concept, it was fitted with old-fashioned cherry cabinets and fancy tile on the floor that reminded me of an Italian villa. It was open on two sides to the living room and a big dining room with a long table. This house was built for lots of people.

Lucille was pulling a roast of beef surrounded by potatoes and carrots from the oven. It looked heavy. "Let me help you."

"No, no, honey, you'll get your nice jacket all dirty." She dragged the large pan to the oven door, and despite her admonitions, I grabbed a potholder off the counter and took an end. We hoisted the pan to the shiny quartz countertop where she basted and added a few more short-cooking veggies and then put the pan back in the oven.

She planted her hands on her hips. "You don't mind any better than Mike."

I laughed. "Funny. That's what my grandfather says. Well, except for the Mike part."

Her eyes went all soft, and she gave me a quick hug. "I heard the reason you went to Crest Lake was to save your grandfather. What a good boy."

I shrugged, my cheeks burning. "He's pretty much my only family now. He's everything."

"Aw." She got a little misty-eyed and waved a hand in front of her face. "Stop. You'll make me cry. So few young people appreciate family these days."

I cleared my throat. "I'll bet you've got an extra apron. I'd like to help."

She blinked at me. "That's sweet, Shane, but really not necessary. Go enjoy the game!"

Tessa turned from dishing out some kind of pasta and gave me an up-and-down look. "Maybe Shane doesn't like football, Ma. Not everyone does."

I laid a finger next to my nose and then pointed at Tessa. "That." I crossed my arms on my chest. "I'm dying in there. Please, please save me."

Tessa laughed. "Oh my God. A male who doesn't like football. Ma, can we keep him?"

Lucille asked. "Well, when you put it like that—there should be an extra apron on the back of that pantry door there."

I found the apron and pulled off my jacket. Tessa grabbed it with a smile that was almost flirtatious and walked out of the kitchen to put it somewhere.

Carlotta raised her eyebrows. "You gave her an excuse to linger over her phone for twenty minutes before reappearing."

"That's okay. I'll take her place." I strapped on the apron, and only once it was tied behind my back did I realize it had big decorative floofs all down the front. Great. As if I needed to stick out more. I grinned and struck a pose as Lucille looked me up and down.

"Aw! You look adorable. So nice to see a man whose masculinity is unthreatened by a few ruffles."

I snorted. Yeah. Not getting into that conversation. "So what can I do?" I glanced around. "Do we need a salad?" Then I remembered the untouched crudités. I whispered conspiratorially. "It might be a way to get something green in the crew." I tilted my head toward the living room.

Lucille's face lit up. "I'd love a salad. Don't bother with a big one, though. Most of the boys won't touch it."

"We'll see about that. I'll apply the Shane Bower magic." I rubbed my hands together.

Ten minutes later, both women were staring over my shoulder as I added a can of hearts of palm I'd found in the pantry and sliced, plus some pine nuts, dried cranberries, chopped apple, and a little blue cheese. I'd gotten good at making salads and a lot of other things when I'd lived with Pops in Crest Lake because he was supposed to eat healthy but hated it. I'd had to make food extra tempting to get him to eat his veggies and other good-for-you stuff. I was a whiz at an Instant Pot.

I dressed the salad with blue cheese in a bottle from the fridge, then set the big bowl on the huge table in the dining room. Brass chandeliers glistened, two over the table where one side was set with chairs and one with two long benches. Heavy white dishes sat on blue placemats.

It was sort of plain, though. It needed something.

I walked back to the kitchen and asked Carlotta for candles. She searched the pantry, and I set up a centerpiece with candles, some of my flowers, and some oranges and nuts I found on a shelf, then folded all the napkins to look like swans just for the fun of it. Creating beauty always made me feel better. Making the salad and decorating the table, I was the most comfortable I'd been since I'd left home that morning. And it gave me something to do.

Lucille walked in behind me and slapped a hand over her mouth. "Oh my word. It's beautiful. Carlotta, come look!"

Carlotta walked in, accompanied by a gray-haired woman of some considerable age and Tessa, who had reappeared. The sport-commentary shouts wafted in from the living room.

Tessa breathed, "Whoa, Shane. That looks epic."

The elderly lady, dressed mostly in black, glanced at Tessa, then at the table. "If epic means beautiful, then you are correct, *cuore mio*."

Lucille sniffled. "I never seem to have time to just make things look pretty." She rested her head on my shoulder for a moment and then said, "Thank you, Shane." She reached toward the older lady. "This is my mother, Luna."

I stuck out my hand, but the small lady grasped my shoulders and reached up. I realized what she was trying to do and leaned down to let her kiss each of my cheeks. "Call me Nonna." She continued to hold me as she pulled back. Gazing intently into my eyes, she said, "You will join this family and will bring us all much beauty and joy. I know. I have the sight."

I registered what she was saying in time to hear the gasp that came from behind her and looked up to see Mike.

FOUR

MIKE

"Hey, Ma. When we gonna eat? I'm hungry." I patted my stomach like an idiot. As if I were speaking to people who needed sign language to comprehend. But I had to say something. Shane, my mother, sister, and grandma were all standing at the dining room table having a moment. And Shane must have decorated the fucking table because it looked like a magazine or something.

Honestly, I think my brain froze. Like, what the fuck was even happening right now?

Ma gave me a weird look. "We eat the minute the game ends, as always! What's the matter with you, Mimmo?"

"Nothin'." I forced a smile. "Just hungry."

"You want me to fix you something?" she asked, looking suddenly worried that I was risking malnutrition.

"Nah. I'll wait. You okay, Shane?" I asked politely, because he was our guest and I was trying to act like I would act if he and I had only worked together that day. And not, like, made out. And that he hadn't featured in a hundred fantasies since.

"Yes, Mike," Shane replied with faux seriousness. "Are you okay?"

"Hey, I could give you a tour of the property, if you want," I offered, without a clue what I was doing.

Shane blinked at me. He started to reply when my mom interrupted. "No, not until after we eat! I don't want you disappearing with Shane right now, and then we can't find you when it's time to sit down. Shane needs some good home cooking. You're gonna love my lasagna." She pinched his cheek and gazed at him fondly, like he was one of her grandkids.

"It smells so good. I can't wait." Shane returned her smile.

"I wanna try your salad," Tessa said firmly.

What, I repeat, was even happening right now?

"Okay. Cool. After dinner then." I managed to say and turned to wander back into the living room.

Donny jumped up and was crowing about some play in the game, so apparently, it was exciting. I didn't care. I liked football normally, but I couldn't focus on it today and had been dying for it to end for the past hour.

Before I reached the couch, a hand grabbed my arm and I turned to see Tessa. "Hey, Mike. C'mere for a sec."

I let her pull me away. We ended up in the front hall.

"What?" I asked her.

"Tell me about Shane." Her eyes danced with curiosity or mischief. Tessa was the family troublemaker, so that was never a good thing.

"What about Shane?" I crossed my arms over my chest. "You were at the ceremony. You know about him. He helped me out the day of the Crest Lake fire."

"Yeah, but… what's he like? What does he do?"

I shrugged. "He's a college student. I guess he does what college students do."

She looked around and lowered her voice to a whisper. "Is he gay? He's gay, right?" She looked delighted.

"How am I supposed to know?" I huffed.

Tessa rolled her eyes. "He's your friend. I know the sexual orientation of *my* friends."

"I met him the day of the fire, and that's it. It's not like we ever hung out."

"So he never mentioned a boyfriend? Or a girlfriend?"

"Yeah, didn't come up while we were *fighting for our lives*."

Tessa relented with a sigh, then studied me thoughtfully. "You should. You should hang out with Shane."

I blinked at her. Did Tessa suspect? About me? "Whaddya mean? Why?"

"Because he's nice! And he's a good guy. He helped you save all those people in the fire, didn't he? And because he's different. It's good to have different kinds of people in your life, Mike—not just stay stuck in the whole Canali thing." She waved a hand toward the living room.

"There's something wrong with the *Canali thing* now?" I said, just to give her grief, but my heart pounded.

"No. But how are you gonna grow as a person if you're only ever around people just like you? You should get outside that whole firefighter bubble, Mikey, while you're young enough to do it, not too stuck in your ways like Dad. Or Gabe. I have all kinds of friends. It's great."

"Yeah, your friends are certainly different," I teased, which earned me an elbow in the arm. Tessa's advice sounded a little high-handed, given that most of her friends were partiers and fashionistas and not exactly profound thinkers or whatever. But her point hit deep anyway. It rang true and even felt… important.

Yeah. Why shouldn't I have a friend like Shane? I hadn't been able to see him and my family mixing in any way. But here he was, obviously getting along fine with my mother, aunt, and sister. I guessed sometimes you dreaded something so much, you built it up in your mind to be worse than it was.

I smiled. Yeah, Shane and I could be friends. I even had a

reason to be friends with him. He'd earned the fucking Medal of Valor with me. A foxhole buddy. My brothers couldn't say shit after that. And if they did, I'd just point out it was like Tessa said—we didn't have to be friends with people only like us. Just because I was friends with someone like Shane didn't have to mean I was gay, either.

It felt like a weight dropped off my chest. The sensation was so strong, I looked down at my feet and was surprised not to see a lead weight lying there.

A chorus of cheers and shouts erupted from the living room. Then I heard Donny say, "I'm starving. Hey, Ma!"

That was the bat signal. The game was over.

I looked at Tessa. "You're right."

"I am?" She looked surprised.

"Yeah. Only you should be friends with Shane too. And help me, ya know, have his back over dinner. With Donny and Gabe and all that."

She grinned and held out a hand for a high-five. I smacked it. "Yes! I got you, bro. Ooh, wait 'til they see Shane's napkin swans! This is gonna be lit."

Napkin swans? Oh dear God.

We were all seated at the big table quickly. The moment a game was over, my brothers wanted food. Well, me too. It didn't matter how much we'd snacked by the TV. Often, we ended up with a kids' table and some people taking their plates into other rooms. It wasn't that unusual to have thirty people here on a Sunday. But today it was a fairly small group—and Shane. So we all fit around the table.

The big old oak monstrosity was loaded with so much food it nearly groaned. God, I loved our family meals so much. Pa looked around the table as soon as he sat down.

"Why so fancy? Did you invite the president for dinner?" he asked my mother.

"No, Shane set the table. Doesn't it look nice?" She smiled

at Shane, but her tone was slightly forced as if she expected pushback.

"*Shane* set the table?" Donny said with a smirk. He looked at Gabe, and Gabe made a prissy expression and waggled his head. Donny laughed.

My face burned. I started to open my mouth to say something when Ma spoke up loudly. "Yes, *Donato,* Shane set the table. Like a guest who knows how to offer help to his hostess. So shut up. Maybe you could learn some manners. You too, Gabe. No acting up at my table, or you can go eat in the yard with the pigs."

"We used to have pigs," Nonno muttered wistfully.

Gabe looked abashed. "Sorry, Mama."

Donny blinked at our mother for a moment, then reached for the bread basket. "Anyone want a roll?" He was in full retreat. *Nice.* I grinned.

I looked down the table at Tessa. She gave me a wide-eyed look, her eyes dancing with amusement. Ma was the one who had Shane's back today.

"I think the table looks beautiful!" Nonna said. "I'm old enough to appreciate nice things. And thoughtful men. Not that I see them very often around here."

"Yeah, it's cool," I said, like it was no big deal. "Hey, Shane, ya gotta try these meatballs. Seriously, they're like little balls of, um, heaven." Shit, I hadn't thought that through. Face burning, I put two on my plate and passed the bowl to Shane, who was next to me.

"Oh, yum." He put two on his own plate. I cringed, but thankfully, the next words out of his mouth weren't in praise of balls. "Thank you so much for inviting me, Lucille. I haven't eaten a big home-cooked meal like this in... well, basically, never."

"Aw!" Ma looked like he'd just told her his dog died. "Did you hear that, Angie? Isn't that a crying shame?"

Pa shook his head sadly. "That's a shame all right."

"You should join the fire department," Tony said brightly. "We spend a lot of time hanging around the station when there's not a fire. And we cook a lot. Big meals."

"And fattening ones," Tessa put in. "It's a wonder any of you can still climb a ladder."

Donny scowled. "Reiger made this healthy cheesecake the other day. Made with cottage cheese or some sh—er, stuff." He glanced at Ma guiltily. "It tasted like crap. Do it right or don't do it, that's what I say."

"Have some salad." Shane picked up a bowl and leaned forward to pass it across the table to Donny, his expression determined.

I handed Pa my plate to get served a slice of lasagna and watched Donny. I bit back a smile, waiting to see what he would do. He glanced at Shane, then at Ma.

"Shane made the salad. Eat some," Ma ordered firmly.

With a grimace, Donny took the bowl. "Thanks, Shane. Looks, um, good." He scooped some onto his plate and shoved the bowl at Gabe.

"Oh, this looks divine! And so healthy. Are those pine nuts?" Tessa said with extra enthusiasm when the bowl came to her.

"Among other things," Shane said cheerfully. He took a bite of a meatball and rolled his eyes in pleasure. Which stupidly gave me a hot flush. "Oh my God! So good."

"Good salad," Pa said, spearing another forkful. "You should make it like this, Lucille."

"It's not bad," Donny took his last bite of it and licked his fork. He eyed the salad bowl as Shane handed it to me, clearly calculating if there'd be enough left for a second round.

I took a bigger portion than I normally would, then gave Donny a big smile, just to piss him off, before passing the bowl on to Nonna.

I took a bite. "Yeah. Wow, Shane, this is really good."

He gave me a grateful smile. "Thanks. But everything here is so good. The lasagna, the roast, Lucille—oh my God."

"Yeah, but we're used to all this amazing food," I said. "The salad is new. Nice to have something different." I shared a glance with Tessa.

She raised her wineglass. "Well said, Mikey. Here's to trying new things. And new friends."

"Hear, hear!" said Carlotta, who was always up for toasting anything.

We all clinked glasses with everyone we could reach. When Shane clinked with me, he only held my gaze for a moment before dropping his eyes. He looked a little self-conscious or something. But I was feeling so optimistic and pleased, I drained my glass in one go and poured myself some more. This wasn't entirely sucking. That was awesome.

"You didn't invite Darlene to dinner? It is still Darlene, isn't it?" Tessa asked Donny innocently.

"Is that the one with all the tattoos?" Ma asked, trying to sound neutral.

"They're *all* covered in tattoos," Gabe snorted. "Donny likes to multitask—have sex and read at the same time."

"Gabriel Lorenzo Canali!" Ma said, shocked.

"The girl I'm dating now is called Mindy," Donny said without much interest. "Darlene moved to L.A. to be closer to her mom and grandma."

"Oh? Well. Isn't that nice," said Ma with surprise. We'd once seen Darlene in Resolute, though Donny had refused to ever bring her to the compound. She was a bleach blonde who dressed like she played a hooker in a 70s TV movie. But then, most of Donny's girlfriends did. "Moving closer to family is nice."

Gabe laughed. "Yeah. Turns out her mom and grandma are both in prison down there."

Aaaand it was Donny's turn in the hot seat. As Ma started in on the value of *nice girls*, I gave Shane a secret smile, but I wasn't sure he saw it. He listened to the family conversation with the rapt interest my brothers gave to football games.

After dinner, Shane volunteered to help do dishes, but Ma shooed us out of the kitchen. "No, Shane, you've done enough for a guest. Go take that tour with Mike. Go on, you two!"

I glanced toward Shane and then the carpet. Donny was giving me a narrow-eyed look, but what the hell? Different friends. And he was our guest. And Ma was making me.

"C'mon, Shane." I led him out the back door.

And suddenly we were alone. Which made my skin tingle and my heart race. Stupid. I needed to learn to chill out around Shane. There wasn't gonna be any more *kissing*.

"This is a huge property," Shane said, as we went down the steps from the big deck and the whole yard came into view.

"Yup. Nonno—that's my grandfather—he bought some of it back when this area was dirt cheap, and he relocated out here from the Bronx. The family added to it over the years. See that house over there?" I pointed to a smaller ranch to the left. "That's where Tony and Viv live. That one over there." I pointed toward a cottage set apart from the main house with a path. "That's Nonna and Nonno's house. And that one down the road." I pointed to a little white ranch with red shutters down a gravel road. "That's where I live. I room with Donny. There's another place in the woods, too, where Gabe lives. Tito's above the garage, and Tessa lives in the main house with Ma and Pa, but Tessa's room is kind of a basement apartment. She has a separate entrance."

Shane's eyes went wide. "Wow. Talk about togetherness. Doesn't that get… I don't know… claustrophobic at times?"

"Nothing's more important than family." I shrugged. "Gabe and Pa built most of the houses on this lot. They're big on the whole family compound thing. But yeah, I want to get my own apartment someday, someplace where everyone doesn't know your business, you know? But it hasn't been a priority, what with my Cal Fire training and everything."

We kept walking, heading to a path that eventually left the property and went down to the river.

Shane stopped walking, his face serious. "Hey, there's something I need to say to you."

"Oh, yeah? What?" My heart slammed. Was I ready for this?

He looked guilty. "I'm sorry I accepted your mother's invitation when you clearly didn't want me to. I shouldn't have invaded your space like this. I was pissed at you, but that's no excuse."

I swallowed. Yeah, I hadn't been happy about him coming here today. But I'd been wrong.

I shook my head. "I don't own you, Shane. My mom invited you. She had every right to invite whoever she wanted over, and you had every right to accept. You can see her, or whoever you want."

"But I know you're…" Shane's eyes shifted toward the house. "I know you're not out, and you didn't want me here. I get it."

I couldn't deny it. "Honestly? I was kind of freaking out about it. But I'm glad you came. It was… okay. And that's a good thing. Maybe I needed to see that."

He gave me raised eyebrows as if to say *oh, really?*

"I mean… it's a little weird," I admitted.

He chuckled. "It's very weird."

"Yeah. My dad and brothers…. Probably not your cup of tea."

"I'm not completely unfamiliar with the type," he said with sarcasm and a touch of sadness.

Yeah. Probably not. Had Shane had trouble with macho guys before? I wanted to ask, but I didn't want to hear the answer.

"So anyway." Shane shook his head as if shaking off a

mood and smiled brightly. "I won't do it again. Invade your space, I mean. Don't worry."

I snorted. "Is that what you think? I've got news for you. Ma likes you. And she's not the type of person who lets things go. You have no idea the badgering she's capable of."

His smile warmed at the mention of my mother. "I can imagine. You have to be stubborn to survive in a household like this. But don't worry. She can't *make* me come over."

Shane was seriously underestimating Lucille Canali. She so could. But that wasn't the point I wanted to make. I hesitated. Was I really gonna say what I wanted to say? Would it be a mistake?

But today had been… intriguing. It made me feel warm and gooey seeing the female side of the Canali clan embrace Shane—even if, other than Tessa, they had no clue that he was gay. And yeah, the guys weren't exactly fans, but they hadn't been as bad as I'd feared. Tessa was right. Maybe it would help them *grow* a bit to be around someone like Shane from time to time. I dunno. It gave me a good feeling. Like maybe if Shane could fit in, they could eventually accept me too?

And, yes, that was selfish. Shane was no John the Baptist. It wasn't his job to *prepare the way*. But if it worked out that way, I wouldn't complain.

"Look, you're welcome to be a friend of the family," I said. "Come any time."

Shane made a highly dubious face.

"No—I mean it. It's fine. *Good,* even."

Shane's expression softened. "You mean that, don't you?"

"Sure. I wouldn't say it if I didn't mean it." But the way Shane was looking at me—or maybe it was the fact that we were alone, or the growing California dusk, made things start to shift and crackle between us. At least it crackled in me. In my oh-too-willing pants. And that couldn't be part of the deal.

"Look…." I rubbed the back of my neck self-consciously.

"About us... obviously, it's complicated. I mean even *more* complicated now. Now that my family knows you and all of that."

Shane frowned and folded his arms over his chest. His eyes did that thing where they seemed to put distance between us. Like they just went all cool and remote. With those clear and open eyes of his, Shane really couldn't hide a thing. I wondered if other people could read them as easily as I did. "I'm sorry. I like you, but—"

"No. I get it. And don't worry. I'm not going to say anything to your family."

I nodded. "I know that. But, yeah, I've got some shit to work out before... well, before I can get involved in anything."

Shane looked away. "So friend of the family, good. Your boy toy, not happening." Shane's tone was cool but not surprised, and he didn't seem upset. He shrugged. "Not a shock after the way you ghosted me."

"I am sorry about that. I just wanna get some time under my belt with Cal Fire. You know? And maybe ease my family into things a bit. Telling them about me, I mean."

He laughed. "Oh yeah? I'll be interested in seeing how you manage to *ease them into it.*" He nudged my shoulder. "I'm not sure tiptoeing up to anything is the Canali way."

"Shut up." I nudged him back. And suddenly it felt okay. It felt really good, in fact. I liked that Shane now knew enough about my family to make a comment like that. My heart got so full I felt it in my toes. He really was a good guy. "But we can be friends, I hope?"

Shane looked surprised. "Like, you and me be friends? Separately from me and your family?"

"Yeah. Why not? You only want me for my hot bod or something?" I teased.

He started to protest, then appeared to realize I was yanking his chain. He smirked. "It's not that hot."

"Oh fuck yeah, it is." I flexed my bicep.

Shane rolled his eyes, but not before he got a good look. "Aren't you worried about what your brothers will say? Being friends with me?"

I glanced toward the house. "I'll just sic Ma on them if they get smart." I smirked.

"Ouch. I'm learning so much about the dog-eat-dog world of family dynamics right now."

We turned and wandered back toward the house.

"Oh, you have no idea. Just wait until we set up the Mexican Train game."

Shane's face lit up with a grin. "Oh baby! I am so gonna beat Donny's ass at that."

I laughed. "Now that I gotta see."

FIVE

SHANE

"Friends? But he kissed you, for pity's sake!" Roland rocked back so far in his chair he nearly tipped it over, and Hissy had to grab his arm to keep him upright. A couple of nearby coffee drinkers gave him a look, and he wrinkled his nose. "Sorry."

It was Friday afternoon at Get Perky. AKA packed. The pumpkin-spice specialties and Halloween-themed baked goods really drew a crowd.

Hissy patted Roland's arm. Yes, we were the Odd Triple— the two gay college students and the almost ninety-year-old lady with pink-and-blue hair, but Roland had gone with me to the book club a couple times, and he and Hissy had bonded over their mutual love of Emily Dickinson, DC super-heroes, and Quentin Tarantino. Now, the three of us met for coffee at Get Perky often since it fit into all three of our sched-ules. Hissy said, "No, Ro. You have to understand how much Mike has to lose." I'd told them about the Canalis and the family compound. "He's jeopardizing his family, his living situation, *and* his job. Triple whammy."

Roland shook his head vehemently. "But he's not even giving them a chance to be his *real* family and love him the way he is." Roland's coming-out experience had been the opposite of mine. He'd tortured himself over what his family would say, and then, when he'd finally gotten up the nerve, they'd told him they'd known he was gay since he was six, loved him since he was born, and always would. Just thinking of it made me tear up.

Talk about luck of the draw.

"But that's not the point," Hissy said. "When he comes out, it will mean he has to renegotiate his place in the family and the fire company with every member, and from what Shane says, that's a lot of people. Some will be accepting. Others won't. Everything will change. That's hard work for a young man who's just finding his place in the world."

"But the longer he hides, the harder it'll be," Roland insisted. "If you're finding a place in the world, it might as well be the right place."

I stared into my tea latte. They were arguing both sides of my dilemma for me. Finally, I held up a hand. "I appreciate your perspectives, but it's decided. Mike wants us to be friends, I think mostly because his mom and aunt and sister seem to like me. It's for the best anyway. The last thing I need is to get involved with someone who's closeted." I sighed. "But it kind of doesn't matter, because he hasn't called me to get together or anything. So I guess we're friends in theory only." It had been five long days since the Sunday dinner.

"You should call him." Roland slapped his fingers on the table. "Hell, friends can call friends anytime, right? So if you're such good *pals*, why aren't you having late-night giggles over your latest dates and favorite, hunky TV stars?" He raised his brows in all innocence, though his voice reeked of irony.

And, of course, that was exactly the problem. Mike and I could call ourselves friends until hell froze over, but we didn't have friend experiences or friend vibes. Jeez, standing out in the Canali compound with him on Sunday, what I'd mostly wanted to do was ask him to show me the inside of that cute little house he shared with Donny and then jump his bones. But friends didn't suck friends' cocks. The truth was, I still had feelings for Mike, big ones, and I wasn't over the hurt of him ghosting me—and now shoving me in the friend zone.

"The thing is... I think Mike really needs a gay friend," I said reluctantly.

Roland gave me a narrow-eyed look. "To, what? Convince him to throw away his ten-year-old sweatpants?"

"No." I kicked him a little under the table. "I just don't think he's been around many gay people. The only thing he's ever been exposed to is that heap of manly manhood in his family. How would you even know how to be queer growing up like that? I mean, not that there's only one way to be queer or that he has to be like us, but hell, I'm not sure some random hookup is a decent example. He needs, I dunno...." It was embarrassing to put my thoughts into words.

"A role model from the land of Dorothy?" Ro said dryly.

"Shane has a good point," Hissy nodded enthusiastically. "We all mirror the behavior of the people around us. It's an excellent idea to expose Mike to other options."

"So you're saying he's never watched *Queer Eye* or Ru Paul?" Ro snorted. "That's not even humanly possible."

I rolled my eyes. And I kind of felt stupid for even bringing it up. I wasn't wrong that Mike could use the exposure. But I highly doubted I was the one to give it to him. I had too many feelings for the boy to be the objective friend he deserved. "Anyway, I better get going, guys. I'm gonna make that chicken and risotto recipe in the Instant Pot for Pops. Come on over if you want to indulge. There will be plenty."

Roland moaned, "Umm. Count me in."

Hissy grinned. "Thanks, but I've got a date tonight. Say hi to Pops for me."

I smiled. It was pretty embarrassing when a ninety-year-old saw more action than two gay men in their twenties. "Come on over about six, Ro." I kissed Hissy's cheek, bumped fists with Roland, and took off for home.

When I keyed my way into the apartment, Pops was chopping onions. That was our deal. I'd make the food if he chopped the onions and garlic since they made me cry. I gave him a one-armed hug from the back. "Roland's coming for dinner."

"I figured. This is one of his favorite dishes. Go get comfy."

I changed into my pink sweats in the bedroom closet and then went to wash my hands in prep for making food. I was glad Ro was coming for dinner since it would be nice for Pops not to have to hear me moan about Mike for yet another meal. He'd given me all the best advice. Told me I didn't have to be friends with Mike if I didn't want to and that I should only stay in contact with him if I wouldn't get my hopes up. Guys like Mike sometimes never came out, he said.

Yeah. Shit. And after five days, that was more than clear.

As I walked back to the kitchen and grabbed the cheese to grate and the chicken to rinse, my phone rang. I peered at the screen. Mrs. Canali. She'd asked for my number before I'd left on Sunday, and, of course, I'd given it. "Hi, Mrs. Canali." I probably sounded some combination of enthusiastic and unsure, which was exactly how I felt.

"Lucille or Mama, dear, remember?"

"Hi, Lucille." I grinned.

"I know this is so terribly last minute, and I completely understand if you are already committed, but if you're free tomorrow, I need you to do a huge favor for me."

"Well, of course. After that meal last weekend, I owe you my firstborn child."

"Hum. At the glacial rate my children are giving me grandkids, I may take you up on that."

I laughed. "How can I be of help?"

"You can come to dinner on Saturday, bring your grandfather, and help me decorate the table the way you did before." I froze, *sure!* and *hell no!* fighting for dominance in my throat. I paused long enough that she rushed on. "You see, Angelo invited his boss from the fire company and his wife to come to dinner, and I thought if we could have some of those beautiful details you added to the table and all, it would give the whole thing a real touch of class. Plus, you met Chief Einnes when you got your medal, so it would be like old home week." She laughed.

Whoa. As if I'd felt at home with that crew of daredevils for one second at the ceremony.

"And I thought if your grandfather could come, he'd enjoy it, since he was involved with the fire also. Plus, that way, we wouldn't be taking you away from him for two weekends in a row. From all Mike has told me, I know he'll fit right in with our crew."

I barked a laugh and glanced at Pops. "You mean because he's the stubbornest human on the planet?"

"Like I said. He'll fit right in!" she said cheerfully.

A million questions crowded my head. *Does Mike know you're inviting me? How does he feel about me being there with his big boss? Do you really want swans on the table for the fire chief?* All I said was, "What time would you like us to be there?" And, "I'll text you a list of what I need."

After a couple more minutes of effusive thanks, she hung up.

I stared at Pops. "Someone up there is getting a big laugh out of my life right now. I swear."

"What'd you do?" Pops asked, eyebrows quirked.

"You won't believe where we're going tomorrow."

———

I maneuvered through Resolute like an old pro.

Pops stared out the window. "This town is a serious throwback. Reminds me of my youth." Before the fire, Pops had lived in an apartment in the town of Crest Lake, which, while small and charming, was way chi-chi compared to Resolute. Crest Lake was ski and tourist country.

Or it had been, before the town had been pretty much burnt to the ground. The thought caused an ache of sadness, but I pushed it off. I didn't need to remind Pops of that.

I feigned cheerfulness. "I know. General Store? Seriously? And that café looks like it could be the only one in town."

"How far is this family house?" He sounded a touch grouchy since I'd seriously forced him to come. He'd argued that there was zero reason for him to attend and, in fact, the firefighters probably thought he was an old codger who'd refused to leave his home and, therefore, made more work for them and had put Mike in danger. He muttered, "I'm certainly capable of spending a Saturday by myself."

"I know, Pops, but, believe me—the food'll be worth it."

"So you keep saying," Pops muttered, but I could practically see him drool. Like me, Pops had a soft spot for a good meal.

I was really happy to have him along, taking some of the focus off me. Plus, I never wanted Pops to think he wasn't a central part of my life. And he needed to get out more.

Fewer cars and trucks crowded the Canalis' parking area this week, probably because it was earlier in the day. Maybe the football game du jour hadn't started yet. Before I could even turn off Mable, Lucille was standing beside my door waving her hands like a kid. She was in a grandmotherly flowered dress, covered by a long apron. When I cracked the door, she was practically bouncing. "I'm so excited that you're here." She took off at a trot and rounded the car, then pulled open the passenger door. "Mr. Bower, we're so happy to have you at our home. Shane is like one of the family."

I was touched by her kindness even if that was total hyperbole.

Pops said, "Call me Bill. Thanks for inviting me." When he stepped out, Lucille enfolded him in a hug, which made his eyes widen. He patted her back awkwardly, but I could tell he was fighting a smile.

She escorted Pops to where I stood and then slid her arm through mine. "Sorry to put you to work the minute you get here, but they're coming at two, and I want as much Shane-ness all over the house as we can squeeze in before they arrive."

I laughed and tried not to wonder what Donny and Gabe thought of a house reeking of Shane-ness. But hell, it was her dinner party.

Walking in the door, most of my impressions were the same as last time. Good smells and a loud TV. But this time there were only three men sitting in front of it—Mike's father, Angelo, Tony, his brother that was married and had two kids, and Giuseppe, the grandfather. Tessa, Tony's wife Viv, and his grandmother Luna bustled around the kitchen.

I asked Lucille, "Where's Carlotta today?" I didn't ask, *Where's Mike?*

"She'll come for dessert. She wanted to be sure there was plenty of room at the table."

I smiled since that was such a family thing to do.

Angelo looked up. "Hey, Shane." He rose from the couch, where the attraction seemed to be some more guys talking about football games that would occur later, and walked quickly over, looking at Pops. "Welcome. You must be Mr. Bower. Bet you're proud of your grandson. Winning the Medal of Valor and all." He shook Pops's hand.

"Call me Bill and yes, I am." Pops smiled. "After all, mine was one of the lives our two boys saved."

Angelo clapped him on the shoulder. "I know my wife's about to put Shane to, er, work, so come on over and meet the family. More Canalis will be here in a while. We're like rabbits." Angelo laughed good-naturedly. Pops gave me a quick glance and then walked over to the couch with Angelo.

I noticed Angelo barely glanced my way. It stung a little. He'd been polite, but I could tell he wasn't a fan.

Lucille mother-henned me toward the dining room, where she showed me all the supplies I'd asked for, including a few bouquets of flowers, candles, colored napkins, blank place cards and holders. There was even a new set of champagne glasses. I grinned. "Perfect." Then I cleared my throat. "Where's the rest of your clan today?"

"Scattered around the compound and running errands for me."

From behind me, Tessa said, "Mike and Donny are picking up ice at the General Store." While I mused on why she'd specifically decided to mention Mike, she slid her arms around my neck and hugged me. "Thanks for coming to our rescue, Shane. Sorry to put you to work again. Ma is really good at sniffing out people's skills and getting them to work for her."

"That's what mothers do. One day, you'll know!" Lucille pronounced.

"I know, Ma. I've been making the family Christmas card since 2003."

Lucille patted her hand. "And you do it so well."

"And you help out with hemorrhoids!" Nonna chimed in.

Tessa went red. "I picked up some cream for her from the drug store *one time*."

I laughed. "Well, it's my pleasure. Though I sort of wish I could have seen the General Store with Mike and Donny. That would be a new experience."

Tessa gave me a doubtful look. "Yeah. It's not that exciting. Trust me."

I'd told the truth about it being my pleasure. Having all the goodies on the table was like a kid with a new box of

Legos. I settled into arranging flowers, pulling vintage glassware and bowls from the china cabinet as I went, and making things look beautiful and special. Time flew by. I was vaguely aware of family members arriving as I accepted grunted hellos and handshakes. Donny went through and gave me a perturbed look, as if wondering WTF I was doing there, but I was busy, and it rolled off my back like rain. I arranged and folded and organized to my little heart's content, primed only for the sound of Mike's voice, which didn't come.

I finally looked up when an arm slid around my waist. Tessa said, "Come with me. You've been working nonstop for over two hours. You need a drink and some fresh air." She handed me a glass of bubbly water.

I took it with surprise. "You remembered. That's so sweet."

She shrugged. "Ma got it just for you. She remembers every drink preference of every person she's ever had in this house. I think it's like a savant thing. Come on."

The air outside was crisp despite the bright sun, but it felt good. We wandered away from the house, and Tessa asked me about college. I told her I was majoring in English and English Lit and how I'd love to go into publishing someday. "What do you do, Tessa?"

"I'm an admin in a manufacturing plant." She made a face. "I wanted to stay near home, and there's not a ton to choose from."

"I can definitely see the appeal of Resolute," I said.

Yells, whistles, and catcalls echoed through the trees. I looked at Tessa questioningly.

She pursed her lips and grimaced. "That, my friend, is the sound of my childhood. And my present, more's the pity."

We stepped through some bushes into a clearing, where the Secret of the Missing Canalis was revealed. Mike, Donny, Gabe, Tony, Tito, and Uncle Ricky ran on an open lawn area, each with pieces of cloth hanging from their jeans. Tony carried a football, and all the others seemed to be after him, racing in every direction like a flight of drugged bumblebees. Some of the guys were shirtless, including Mike—and, oh shit, I couldn't look away. He was sweaty and dirt-streaked, but his olive skin glowed in the sun, lean muscles rippling like some old movie where the hero ran down the beach toward his lover. My mouth literally watered as I stared. Mike took off after Tony, dodging and weaving. Tony tore toward a big tree that had a piece of cloth on it, which I gathered was some kind of goal line. The look of desperation on Mike's face increased until finally he made a huge leap through the air, arms reaching toward the piece of cloth on Tony's belt. He missed Tony entirely, slammed into the trunk of the tree, smashed to the ground, and lay there sputtering around a mouthful of dirt with blood on his face.

I didn't think for one moment, even when Tessa's hand gripped my arm and slid off as I pulled away. "Mike!" I literally screamed it as I ran toward the fallen body by the tree. When I got there, he was struggling to sit up, and deep red blood dripped from his chin. "Mike, Mike. Oh my god, are you badly hurt?" I ripped the apron I was somehow still wearing from around my neck and started mopping his face.

My focused brain picked up two things at once. One was the guys behind me laughing hysterically. And the other was Mike trying desperately to scoot out of my grasp, eyes panicked.

My mopping hand froze in midair. I felt shame for a hot second. Then...then I was pissed. I stood up, hands on my hips, and glared at the gaggle of idiots. "You think this is funny? Your brother with blood pouring down his face? He could have been seriously hurt!"

I turned to look at Mike, who was staring up at me with wide eyes. I wadded up the apron, which was ruined with blood anyway, and threw it in his face. "Clean it up before your mom sees you and freaks out. Jesus, you don't need a nurse; you need a washing machine."

I turned and marched toward the house. But not before muttering, loudly, *"Assholes."*

Tessa scampered to keep up with me. "Good for you, Shane. You tell 'em."

Still, I knew she could feel me shaking.

SIX

MIKE

"Ouch!"

"You shouldn't play football out there if you can't watch where you're going!" Ma groused, dabbing at the cut at my hairline.

We were in the downstairs bathroom where, because she had six boys, Ma had a cabinet of first aid supplies that rivaled that in an ambulance—which had been confirmed by our cousin, Blake, who was an EMT. The cut didn't need stitches, she'd declared, but it had bled like a bastard, and there was gonna be a nice bruise on my forehead too.

"You have too many veins in your forehead," she said, clearing more blood.

"I'm sorry. I'll try to do better next time I'm born," I said sarcastically.

"It's this Canali hair. Takes a lot of blood vessels to support all this hair. It's your father's fault."

I snorted. "We all have your hair, Ma."

"You do not! My hair is reddish."

This was a conceit of my mother's, that her dark hair had

red in it. Which, frankly, it did not. It was as deep, dark brown/black as the rest of us.

"Okay," I said, knowing better than to argue when it involved Ma's vanity.

"Sit still, Mike. Stop fidgeting," she ordered.

"I'm not fidgeting." I made like a statue. And while she worked, my mind wandered, replaying that scene at the tree. I felt like shit that I'd recoiled from Shane when he was just trying to help. Only with my brothers there, Shane touching me and acting all worried about me felt like it laid everything bare. It had been a knee-jerk reaction to pull away, hide.

Which said a lot. I'd acted like a coward, and that didn't bode well for me ever being able to come clean with my brothers. Another reason to feel like shit. What was wrong with me?

"There. Now be more careful," Ma said, giving me a kiss on the forehead, which I normally would have ducked away from, a habit leftover from my teenage years, but it landed this time thanks to my distracted brain.

"Thanks, Ma." I hopped off the counter and looked in the mirror—the butterfly bandage was kind of dashing—and left the bathroom.

Priority one was Shane. I finally found him on the front porch. He was sitting in a rocking chair staring blankly out at our driveway and the woods which surrounded it. I slumped into a chair next to him, biting my lip and wondering if I'd ever stop fucking things up.

"I'm sorry about what happened back there. I… I just overreacted," I said.

"I get it." Shane didn't look at me. His *I get it* seemed to imply more than that incident. It implied he got my whole sorry-ass life.

"Anyway, you stood up to Donny and them. You did good."

He shrugged. "They're not the first people to laugh at

me." He winced. "God, that sounds so victim-y. I just mean I've dealt with their type before. I can handle your brothers."

Yeah, he could. Me, not so much.

"Cool." I sighed. "It's just… weird. Seeing you here. Being around my family. We should go do something somewhere else. Would you want to? Hang out with me sometime?"

Shane pursed his lips. "Well. You have my number."

There was an edge to his voice. Did he think I was just yanking his chain? I had ghosted him before. "I also have you right in front of me. Unless you're a very clever illusion."

That earned me a slightly amused glance.

"So how about tomorrow night?" I suggested. "I'm not on duty again 'til Monday. We could go see a movie or something. I could drive down to Sacramento."

Shane looked at me doubtfully. "Really?"

"Yeah. Totally. You free?"

"I could be…" Shane said slowly. "But not for a movie. How about I pick what we do?"

"Sssure. As long as it doesn't involve public humiliation?" I gave him my best charming smile—and was gratified to see his eyes warm a few degrees.

"So private humiliation is on the table? Good to know."

He was teasing, which meant maybe I was out of the doghouse. My chest opened a little, and I could breathe. Why did his opinion mean so much to me? Maybe because he was a genuinely good guy, and he'd been so brave and smart during the Crest Lake fire. He'd insisted on helping me, even when it put his own life in danger. I really would feel like a heel if I hurt him. But, yeah, that wasn't all there was to it.

We were alone, so I gave in to the urge to study him. Those dark lashes and so-blue eyes, that creamy skin and full lips. Fuck me. Why did I find him so attractive? It wasn't like he was a magazine model. He was just a cute guy, a boy-band type of guy maybe, like a young, gangly Harry Styles with a definitely femme edge. But… damn, everything about him rang my bell—or my two bells and eager clapper. I couldn't be this close to him without wanting, badly, to kiss him.

Just friends, I reminded myself. *Just goddamn friends.*

"What time you want to meet tomorrow?" Shane prompted.

"I could be there at seven?"

"Deal." He took out his phone and texted me his address.

It made me feel so happy. I had a date—no, a friendly meetup—with Shane. In Sacramento. That would be fun. I could really use a fun night out away from the fam.

"So my ma got you to help decorate, huh? She always gets kind of manic when there's a guest she thinks is *important* with a capital I coming over. Like Chief Einnes."

"Yeah. I told her me and Pops didn't need to stay for dinner, but she insisted."

I wasn't sure how I felt about Shane being my mother's personal party decorator. But, if it made them both happy, who was I to complain?

"It's weird how much she likes you."

Shane gave me an insulted raised eyebrow.

"I mean, you're great. But… you know what? Never mind."

"Wise call. Personally, I think she's really desperate for help setting the table."

"No, she does. Like you, I mean." It had been a bit of a surprise how quickly Mom, Nonna, and Tessa had taken to Shane. Was it the Medal of Valor award? The fact that he'd helped me during the Crest Lake fire? Or were they just charmed by him?

Unfortunately, the guys in the family were a different story.

"You're lucky to have a mom like her. You know that, right?" Shane asked, his tone a little dark.

I remembered that his own mom had disowned him for

being gay. My heart gave a sympathetic throb. "Yeah. I am lucky."

Shane stood up and stretched. "That's okay. Donny makes up for it." And with that parting shot, he went inside.

I smiled. Yeah, Shane could hold his own.

Ma made us all put on button-down shirts and slacks for dinner—which we bitched and moaned about. But we did look pretty spiffy as we sat down to a table groaning with Italian beef, fresh rolls, gnocchi, and a suspiciously Shane-looking salad.

Chief Einnes and my dad told stories—some harrowing ones about fires and some ridiculous ones about the crazy shit that went on in fire stations. There was the legendary Sparky, a fire station dalmatian who hated the postman so much that he could escape any room or collar to run out and bite the poor guy. There was that Christmas when some nice neighbor had dropped off gallons of homemade eggnog in the spirit of the holiday—only it was bad, and Dad's entire station vomited for two days straight.

That story never got old. Shane and Pops gasped and laughed along with everyone else.

Chief Einnes turned to Shane and Pops, who were at one end of the table. "So, Shane… I didn't realize you were part of this crazy bunch. Don't tell me you're another feather in Angelo's cap?"

"Oh, no. I can't claim credit for Shane," my dad said quickly. Maybe a little too quickly.

"Yeah, no. Shane's no Canali," said Gabe flatly.

"We're just getting to know Shane!" Mama said brightly. "I invited him over after the award ceremony. He's been a joy to have around. Such a sweetheart. I hope he becomes a regular around here."

"He will. I know," pronounced Luna in her spooky *I know things* voice. She tapped her forehead.

I shared a smile with Tessa. Grandma was hilarious.

"Well isn't that nice," said Margaret, Chief Einnes's wife. "I suppose these boys have a lot in common." She glanced between me and Shane. "Both of them are so brave and willing to help others. It's a rare thing these days."

"Not that rare," Chief Einnes said contrarily. "We have excellent young men in Cal Fire."

"Not saying you don't," Margaret agreed. "But these two are so young. Shane's a civilian. And you only just joined the department, didn't you, Mike?"

"Yes, ma'am, that's true," I said.

"So brave and so sensible too," Ma mused. "Bravery doesn't always come with common sense. Or compassion."

"Or artistic talent," Tessa added, giving Ma a knowing look.

Ma's face lit up. "Yes! Just look at the table. This was all Shane's doing. Like using that old tin pitcher for the roses. That thing's been in the cupboard for thirty years, and I never would have thought of that, but it's perfect. I so envy people who have an eye for mixing and matching. We have a lot to be grateful for in this family, but one thing the Canalis are lacking is artistic talent. Shane's got it in spades."

"If that's what you wanna call it," Donny snarked, aggressively cutting up the beef on his plate.

Gabe snorted. "Or something." He gave Donny a knowing smirk.

I felt my cheeks flame. I picked at my food, hoping the conversation would move on from Shane.

"Oh now, Ma, you're forgetting the masterpieces Tony used to make with seashells," teased Tessa. "There are still bits of shell all over the attic."

"Hey, free materials, baby!" Tony shot back. "Recycling. I was into the green movement before it was hip."

Tessa rolled her eyes. "It's been hip since at least the 70s. You're not that old."

"I was there that day. At Crest Lake," Pops said loudly.

He'd been so quiet all through dinner. He looked pointedly at Donny and Gabe. "Both Mike and Shane put a whole lot of strangers' lives before their own. I doubt any other firefighter could have done as well, no matter how long they've served."

"I agree with you there." Chief Einnes nodded. "Cool heads under pressure. They deserve all the accolades."

Pa patted my shoulder, his face proud. "Mike always has been one of the most level-headed of my sons. Follows his own star and doesn't bow to pressure. Why, when he was just a little tyke, his brothers had him referee their games."

"Oh, man! I remember that!" grinned Tony. "You took it so damned seriously, Mikey."

Donny laughed. "Yeah, Pa. That was so we didn't have to have him on our teams."

I gasped in outrage. "What?"

Donny waved a hand. "Come on. You were, like, five. You're the baby of the family, so you don't know what it's like having a little kid who always wants to play and slows down the game. Making you the referee was a stroke of genius. Anyway, you loved it."

"That's not the only reason," Pa countered. "Mikey made a great referee. He stayed focused on the game like his life depended on it, and when he had to make a call, he was always sharp and fair to a fault. I wish we had refs like him in the major leagues."

Donny looked ready to barf, so I gave him a serene smile.

"I can see that," Shane put in, studying my face. "What is that verse? *And a little child shall lead them*. I can picture five-year-old Mike blowing a whistle and doing that arm motion thing. Oh, for video!"

"There is no video." I gave him a faux glare, then smiled.

"You know your Bible, Shane?" My mother looked impressed.

Shane fidgeted. "Uh... My parents took us to church a lot when I was little."

Oh, no. Don't ask about Shane's family.

Saved by the bell. From the front hall came the sound of the front door opening and closing.

Nonna spoke up. "That's Tito!" She pointed to her forehead and said to Margaret in a confidential whisper, "I have the sight."

Ma harrumphed. "Nonsense, Nonna. We're a good Catholic family." This was so clearly for the benefit of Chief Einnes and his wife that I had to bite back a smile.

Carlotta walked into the dining room.

"Damn," Nonna muttered.

Everyone greeted Carlotta, and Ma introduced her to the chief and his wife.

"Nice to meet you," Carlotta said. "I'm so sorry to interrupt. I thought sure you'd be done with dinner by now." She eyed the table longingly.

Ma sighed. "Get yourself a plate. There's plenty. You can squeeze onto this corner by me."

"Oh no! I wouldn't dream of it. I can eat in the kitchen." She got a plate and proceeded to walk around the table, loading it from the various dishes while Dad and Chief Einnes talked about a recent referee call Dad was still pissed off about.

Carlotta leaned past Margaret to get some garlic bread and said, "What a lovely green sweater. It reminds me of the ocean. I bet you're an Aquarius, aren't you?"

"Me?" Margaret blinked. "Uh... Scorpio, actually."

"Carlotta's joking." Ma waved her hand and shot Carlotta a warning look.

After dinner, Shane and Pops got ready to leave. I hadn't had a chance to talk to Pops yet, so I went and shook his hand.

"Glad you could join us," I said. "You're looking a lot better than the last time I saw you." He was much pinker and less gray and drawn than he'd been that day of the fire.

"You too, son."

"Were you able to salvage anything from your place?"

Pops grimaced. "Eh. Our building was one of the few to survive. Maybe it's because the building is so damned old and ugly even the fire wouldn't touch it." He laughed. "But there's nothing up there now. All the businesses burned down or closed, and it looks and smells like a hellscape in town. I've been staying with Shane."

"Oh. I'm glad to hear you didn't lose your things."

He shrugged. "To be honest, I wouldn't miss most of it if I never saw it again. But it'll come in handy when I go to get my own place. Once I figure out where."

"No hurry," Shane said stubbornly.

I smiled. "Well, nice to see you again, Pops. Talk to you soon—" This last was to Shane, and we shared a secretive look that had me smiling all the way back to the little house I shared with Donny.

I'd just kicked off my shoes and unbuttoned that torturous button-down shirt when Gabe and Donny came in.

"Hey. We need to talk," Gabe said seriously.

"About what?" I wandered into the kitchen, needing a beer.

We all grabbed one from the fridge and stood around our small kitchen, taking the first sip. The cottage had been built by Pa and Gabe years ago, with some help from contractors. The cabinets were pine, the appliances plain white, and the whole place was bland and messy, given that neither Donny nor I were into decorating or, you know, cleaning.

Donny and Gabe shared a look. "It's about Shane. Is he gonna keep coming over here or what?"

"Yeah," Donny said. "He's not part of the family."

I rubbed the back of my neck. Great. I wasn't exactly surprised by this ambush, but I wasn't in the mood for it either. "I don't know if he will or not, but you see how Ma's taken to him. If she keeps inviting him, then I guess he'll keep coming."

"Ma doesn't get it," Gabe said with a sneer.

"Yeah, she's totally naïve," Donny agreed.

"What is it that Ma doesn't get?" I demanded, though I knew exactly what they were talking about.

"That he's a fag," Gabe said with exasperation.

"Yeah, she thinks he's just *artistic* or something," Donny snorted.

"Maybe he is," I challenged. "Just artistic."

"Oh come on," said Gabe. "That guy is so light in the loafers, he's practically flying."

"I can guarantee he wasn't *flying* the day he earned the Medal of Valor with me," I shot back.

Donny got an angry frown. "Come on! I saw him at that barricade. He was fucking crying. However it went down out there, I'm sure it was ninety-nine percent you."

"No, it wasn't!" I was getting ticked off. "Shane could have stayed at the boat rentals with his grandfather. I *told* him to stay there, that it wasn't safe. But he insisted on going back with me to warn the others. He was out in that choking smoke every second as long as I was, running to cars and telling people to go to the lake. You could *feel* the fire coming. I really thought we were gonna die. Pops was right. He was just as brave that day as anyone in the fire department, so don't run your mouth about things you know nothing about. You don't fucking know shit." My voice was rising along with my temper.

"Okay, okay." Gabe held up his hands. "I get it. He did good that day, and you feel obligated."

"I don't feel *obligated*. I like him. There's nothing fucking wrong with Shane. We can be friends with different kinds of people, you know. Not everyone has to be like us."

Donny's frown grew. "I have different kinds of friends."

"Yeah, like biker chicks and meth addicts, your floozy girl-friend being exhibit A. Real classy there, Donny."

"Shut up!" Donny said, taking offense.

"Both of you shut up," Gabe barked. "Don't get off the fucking subject. Mike, I get it. You guys, like, bonded over that fire incident. I worked with guys on the force that I wouldn't exactly wanna hang out with in real life, but they're solid work buddies. But the rest of us, we don't have that link to Shane. Okay? So we don't want someone like him hanging out here all the time like he's part of the family or something."

"Yeah, like he's part of the family or something," Donny echoed.

"And people start seeing him as one of us. Like Einnes at dinner, man. That's not cool."

"We don't want a queer in the family," Donny said flatly.

Fuck. That hit deep. I took a long draw from my beer and stared at the fridge, swallowing down the sharp pain in my chest. I wasn't gonna let them see it.

"Mike?" Gabe said.

I shook my head. "It's Ma and Pa's house. Whaddya want me to do about it? I'm not in charge of Ma's social calendar."

"You could talk to Shane. Edge him away from coming over here," Donny suggested.

I gritted my teeth and swallowed hard. I never took a stand against my brothers.

Maybe it was time I did.

"Well, Ma wants him here. And Tessa. And *me*. So I guess you guys are just gonna have to learn to deal with it." I threw my bottle in the sink and stalked out of the house, slamming the door good and hard behind me.

SEVEN

SHANE

"Oh my god, when is he going to get here? I'm so excited." Winston's soft Jamaican syllables surrounded us as he literally bounced in his chair, and Chas put an arm around his shoulders.

"Soon enough, love."

Roland gave me that stare again. "You're sure about this? He's not going to walk in here, take one look at us, and run screaming for his macho buds to—" He waved a hand. "—I don't know, go out and chop down a tree or something?"

I huffed out a breath and put on my *patient* face. I was realizing maybe I told Ro too much about Mike. "No, of course I'm not sure about this, and I have no idea what Mike's going to do. I told him I was choosing the activity tonight, and I told him to wear *hitting the town* clothes. He said he didn't have any. I told him to improvise." I released a breath as softly as I could manage. "That's all I know. News bulletin complete."

Roland shook his head. "You should have gone for the movie, Shane. Easy peasy."

"No. I shouldn't have." I tapped the side of my glass, looking for the words to explain what I felt. I shifted in my seat. "I've been in Mike's world—at least the family part of it. The poor guy's surrounded by men who think sweats are the height of fashion and watching football together is the best way to spend a weekend. Do you guys remember what it was like the first time you went to a place where gays were just out and free?"

Winston sighed, his face lighting up. "Yes, ma'am. I was sixteen, and my friend and I snuck out of our rooms and walked two miles to catch a bus to the city and a gay club. I thought I'd died and gone to heaven—and that's no exaggeration."

"I remember," Chas nodded. "I was older, but, yeah, it was completely eye-opening."

"I want to give Mike that," I admitted. "How can he ever find himself if he only has his dad and macho brothers as an example of what's possible in the world?"

Winston sniffled. "Stop it. You're gonna make me cry. He's just a gayby!"

"Or he could just hate you for pushing him out of his comfort zone," Roland said cheerfully, taking a sip of his rum and Coke. He stared toward the door of the Rusty Scupper, the bar where we were all meeting up. This was the door through which Mike Canali would presumably walk at any minute. I'd given Mike directions to the bar, but hadn't told him it was only a waystation on the road to the real destination. Ro muttered, "I don't know why you're so wound up over this guy. I mean how *all that* can he be?"

"You didn't have to come, Ro." Yes, he was trying my patience, and I had little to spare. I had no idea how Mike would react to my plans for the evening, and Ro's chiding was getting on my last nerve. I knew he was just being protective, but I couldn't deal at the moment.

"The myth, the legend... Mike Canali. I wouldn't have missed it," he snarked.

Ro just might have gotten a Cosmo in his lap, but at that moment, the real Mike Canali did in fact walk through the door, glancing around anxiously. Oh wow. He'd translated my request to dress up into black jeans and a tight black T-shirt that he'd covered with a Sherpa-lined jean jacket, hanging open. The ensemble was butch as hell and looked mighty fine with his dark hair and eyes and killer bod. Be still, my gay boy heart.

Across the table, Winston turned his head toward the door, his lips parted, and he whispered, "Oh my." Winston, who set new records in femme, loved super-masc guys, as was evidenced by his honey, Chas, an ex-NFL tight end. But as Winston was first to point out, he might be attached but wasn't blind, and his level of aesthetic appreciation was profound.

Even though my heart beat like a Lil Nas anthem, I had to smile at Ro. Snarky and protective or not, his eyes were popping out of his head right then. "Holy shit, Shane. Your hang-up on this guy? Totally, totally get it now."

I stood and waved at Mike, who smiled hesitantly and made his way through the people lined up at the bar toward our table in the back. As he got closer, I blinked and saw our group from his point of view. For a club night, I was positively lowkey in tight pink jeans and a see-through silver shirt, but I'd covered it with a white button-down dress shirt for camouflage. Yes, the Rusty Scupper was used to having some clubbers among their clientele. After all, it was in Lavender Heights, but most of the people in there were cishet, and shoving queerness down their throats was frowned upon. Chas also looked like a regular guy in his black leather jacket and blue jeans. Old Levi Strauss could be used to cover a multitude of sins. Ro hadn't taken off his trench coat, so heaven only knew what it concealed. But then there was Winston. Even at two p.m. on a Tuesday, in the law library of the firm where he was a partner, Winston just stuck out with his beautiful halo of black hair and painted nails.

Suddenly, I was second-guessing all this. The truth was I still really wanted Mike to like me, and this night could nix any chance of that for good. Hell, I hadn't needed Ro's needling to make me worry.

But I was committed now. I sighed softly. Besides, if he couldn't like me like this, he couldn't like me. Better to know now.

Mike arrived at the table where I was still standing. If I was nervous, he looked terrified, and my compassion overcame my butterflies. I tried to sound casual. "Hey, Mike, I wanted you to meet some of my friends. This is Roland, or Ro, my best friend from school."

Ro waved a hand at him, still staring wide-eyed, and Mike nodded.

I pointed across the table. "That's Chas, who I also met in school. He's getting a master's in English literature so he can teach."

Chas held out a fist, and Mike bumped it, looking fairly comfortable with the hunky guy.

I continued. "And that's Winston. He's a lawyer and Chas's significant other."

Winston stood—and stood and stood, revealing six-foot-five of willowy perfection encased in a gold lamé sheath over skin-tight dark jeans. His curled hair almost concealed the gold earrings that hung to his shoulders. He extended a graceful hand with brilliant red fingernails and said in his island lilt, "Aren't you a sight for sore eyes?"

Mike took Winston's hand and gently shook it. "Pleased to meet you." I could actually see his pulse thumping in his neck, but he smiled. "I'm glad to meet Shane's friends."

Well good for him. Making a real effort. I refrained from

kicking Ro under the table since Mike was clearly not running screaming from anyone.

Mike sat in the empty chair we'd left next to me. "Sorry I'm late. I didn't leave enough time to find parking. I'm not real familiar with the, uh, Lavender Heights area of Sac."

Winston rested his chin on his hand and fluttered inch-long lashes. "Welcome home, honey."

"Uh, thanks." Mike's Adam's apple jumped, but his smile was genuine.

He pulled off his jacket, showing off that torso that made my happy gay cock do a Charleston, and finally turned his head and met my gaze. Maybe wishful thinking, but his expression softened. "Hi."

"Hi." Be still my foolish heart. "Want a drink while you can still hear yourself think?"

"What?" He cocked his head.

"You'll see."

The waitress appeared and smiled at Mike way too warmly to suit me. "Hey, handsome. What can I get you?"

"Beer's fine. Whatever's on tap." He looked right back at me even though she was blonde and pretty, which I, of course, ate up. I might have preened a little.

Chas said, "So I hear you're a firefighter. Must be a tough job."

"Yeah, but I like it." He shrugged.

Ro's eyebrows shot up. "Really? What do you like about it?"

Mike looked thoughtful. "I originally studied fire science in school mostly because it's a family tradition, but when I actually got into the field, I found out it's a special kind of challenge." He cringed like he thought he sounded dorky. "It's hard to explain."

Chas jumped in. "No, that's interesting. In what way special?" He seemed genuinely interested.

The waitress brought Mike's beer, and he murmured,

"Thanks," but he didn't even look at her. To Chas, he said, "Well, we spend a certain amount of time doing nothing, especially in the winter, but when we're actually fighting a fire, it's like you can't think about anything else. It's one-hundred percent riveting. Consuming."

Ro said, "Otherwise the fire consumes you, right?"

"Exactly. Not everyone wants to put themselves in life-and-death situations on purpose, but that's what the job is, and I found out I like it. Your brain goes into this intense problem-solving mode, and every crackle and flare of the flames is like a piece of a big puzzle."

"A puzzle that can kill you, hmm?" That statement in Winston's lilting voice made me shiver.

Mike nodded. "Absolutely. Every little detail becomes important since it can become a big problem."

"Quatti buy chubble, hunjed poun'cyaan pay farri."

We all stared at Winston and the interesting sounds coming out of his mouth. Only Chas looked a little clued in.

He said, "Winston has about a million old Jamaican proverbs he loves to quote."

I asked, "What does it mean, Winston?"

In his perfectly modulated speech, Winston said, "It means a penny can buy trouble that a hundred pounds can't pay for."

Mike's face lit up. "Wow. That's it exactly. What a great proverb."

Winston smiled. "My Jamaican mama had a great deal of wisdom." He leaned back in his chair, and his smile tightened. "Unfortunately, my Jamaican papa had no use for a battyboy like me."

Chas slid an arm around Winston and gave him a hug. "And that's how you became one of the best civil rights lawyers in California."

Winston nuzzled against Chas. "Mi luv yuh."

I glanced at Mike. Interestingly, he gazed at Winston and

Chas with an intrigued expression and a funny little smile. Then he let out a breath that seemed to stir us all to action.

Roland said, "Okay, boys and girls, time to get the proverbial show on the road. We've got worlds to conquer." He gave Mike a quick glance as he slid money on the table.

We all did the same, but Mike looked at me questioningly.

I said, "This was just our meeting place. We're moving on."

Mike glanced around but pulled money from his pocket and put it on the table like the rest of us, chugged the last of his beer. and then pulled his jacket back on over his T-shirt.

Ro led the pack, his trench coat swishing, and Winston and Chas followed. I motioned for Mike to go ahead of me, and I brought up the rear of the line.

By the time I got outside, Ro was already preparing to dodge traffic to get across the street to where the action was. He waved at us and started to run. I grabbed Mike's arm and pulled him with me, a couple cars honking their displeasure at us as we hauled ass.

When we hit the other sidewalk, he snorted at me. "I think it's a good thing I'm working on my EMT."

I just grinned at him and stepped closer. People crowded the space in front of our destination, some in small groups and some in a line. There were a few that appeared to be female, but most were male or nonbinary, and some of their outfits made Winston look tame. Coats and jackets covered the most outrageous—or bare—bits, but heavy makeup, glitter, and teased hair were everywhere.

Ro, Winston, Chas, and I were super familiar with the drill. Chas led the way to the giant guy at the door. He reached out a fist toward the doorman AKA bouncer that I knew had a fifty in it, or maybe more, and said, "Hey, Bruce."

"Oh hi, Chas. Great to see you." The fist bump became a bill transfer, and Bruce unfastened the rope in front of the door and let the five of us through, ignoring the grumbling of the people behind us.

Mike gave me a wide-eyed look.

I said, "Chas was a pretty well-known football player a couple years ago. He still has a lot of fans."

"Fifty-dollar bills have a bunch of fans too." Ro grinned.

I nodded. "You need both the clout and the bread to get in this place."

Mike glanced around. "Where are we?" We'd stepped into a small lobby where a coat check was doing big business. Through the double doors, guarded by another big man, sounded the thumping of a bass.

"The club is called *Friend of Dorothy* in honor of one of the code words gay men used to identify themselves back in the day. I think you'll like it. It'll give you a feel for the culture without being too cray-cray." I hoped.

"The culture?"

I shrugged. "Gay culture. Your community. Your people."

He nodded. "Got it." But boy did he look like he wanted to run back to Resolute. "So, an *educational* night then."

I gripped his arm, and for a second, he slid his hand over mine as I guided him. I tried not to read anything into it, but it sure felt nice.

We dropped our coats at the coat check, handed the cute twink a five to hold them, and headed toward the double doors where Ro, Winston, and Chas stood. I grinned because boy, did they look different. I hadn't been that much of a surprise to Mike I was sure, since he'd seen me in tight jeans and shiny stuff before, though his eyes had lingered on my chest in my sheer blouse. Ro was dressed pretty much like me, though he wore silver tights rather than jeans, and his shirt was silver mesh. Winston had taken off his jeans and donned five-inch heels that put him at a towering six-foot-nine of gorgeous legs and shimmering lamé, a regular Diana

Ross, size extra-large. Even Chas was nearly half a foot shorter.

But while he might not have been the tallest in our group, oh my, Chas was the most spectacular. Somewhere in that cloakroom, he'd ditched his jeans and jacket. Now, dressed in a blue leather bikini and harness that showed off his ripped body, Chas had stepped away from the regular macho guy image he'd displayed across the street and was likely the cause of the streak of hot pink on Mike's cheekbones.

Ro yelled, "Ready to party?"

The big man opened one of the doors, and we filed in.

Whoa.

I considered *Friend of Dorothy* to be one of my more middle-of-the road clubs in that it wasn't all leather daddies, BDSM types, or a full-on drag scene. This club had something for everyone. What it didn't have were tons of drugs or a dark room. Sure, there were hookups in the johns, but mostly, the club was about dancing and good fun. Still, looking around, it was likely a lot for somebody used to the Resolute Café.

Straight ahead and up a few steps, there was a demonstration dance floor where the really good dancers, including professionals who were in shows around town, showed off their skills. A couple steps down from that floor and surrounding it was the regular dance floor, crowded with bodies as Mykki Blanco's "Free Ride" thumped through the sound system.

Yeah. It was a lot.

Mike hung back toward the door as if the wall of music, smell of sweat and perfume, and the waving arms were pushing him there by psychic force.

Well crap. I'd brought the man here with some vaguely formed ideas of showing him the world he could inhabit if he wanted to, or, at least, that all kinds of people were queer, but what the fuck did I do now? If he didn't have hitting-the-town clothes, then maybe he couldn't dance. And even if he could, me taking him out on the floor promised new milestones in totally awkward. Jesus. I didn't want to leave him, but....

Walking out of the crowd like some kind of regal ancient queen, Winston stalked toward me. No. Make that toward Mike.

Mike's eyes literally bugged out, but Winston kept coming. When he got to Mike, he held out a bejeweled hand.

As if facing a force greater than the Dixie fire, Mike succumbed, took Winston's hand, and walked into the heat of the dance floor. I stared, utterly mesmerized.

Ro came bounding up like a silver puppy. "Come on, bestie. Let's dance."

I held up a finger. "Wait. I've got to see this."

Winston could be spotted in any crowd, and Mike was tall enough that I could see him above most of the bodies. I took a few steps closer, and Ro followed.

For a second, Mike just stood there staring at Winston, but Winston began to move. Not complicated, which I knew he could do, but simple steps. Hips moving, arms weaving, Winston smiled.

Mike smiled back and moved too. Not exactly Fred Astaire, but hellfire, pretty darned good. His hips led the way, and his feet followed, sliding sinuously around Winston, looking over his shoulder, that gorgeous smile flashing.

Ro said, "Son of a bitch, who'da thought?"

"Yeah." But weirdly, my enthusiasm was dampened by a stab of jealousy.

"Come on." Ro grabbed my arm and pulled me into the crowd, though I tried to keep my eyes on Mike and Winston, which was making for complicated dance patterns.

Ro huffed and danced away with another guy, leaving me on the floor staring at Mike until two other men grabbed me and pulled me into their dance.

The music stopped, and I paused, staring to see what

Mike would do. Yes, I was hoping he'd come toward me or at least look for me. But before anything else could happen, a really hot guy in black jeans like Mike's and a plain white shirt that hung open over his bare chest walked up to Mike, said something, and they began dancing as soon as the music started up again.

Okay, Winston was one thing, but gorgeous strangers turned out to be quite another. Yes, I'd wanted Mike to experience all kinds of people being gay or some stripe of queer, but the reality? Not quite so altruistic.

A guy started dancing with me, and I moved along as an excuse, but that's all it was. I practically counted the beats until the damned song ended, my heart thudding sickly and little green devils dancing in my brain. I wasn't a violent man. Uhh. Right. But Mr. Bare Chest might have to watch himself in dark alleys.

EIGHT

MIKE

Holy shit. This was wild! And also? I needed a lot more alcohol. Right now.

I'd never been to a gay club before. When I drove to the city—Sac or San Francisco, I always had someone with me, usually Donny, and he wanted to go to a sports bar. When I'd been at Butte College, one of the best schools in the area for fire science, everyone there knew my family since all my brothers had gone there too. So I couldn't exactly get my freak on there either.

Hell, I didn't even know I *had* a freak. I still wasn't entirely sure—definitely not compared to most of the people in this place. But it was possible I had a baby freak. And it was possible it was waking up at this moment.

Winston danced up next to me with his partner, Chas. The gesture reminded me of my brothers—he was keeping an eye on me, in a protective sort of way. That was the *only* way he reminded me of my brothers, though. I'd thought Shane was flamboyant, but he was nothing compared to Winston. The guy was well over six feet, and under his finery he might have looked masculine, yet he wore heels and makeup and feminine clothes. He was a walking reminder that anybody could be gay. He'd weirded me out at first, truthfully, but his eyes were kind, and he had a soft edge to him that was so likeable. And the way he watched out for me here at the club was really sweet, considering the fact that he didn't know me at all, and he had his own partner to focus on. Yes, I liked Winston.

As we danced—me with a hot stranger in black jeans and a white shirt over an impressive six-pack— I stole glances at Winston and Chas. A feeling crept up on me, warming me, that I realized was admiration. Winston had the courage to be exactly the way he wanted to be, regardless of what anyone else thought. And regardless of how it fit or didn't fit the body he was born with. That took major cojones. And Chas... he obviously didn't feel the need to match Winston. He just did his own thing. Both of them were completely comfortable in their skin. Of course, this was a gay club, so they were probably dressed up for it. But it was hard to imagine Winston conformed very much in his real life. And I'd bet Chas didn't hide the fact that he was dating a big, effeminate gay man.

Yeah, but they live in Sacramento, not the Canali family compound in Resolute.

That excuse didn't entirely ring true, though. Or maybe it didn't make their self-confidence any less impressive—just more enviable.

The guy I was dancing with got my attention by grabbing at my ass and pulling me in for a grind, his eyes promising anything I wanted. He was good-looking, but I wasn't feeling it.

Before I could extricate myself, Shane was there. He stared daggers at the guy I was dancing with and shouted over the music. "Can I cut in?"

The hot guy sort of sneered, like he wouldn't move, but

when I grabbed Shane's hand and turned to him, Hot Guy got the hint and moved off.

"Hey!" I gave Shane a big smile. I'd been so distracted by Chas and Winston, I hadn't taken a good look at him without his coat, but now, under the club's colored lights, I noticed I could see his slender chest and nipples under a see-through shirt in a silvery color. And his jeans were practically painted on. I couldn't help staring. Heat pooled in places the Hot Guy had left cold. Oh, yes. Shane was much more my type. Noted. For research purposes only.

Shane spun around as "Juice" by Lizzo played, and I managed to get my eyeballs back into my head. *Chill, Mike. It's not like you've never seen nipples before.*

Shane shimmied at me, arms out, his expression amused, and I did my best to copy him and shimmy too. I put my hands behind my head and did it again.

Shane laughed and leaned in to be heard. "Smooth moves!"

I shook my head. I was no dancer. But I was drunk. Or semi-drunk. On third thought, I was not nearly drunk enough. I took Shane's elbow and jerked my head. "Let's get a drink."

He nodded, and we made our way to the edge of the dance floor. I signaled a passing waiter, and he gave me an appreciative onceover and a smile. "What can I get you?"

I needed something with a serious kick. "A boilermaker!" I looked at Shane, eyebrows raised. "It's on me."

"Cosmo," he shouted at the guy.

The waiter took off, and we stood there and watched the dancers.

Shane leaned close to me so he could talk in my ear. "Is this okay?"

I hesitated a moment, then nodded. "Yeah. It's pretty cool. Thanks for bringing me. I've never been to a gay club."

"You don't say." Shane pulled back far enough to give me an amused look.

I shrugged. It was too noisy in here to list all my excuses out loud.

"Cute guy you were dancing with," Shane said, studying my face.

I gazed over the crowd and saw Hot Guy. He was dancing with a redhead now, but his gaze was fixed on me. I shrugged.

"Just, uh, you know, have a good time," Shane said, still close enough I felt his breath on my ear.

What was he suggesting? I glanced at Shane, who seemed to be working hard to keep his expression neutral, and then my gaze stayed on Hot Guy for a moment. But no. The idea of getting laid tonight was tempting. God knew it had been a dry spell what with my training and the fire season in full swing. And between the beer, the dancing, and the visual and mental stimulation, my body was a prickling, tingling, horny energy ball. But I was here with a group, and I liked them. I liked them a lot. I thought maybe we could all be friends. Tessa was right. I needed friends outside my bubble. I could be myself with them—or at least, I could once I figured out who I was in a scene like this. I wanted that. I wanted to figure out who *gay Mike* was, and I knew this was the path to do it. I didn't want to leave a bad impression on this potential new tribe by dumping them to run off with a hookup the first time we'd gone out together.

I inhaled.

Okay, truth. My horniness at the moment, and for the past few weeks, was about Shane. Shane with those eyes so clear and gorgeous and knowing. I didn't want to hook up with another guy in front of Shane, even though we were supposed to just be friends. Looking at Shane, everyone else in this club faded into the background.

I shook my head. "I'm just here to have fun."

Shane was about to say something when our drinks arrived. I tossed back the shot and took a big swallow of the beer to wash it down. Then I chugged the rest of the beer in a few gulps. I was tempted to order another. I really wanted to feel loose tonight, forget everything. But I didn't want to overshoot it and end up stupid-drunk.

Shane sipped his drink, gaze roaming the crowd. It occurred to me that *he* might be wanting to hook up tonight. A slick of icy dread washed through me. Fuck that!

"Let's dance!" I leaned in close until his dark hair tickled my cheek.

He gave a tiny eye roll at my impatience and downed his drink, setting his glass on a table with a pointed thud. I grinned, grabbed his hand, and tugged him onto the dance floor.

We staked out a spot next to Winston and Chas.

I waited for the alcohol to kick in and realized it already had since my moves felt smoother and more natural. Roland joined us with a guy wearing a leather chest harness, a bushy beard, a friendly smile, and very little else. The six of us danced to "Bad Romance," "All for You," and "Heaven is a Place on Earth," and I lost myself. With every beat of the bass, some tightly wound coil inside me slipped another fraction of an inch. When the crowd threw up their hands and chanted *They say in Heaven, love comes first,* I did, too, totally into it.

Your culture. Your community. Your people. Shane's words wove in and out of my mind, chased by the music. My people.

Were these really my people? I'd always thought of my people as my whole, extended family, the Canalis, AKA the Hot Cannolis—we were a tribe. And then firefighters in general. But maybe they weren't my people. Or, at least, not my *only* people.

I looked around. This tribe—gay, queer, LGBTQ of all sorts. That was me too. But I'd always been pretty much alone with that. Alone inside my family. Alone inside the world, other than the few times I'd hooked up with someone or gone out for a few hours—in a much smaller way than this—before going back inside the closet and turning the key once it was over.

Was this really who I was? This? I looked at this crowd, seeing them through Donny's eyes. He'd say they were aberrant freaks. But perspective was everything, isn't it? It *was* a culture, just like the firefighter's culture. Or cosplayers, or anything, really. They dressed up and egged each other on to be more and more outrageous and came to places like this, where such outrageousness was celebrated.

And why not? There was something powerful in saying, *this is who I am: I'm queer, and I'm fucking happy about it!*

I could see it and appreciate it, even envy it. But was it really me? Mike Canali? Angelo's son? A proud member of Cal Fire—tough guys, public servants, heroes.

I felt a twinge of yearning for it, an ache of want at the idea of having a place where I could be anything I wanted, go as far with my desires and kinks as I cared to go, without judgment. But what would be the cost? Would I have to give up my family? The brand-new career I'd wanted all my life? That was never going to happen. I loved my family, and I was damned lucky to have them. They were a gift few people got in this world. And I wanted a life in Cal Fire too.

Was there a place for me somewhere in between?

Shane grabbed my hand and yanked hard to get me to look at him. He was frowning. "Stop thinking!" he mouthed.

Oops. Yeah. My groove had slowed down considerably. I shook my head. I didn't have to decide anything tonight, didn't have to do anything except get drunk and enjoy myself for once.

The music changed to Eric Clapton's "Wonderful Tonight." A few dancers left the floor, and the rest coupled up. On impulse, more to stop my churning brain than anything else, I pulled Shane close to me, my arm going around him and pressing my palm to the center of his back, his chest grazing mine. I froze at the sensation. Part of me wanted to make it a momentary hug and back off again, laugh it off. But I couldn't make my hands let him go. Not when the music was sweet in my ear, and Shane was so warm in my arms.

With aching slowness, Shane's arms slid up to my shoulders, and both my arms went around him, settling in. This was fine. I could have this. It didn't mean anything. Everyone was doing it. I closed my eyes, wanting to focus on the feel of him—the light brush of his chest, his palms warm on my shoulders, the humid heat that radiated off him, the tang of cranberry juice and sweat and something earthy and warm.

His presence in my arms felt so natural and at the same time so important, monumental. My chest grew tight.

Another eye-opening thing about tonight? In a group of five super nice and attractive gay men, and an entire club full of every type of man you could think of, Shane was still the one I wanted. He was the one temptation that could follow me out this door and be more than a quick means to get off. The one shining star that wanted to burrow under my skin and stay there. Maybe it was just because I knew him. I knew he was funny and smart and brave and resourceful, that he loved his grandfather—that he loved books and words. Maybe it was only that familiarity... but I doubted it.

He liked me, too, even if he was annoyed at me a lot. Holding him like this, I could feel the emotion in the slight tremble of his touch, in the way his body seemed to arc toward mine. I remembered the way he laid against me in that canoe, his face pressed to my chest, warm and surrendered. Which made me remember his kiss—how good it had been, how perfect. The sweetness of his taste. The sensual sucking of his mouth.

Oh fuck.

I put my hands on his waist and moved him back a little, just enough so our chests weren't touching, and he didn't feel my reaction. I swallowed hard.

His gaze met mine. Those incredible, amazingly clear eyes of his had gone a darker navy, and they told me he wanted to be kissed again, very much. I wanted to obey. I looked away over the crowd, my hands gripping him a little harder—more in warning than in passion.

Shane was now friends with my family. With my sister Tessa, my mother, my grandmother, for God's sake. And he came to the family compound. Being with him, starting up something with him, would be so fucking complicated. We'd have to hide it around my family. Would I be able to pretend? Would he? And would he hate me for it?

Just take it slow. It's okay. You can be friends for now.

My father always said, *You don't have to jump into the deep end.*

No, I didn't. Shane was opening up a new world for me. A chance to explore this side of myself. I wanted it so much, suddenly, that I could hardly breathe. But we could take it one step at a time, couldn't we? That would be the smart thing to do. The wise thing. Oh wisdom, thy name is Canali. Ha!

The music ended, and I dropped my hold on Shane and turned to the others in our group with a big smile. "I need another boilermaker. Anybody else?"

NINE

SHANE

I raced out of my advanced composition class and down the stairs of the building toward the parking lot, focused on getting home to make tacos for Pops and me. The buzz in my hip pocket made me stop and grab for my phone.

Uhh, yeah. It was Lucille Canali. I hadn't seen her, or any of the other members of the clan, since that dinner with Chief Einnes and his wife. She'd invited me to Sunday dinner the week after that, but I had tests I had to cram for and an editing job to do, so I'd declined. But what I lacked in Canali family communication I was making up in Mike contact. We'd been out three times in the past two weeks. That wasn't quite as exciting as it sounded, since it had always been with Ro, Winston, and Chas, but I was thrilled that Mike thought so highly of my friends. And we'd all had fun at the Halloween bash at Friend of Dorothy. All of this, however, I was pretty damned sure, no one in the Canali family was aware of, and it made me antsy. Where Mike told his family he'd been on his nights out, I hadn't asked, and he hadn't volunteered. But what if Lucille were to question me on that topic and wanted to know where Mike was and what he was—

Crap! I clicked the phone fast before it went to voicemail. "Hi, Lucille. I just this second walked out of class."

"Hi, Shane, dear. You're so busy. We haven't talked in ages."

Oh good. Maybe she just wanted to chat. "I know. I'm so sorry. How are you? How's the fam?"

She took a breath, and my stomach did a flip. "That's why I called, actually. Uh, you remember my son Gabe? The oldest?"

"Oh, yes, of course." The one, along with Donny, most likely to look at me like a pink powder puff covered in dogshit. I wasn't about to forget.

"Well, you see, Gabe is a policeman, but he's been studying IT, and he's hoping to get a job connected to the police department, but not actually on patrol."

"That sounds interesting." I had no idea if it was.

"The problem, dear, is he needs a really good résumé, and none of us are writers." She gave a little chortle. "So, of course, I thought of you."

Me and Gabe? Holy shit! Not a match made in heaven.

She rushed on. "I mean, I know you're so busy, but he could come to you in the city, or you can come to dinner Sunday, and you can help Gabe rather than letting Tessa wrangle you into working in the kitchen."

As if it was *Tessa* who wrangled me into things. Lucille was hilarious. But anyway, the prospect of being closed in a room with that sneering alpha male made my palms sweat. Still, I'd have a reason to be there. Not like I'd have to come up with small talk. *How about them Giants? Yeah. No.* "Uh, does Gabe know you're asking me to help him?"

She spoke softly, like she might have people around her. "No dear. I don't want him to get his hopes up if you're not available."

Yup. Totally hilarious. "Tell you what. How about you ask him if he wants my help. I, uh, wouldn't want to embarrass him."

"Oh, Shane, you're so thoughtful. I wish I could teach all my boys to be so considerate. Okay, I'll tell him, but I'm sure he's going to be thrilled."

And I was sure he would vomit at the mere suggestion.

"Thank you. Thank you, Shane. I'll call you as soon as I hear from him!" She sounded so excited, like she'd won a sweepstakes or something. She hung up.

I chuckled as Mable and I negotiated the few blocks to my apartment. Hell, I was so sure it wasn't going to happen, I didn't even bother to tell Pops.

———

"I can't believe you're going to spend the next couple hours with Gabe. Shit, Shane, be really careful what you say, okay? You know what he's like." Mike's voice rang tinnily on my cell phone from where it lay on the passenger seat of the car. Yes, I *was* driving to Resolute for dinner with the Canalis. Yes, I *was* about to consult with Gabe Canali on his fucking résumé, assuming he didn't shove it into my dark and intimate recesses before then.

Mike huffed, "I can't believe you didn't talk to me about this before promising my mother."

My hands gripped the steering wheel. I hadn't considered how Mike would feel about this arrangement, but in truth, I never dreamed he'd be this weirded out. It wasn't helping my own nerves. "I was so sure he'd say no when she asked him if he wanted to work with me. I never gave it much thought."

"She never told him."

"What?" It was a good thing there was no one behind me as I drove through the little town of Resolute because my foot stomped the brake reflexively.

"She told him she'd called in an expert. He was desperate for help, so he agreed. It wasn't until today she told him the expert was you."

"Great! That's perfect. Maybe I shouldn't come?"

Mike paused long enough that I was looking for a place to turn around. Then he said, sounding resigned, "No. He really does need help. I know you can do a way better job than any of the knuckleheads around here."

"Your words say *yes*, but your tone says *danger, Will Robinson!*"

He chuckled. "I'm sorry. I'm just—shit, I'm feeling paranoid. Gabe and Donny are really close, and I live with Donny, and he's asked a couple times where I'm going when I leave. I've been saying I've got studying to do for the EMT, and he keeps asking me what I've learned and, I'm, I don't know, I'm—"

"You're freaked." I took a deep breath and pulled to the side of the road in front of the Resolute Cafe. This was no bueno. Mike and I had been becoming friends—not in theory, not in a *I'll call you, maybe* sort of way, but in living technicolor. And, more importantly, his going out in the gay scene was good for him—good for his identity. I felt that in my toes. The last thing I wanted was to fuck that all up and have him retreat to the back of his closet. "Seriously, Mike. Maybe I should just disappear when it comes to your family. You and I can hang out, but I'll stop seeing them."

He snapped, "And how do I explain that?" His voice sounded edgy, like I'd created this whole mess, which I guess I kind of did when I accepted Lucille's first invitation.

"You don't have to explain anything. I'll just say school is intense. Which isn't even a confabulation."

He laughed. "Pops is right. You use big words when you lie."

I pressed a hand to my heart even though he couldn't see it. "Heaven forfend I should ever prevaricate."

He laughed at my joke but then sighed, "No. My family really likes you. I don't want you to hurt their feelings."

I rested my forehead on the steering wheel. "Your mother likes me, and your sister. They don't constitute a quorum."

"And my grandmother and aunt, and…."

"And?"

"Tony and Viv like you okay, I think. And Nonno? Though I'm not sure he knows who you are."

Thinks. Right. I reached to put Mable back in gear. Time to go home. I hadn't missed the way, earlier in the conversation, he'd seemed to blame me for the complication with his family. And he wasn't wrong. "Look, Mike. I'll call your mom and apologize and—"

The hard knock on the window made me jump a foot, and I stared toward where Tessa stood on the sidewalk peering in at me, smiling, a giant shopping bag looped over her shoulder. When our eyes met, she waved.

I grabbed the phone. "Too late. Tessa's outside my car. I'll be there in five minutes." I hung up as Mike sputtered, and then I rolled down the window. "Hey, Tessa, I'm on my way to your house. Need a ride?"

She grinned. "No thanks. I've got my car. So you're going to help out Gabe, huh?"

"Ye-es. That's the plan. As it's been relayed to me."

"Ah. So nice of you." Her smile looked a little dubious, but I had enough doubts of my own, and now Mike's, so I just shrugged.

"Happy to help."

"It'll be good for him." She waved again. "See you at home." Hefting the bag, she walked across the street.

I stared after her. Yeah, cod liver oil was good for you. Kale too.

———

Okay, what the hell?

Forty minutes later, I sat in one of the rooms the Canalis used as an office at a smallish round table with résumé attempts and a laptop spread out in front of me—and no Gabe.

I'd been welcomed effusively by Lucille and Carlotta, but all the male Canalis were notably missing, even Mike. Lucille had put me in this room, and nothing else had happened.

I glanced through the various revisions, which were, admittedly, dreadful with a capital D, but I wasn't prepared to put together Gabe's résumé by myself. Prepared or willing. I mean, what qualifications did a police station IT guy even need? I sure wasn't getting the answers from the junk on the table.

The only good things happening were the smells wafting in from the kitchen. At least I'd get a delicious meal I didn't have to cook. Still, I was ready to throw all the Canali brothers out an upper-story window at the moment. I was trying to do Gabe a favor, and I was being treated like my time meant nothing.

Suddenly, the door opened, and in walked Gabe, tall, dark, and glowering. He had a rounder jaw than Mike, and his eyes were closer-set and meaner, but he was still a damned handsome man. He marched to the table like it was the last mile, sat across from me, and said, without looking up, "Thanks a lot for doing this. I really appreciate it."

I wasn't sure whether to laugh or throw the résumés at him. How long had he rehearsed that speech? I could practically see Lucille moving his mouth like he was a hand puppet.

"Sure. No problem. Let's do this." I just wanted to get it over with.

"Yeah, okay."

I put on my best professional voice. "So, you want to do IT for the police station, and—"

"Yeah, it's a really good job." He sounded super defensive.

I blinked. "I'm sure it is. Everyone needs good IT."

"Right. Tell my brothers that." He snorted.

Ah, so that was the source of the frown. Or at least one of them. "Your brothers can't figure out why you'd rather chase software glitches than bad guys?" I smiled and shuffled through the attempts at résumés for some content I could reuse.

"Yeah. If you're not running into a burning building or stopping a bullet, what good are ya anyway? Knuckleheads." But there was reluctant admiration in his tone.

Apparently, *knuckleheads* was the intra-family term for the Canali way. Yep. Fair enough. And it dawned on me that Mike wasn't the only one who felt pressure to conform. Gabe was the oldest, but he still worried about what his brothers and dad thought. I filed that away for later.

"What about what *you* think, Gabe? Why did you decide to go this route?"

The big crease popped back between his dark brows, and for a second, he didn't say anything, just studied me, as if deciding what he could say. Then he rushed through the words. "Anita really worries when I'm on patrol. She's a dispatcher, so she knows everything, and I can't hide the hard shit from her." He gave me a quick look. "It's tough being a good cop when you know someone's sitting there white-knuckling for you every minute." He shrugged. "It gets to me that it gets to her. Like, it makes me think about what could happen. You can't overthink that shit."

Damn. Gabe was F-ing scary, but I was still kind of touched. "That's a good thing you're doing. For Anita. And you."

"Don't say anything all right? My brothers'd think I'm pussy-whipped." He stared at his hands.

Okay, first of all: that term was soooo offensive. But this wasn't the moment to give Gabe that lesson. Nor would any moment be, if I wanted to live.

"Tell your brothers that there are way more good jobs in IT than in law enforcement and they pay more. Lots more. Regular hours, nights and weekends off…" I was kind of making this up, but I was pretty sure I was right. "You'd be able to get a position anywhere, not just with the police. So they should fuck off." I smiled sweetly.

"Ha!" He stared at me for a second and then chuckled as if surprised. "You've got some balls."

"Believe me. Looking like this, you have to." I poised my hands over the keys of Lucille's laptop that she'd loaned me. "Okay, first tell me the databases and software programs you've learned that aren't specific to law enforcement and then tell me the cop-related ones."

"Oh, okay. Well, Amazon S3, of course."

I nodded like *of course*, although I understood zip about it, but I had heard the words and knew they were important.

"I just finished my course in SQL, and the instructors say that's a real big deal."

I kept nodding, and he kept rattling off his proficiencies until even I was impressed. "Hey, you've really worked hard at this."

"Thanks." His lips turned up only slightly, but his eyes said he was pleased with the compliment.

"So what's your goal?"

Frown was back. "What do you mean?"

"If a police department gives you a job, what do you want to accomplish for them? Maybe something you learned being on the cop end of things?"

The crease between his eyebrows this time reflected concentration, not annoyance for a change. "What I noticed as a cop is that having the databases really makes locating suspects and catching perps easier. It also prevents a lot of mistakes. I figure having the very best information and being

able to get to it fast and reliably makes everyone better cops."
He looked up at me for approval.

I said, "So you could say your goal is to see to it that the
cops on the street have the best possible access, right?"

"Right." He grinned. Jeez, real teeth. "Right!"

I started typing, and Gabe watched me like a hawk for a
while, as if I might try to intentionally sabotage him or something. But I just focused on the task, and after a while, he
started scrolling through his phone.

I got to the bottom of the page, cut some words, added a
couple more, prettied up the formatting, and hit print.

Gabe looked worried as he walked to the printer and
pulled off the single sheet. Big frown this time. "Hey, it's one
page. All that shit for a single-pager?"

I nodded. "Résumés can be one or two pages, but my
recommendation for you is to keep it short. Your replies are
impressive. If we stretch it out, it will become more obvious
that you may be an experienced cop, but have no work
history in IT. The right words should pop out on this résumé.
Hiring managers are busy. If they ask for more, it's a good
sign."

He gazed at me levelly, glanced for a second at my T-shirt,
which was totally low-key in royal blue and said, *I may be
wrong, but I doubt it,* and then looked back at my face. "You're
pretty smart. How do you know all this shit?"

"I do a lot of freelance editing, and people often ask me to
edit résumés, so I had to learn the rules."

He gazed at the page again. "You know. I really like this. It
doesn't make me sound like an idiot."

"You're obviously not, Gabe. Remember when you get
called in for interviews that all they care about is themselves,
their company, and their problems." I flashed some teeth.
"You know. Like everybody. Especially knuckleheads, so you
should be used to it with your brothers." I didn't know what
came over me, but I winked.

He barked that laugh again. "You got that right." He stood. Tall. Very tall. "So can I show this to the clan?"

"Whatever you want." I started straightening the papers on the table.

There was a pause as he walked to the door of the room, and then things got quiet. He said, "Pretty stand-up of you to help me out when I haven't exactly been nice to you. Thanks, Shane."

I wanted to scream, *Then stop talking trash about me to your brothers!* But I hoped that was a given. I just said, "It's my pleasure. Your mom's been great to me."

"Yeah. She's like that." He shuffled his feet. "Thanks again." He walked out of the room, leaving the door open. I could hear the TV and the shouts of the Canali men coming from the living room.

I shut down the computer, gathered my notebook and fave pencil I'd brought with me, and headed toward the living room, kind of dragging my feet. Canalis in groups could be a lot, and I wasn't quite up to it at the moment. Oh well. I'd help Lucille and Carlotta.

When I stepped out of the hall into the living room, a rowdy cheer went up from the guys who were standing around with Gabe, looking at the résumé.

"Good job, man," said Tony.

"Nice résumé. Looks impressive," said Angelo, looking surprised.

"Good thing, 'cause Gabe sucks," said Donny, which earned him a thrown elbow from Gabe.

Jeez, even freak-out Mike was smiling at me. I couldn't help but smile back. Relief washed over me. I was so glad this whole Gabe thing hadn't turned out to be another huge misstep on my part.

Lucille came rushing over and hugged me. "Thank you so much, Shane. What a great job. When you want a job done right, call an expert. That's what I always say. I made a strawberry shortcake just for you, and you don't have to share it with anyone."

"Hey now, hang on." Donny was aghast.

"You really made just the one?" Angelo asked, sounding hurt.

"Yes. But there's pie, so shut up, all of you. When have I ever let you starve?" scolded Lucille.

Carlotta yelled, "No macking on Shane's shortcake!"

Tessa grinned, standing by the kitchen island sipping a soda. "Thanks, Shane. That was above and beyond the call of duty. Only now you'll be doing the Canali family résumés until you're in your grave. You know that, right?"

I smiled back, feeling heat in my cheeks at all the praise. "I don't mind."

Grandma Luna, who insisted I call her Nonna, stepped to the middle of the room. She raised a hand, which caused most of the fam to quiet down in deference to her age. She spoke slowly, but loud. "I know that it is now time."

Carlotta got a little indulgent smile. "Time for what, Nonna?"

"It is now time for Shane to start courting Tessa. I have seen it. I have the sight."

Tessa spit soda all over the kitchen island.

TEN

MIKE

"Where did you find that piece! I've been looking for that for two days!" Ma slapped my arm playfully.

"It's my superior jigsaw puzzling skills," I deadpanned.

"You get that from me," Ma stated matter-of-factly.

Probably true, since my dad hated jigsaws. My brothers too. Pa, Donny, and Tony were watching football in the living room, but I hadn't been feeling it. I'd wandered into the dining room, where Tessa, Ma, and Nonna were working on a jigsaw. I'd only meant to put in a few pieces, but I got fixated on finishing this one area of wall on the villa in the image.

"Try turning it the other way," Tessa said, eyeing the piece I was trying to get to fit. I tried it. It slipped in easily.

"Show off," I said.

She smiled, then glanced toward the living room. "Not into the game?"

"Nah. Tampa Bay's gonna win. Not much of a contest."

She smiled. "It's nice having you join us."

I gave her a sharp look, sure she was yanking my chain.

But no, she seemed sincere. "I mean it. This family, I swear, it's segregated worse than a conservative Jewish synagogue."

"What do you know from synagogues?" Lucille asked sharply. Then, to me, "We're a good Catholic family."

Tessa rolled her eyes. "Ma, you know my friend Mindy's Jewish. But that's not the point. The point is it's always the boys versus the girls around here."

"Which is why it's nice to have Shane around," Ma pronounced as she popped in a puzzle piece. "He doesn't care about all that. Such a smart boy. And so helpful!"

I wasn't touching that one. I said to Tessa, "You could always watch football. No one's stopping you."

"Yeah, except then I'd have to gouge my eyes out." She stuck out her tongue in distaste.

I shrugged and kept working. But it *was* nice. We all had tea, and it was relaxing sitting at the table with them. No talking, no yelling at the TV, just everyone working together on a project. Sometimes, my mom would hand Nonna a piece wordlessly, or Nonna would lean over the sky that Tessa was working on and nudge a piece into place. After the three days of duty I'd had that week, which had included a dangerous brush fire and the tense rescue of some horses at a ranch, it was good to chill.

I looked up and caught Tessa watching me again. She quickly looked away.

What? It wasn't that weird for me to join in on a jigsaw puzzle, was it?

Except maybe it was—at least when my dad and brothers were in the house. I thought about that. Normally, I wouldn't do this because I wouldn't want to deal with the ribbing that was bound to come my way. But so what? I wanted to work on the freaking jigsaw. So I would.

Which made me think: was this what Shane felt? When he hung out in the kitchen with the women in the family? More relaxed and at ease? What did it mean that I was doing it now too? And why did it have to be the men and the women doing separate things anyway? Like everything had to be black and white. Working a jigsaw or setting a table didn't make you female. And why worry about gender shit at all? Do what you like.

A few weeks ago, I might have freaked out thinking that and run back to the living room with the guys. But I'd hung out with Shane and his friends in Sacramento, like, four times now, absorbing, as Shane called it, the *gay culture*. I'd never be as femme as Winston or even Shane, but I *was* different from my brothers. At least I could admit that much. It was fine to be different. Right?

Maybe I liked different things, had broader interests. Maybe I liked hanging out with Tessa more than Gabe. So what? I was twenty-two. I didn't have to copy my dad and brothers like some hero-worshipping kid anymore.

"So what's the best way to fix up Shane and Tessa?" Nonna mused to Ma, holding up a piece at arm's length and squinting her eyes at it. She gave a soft grunt of approval and snapped that sucker right into place.

Tessa and I exchanged a look. The topic made me itch, but at least Tessa wasn't likely to say yes.

"They would make a darling couple," Ma replied, not looking up. "Shane would make a wonderful husband. So thoughtful!" She tsked. "But Tessa likes those bad boy types. Maybe it's her age."

"I'm sitting right here!" Tessa said loudly. "And I do not like bad boys."

I was taking a sip of tea and nearly choked on it.

"What?" Tessa glared at me.

"The last one had a motorcycle called Satan, and he wanted to give you a dog collar."

Tessa gaped. "How do you know about that? Anyway, I broke up with him over that stupid collar. I have too many brothers to ever put up with that sh—er, nonsense."

"I know. Fido." I grinned.

She kicked me under the table.

"We could arrange a nice dinner at a restaurant and act like everyone's coming, but then only the two of them show up," Nonna plotted.

"Sitting right here, Nonna!" Tessa said again. "Anyway, I don't think I'm Shane's type."

"Of course you are. I saw it." Nonna tapped her temple knowingly. "I had a vision of a family wedding. I'm never wrong!"

Tessa and I exchanged an amused look. No one in the family took Nonna's predictions seriously. Mainly because they were *always* wrong.

"It's time to consider settling down with someone nice," Mama scolded Tessa. "You've had your fun. You're not getting any younger, you know."

"I'm only twenty-three!"

"And I'd had Gabe at your age. I'm not nagging! Simply stating a fact. Mike, look at this piece. Does this look blue to you? Or green?"

I looked. "Green. I think it might be part of a shutter." I took the piece from her since I was working the villa.

Mama went on. "You need someone reliable who'd be happy to help around the house and with the kids, as well as being smart and a good provider. I love your father, but he's so old-fashioned. If I were you, I'd jump on Shane before someone else gets him. I would have loved to be married to a man like him!"

I knew Mama was talking up Shane at least in part to get Tessa on board, but it was still ridiculous. Shane and my mother... or even her younger version? I had to choke back a belly laugh. Now that was funny.

"Well, you can always propose to him, Ma," I said, trying to sound serious. "I'm sure Dad would agree to a divorce if it's really what you want."

She nudged my arm. "Oh stop it! You know what I mean."

"It's fate, Tessa," said Nonna in her spooky voice. "You can't fight fate."

"Now, Nonna, stop. You know Father O'Brien doesn't like that kind of talk," Ma tsked.

"So? It's God's plan then. Same thing." Nonna waved a dismissive hand.

Tessa put her head down on the table and bonked it against the wood lightly. "Ma, Nonna, I'd be thrilled to date a guy like Shane. Trust me. The problem is I'm not *Shane's* type. I mean, hello? He's gay."

My heart stopped. Literally, everything inside me froze. I knew Tessa suspected Shane was gay, but, damn, I never thought she'd blurt it out like that.

Shit. What would my ma do? Would she decide she didn't like Shane after all?

I watched her blink at Tessa as if that didn't compute. Then she made a face and shook her head. "Oh, you! Just because a man likes to cook and decorate, that doesn't make him… him gay. My hairdresser, Andre, has six children. Six!"

Tessa looked exasperated. "Andre may be straight, Ma, but Shane is really very gay. Tell them, Mike!"

I drew back. *Me?* "Um…" I said.

"I swear I saw him with Tessa," Nonna complained. "I'm never wrong. Maybe he swings both ways."

"Nonna!" Mama gasped. "Have you been getting into the cooking sherry today, or what? Don't say things like that. Mike, Shane's your friend. Is Tessa right?"

All three of them watched me intently. I thought about lying. And I thought about saying *he's not my friend*. But then I thought of Winston. And Chas. And Roland. And, most of all, Shane. What would Shane want me to say to my mother and grandmother?

He sure as shit wouldn't want me to lie, not about this.

"He's gay," I said. Then I picked up my tea and sipped it,

tense as fuck. I felt like *I'd* just come out, which was stupid. But their reaction would tell me a lot about how that might go —eventually.

Mama put down a puzzle piece to pick up her cup with both hands and sip thoughtfully. "Oh. You're sure?"

"Yup. Pretty sure."

"Mama, you think Shane's a great guy, and the fact that he's gay doesn't change that," Tessa said stubbornly. "He was just born a little different. Some people are."

Mama gazed off, still sipping her tea. "Well. We've never had anything like that in our family. Maybe because we're Italian."

"My Uncle Spanzo. You didn't know him," Nonna mused, her tone fond. "Such a talented chef. I remember his *roommate* had the prettiest golden curls for a man."

Ma looked interested. "Was this in the old country, Nonna?"

"Yup. The Bronx," Nonna said.

Ma sighed. "Well. I must say, this news is disappointing."

I felt a stab of bitterness. "Like Tessa said, people are just born that way. Imagine, Ma," I went on passionately, "if you'd been born into a world where everyone was supposed to like the same sex, only you loved Dad, and you couldn't tell anyone."

"And you had to get married to another woman you didn't like that way. And have sex!" Tessa was getting into it now.

"Exactly!" I said. "That's the way a gay person feels all the time."

Mama folded her arms over her chest and raised her eyebrow at us. She looked at Nonna. "Nothing makes you feel quite so old as *kidsplaining*. Yes, thank you, my children. I do know what being gay means. I saw *Christopher and His Kind*, you know."

"You did?" I said, surprised.

"But you said you were disappointed," Tessa pointed out.

Mama waved a hand. "I'm disappointed because I wanted him for *you*!"

"I could swear I saw it." Nonna shook her head mournfully.

"Do you have any other nice, considerate friends, Mike?" Ma asked, hunting around for pieces again. "Or are they all gay?"

I wiped my hand over my face. This was too weird. I stood up. "I need more tea… or something."

I managed to escape to the backyard. The November day was overcast and gloomy. I decided to go for a run to clear my head.

I trotted to the house I shared with Donny and headed to my room to change. The door to Donny's room was shut, which meant he'd come back at some point from the main house and was probably watching porn, which he did a lot. I bet he figured he had the house to himself. Yeah. No. I definitely didn't want to linger. I changed into running gear, then took off. You could cut through the woods on our property to reach a country road and then a path along the canal. There was sparse vegetation along the canal, and everything looked flat and brown in the light of the cloudy day. I ran hard.

We've never had anything like that in our family. Maybe because we're Italian.

Okay, so they were naïve. But Ma and Nonna hadn't freaked out. And they hadn't acted like they hated Shane now. Nobody made it seem like that big a deal, honestly. Well, except for Nonna's failed prediction.

How would Nonna and Mama act around Shane next time he was at the house? Would Ma call and invite him again? Would they treat him the same? Would they still think he was the best? If they did… if they did… My heart wanted to plummet and soar at the same time. This whole day felt surreal. Somewhere between the red and the blue pill.

Shane coming into my family's life was turning out to be really, very fortunate. Like a test pigeon. And, more than anything, I wanted to see him fly.

I loved the feel of my running shoes striking the dirt. The rhythm pounded through my blood, making me feel alive, while my mind replayed the conversation over the jigsaw puzzle.

There was still a part of me that wanted to feel paranoid about it, but I breathed deeply and tried to take in positive energy with each breath like Aunt Carlotta always said I should do. Ma and Nonna had been cool with it—stick to that.

A drip of sweat fell off my nose, and I wiped at it.

And I had a great uncle who'd been gay? That kind of blew my mind. Imagine all those men back in the day who couldn't be gay or they'd be thrown in jail or worse. Shit. I shuddered. But even back then, with their lives on the line, they'd met in secret to hook up and fall in love. To kiss, rub their bodies together, suck each other off, and fuck. Fucking the right body, the right gender, the right person was that important. I wanted that. I needed that.

I stopped to catch my breath, leaning against a tree and closing my eyes. Imagine doing that shit with Shane. This time, my shiver was the best kind. *Man, I'll bet he's good at it. Those lips.* An image of seeing Shane on his knees with his mouth wrapped around my cock flashed in glorious Technicolor all over my brain, so real I actually glanced down. I barked a laugh when all I saw was my glorious boner sticking out like a tentpole. If I planned on going home, I better find another train of thought, like multiplying by eight.

Methodically, I started walking, but my imagination wouldn't get with the *do your times tables* program. It kept throwing up pictures. Me and Shane in the shower. Me and Shane frotting like hamsters in the back seat of his car. Oooh, man, me fucking Shane so deep he was begging for more.

My steps faltered, and I stopped. God, that sounded so good. I'd seen my share of gay porn, always careful to be super-discreet, and I'd done a lot of what I'd seen, but anal? Nope, not yet. I knew some guys didn't like it and never did it, but for some reason, the idea gave me goose bumps. Maybe Shane fucking me? Whoa. What would that feel like? It had to be so—gay. I loved that idea.

I started walking again, a bit faster. A lot of gay guys used dildoes to try fucking themselves, but I never had. Explaining to Ma why you had a dildo in your closet was not happening in this lifetime. What if Donny found it? That made me swallow hard. Sure, I'd fiddled around a little with a finger or two, but that didn't do much except feel weird and unsatisfying.

Suddenly, I was running, and I knew right where I was going.

A couple minutes later, I barged into the back door of my folks' house. The sound of football echoed, and Ma, Nonna, and Tessa were still bent over the puzzle. I yelled, "Hey, Ma, I gotta take a shower. I'm grabbing a snack to tide me over."

She looked up from the table. "You want a sandwich, Mimmo?"

"No thanks, Ma. I'll grab a banana."

"They're still green."

"Uh. That's okay. I like them that way." I turned, took a breath, grabbed a banana from the stand where Ma hung them to ripen, and hurried out the back door. Jesus, I didn't know whether to laugh or barf.

Inside my house, Donny's door stood partly open. I listened. Quiet. Holy crap, he was gone. I had the house to myself. One glance at the banana actually made my cheeks heat, but it also made my dick throb. I slipped into my room and closed the door. Did I dare lock it? If Donny came back and tried to get in, how would I explain that? Fuck, I'd worry about that if it happened. Click.

Already breathing hard, I grabbed a towel from my bathroom and laid it on the bed, then fished out a bottle from the back of the bedside table. It was a bottle for a macho-branded body lotion, which I'd refilled with clear lube. The tricks you learned living in a big family with a nosy mother. *Here goes nothing.*

Lying on my back, I started working on my cock like I regularly would, stroking with two slippery hands. It didn't take much to get rock hard since I was more than halfway there, and damn, it felt good. With my eyes closed, it only took a second to change my big, rough hands into Shane's slender ones, and I moaned as he stroked me senseless. Still working the dick with one hand, I scooped some lube onto a couple fingers and slid them into my channel. Holy shit! The pressure felt hot and a little uncomfortable, but tingles and zips of energy shot out into my balls, and I nearly came. *Wait. Not too fast.*

After a couple deep breaths, still stroking my cock, I added more lube and another finger. It took a minute to get used to that as my body relaxed around them, but like before, it was awkward reaching back like that, and I couldn't get a good angle.

Feeling only a tiny bit silly, I squirted heavy lube on the banana, and before I could even think, I pulled one leg up, positioned my makeshift dildo, and pushed.

The burn at the entrance shivered through me, but I was so slick and so ready the damned thing only resisted for a couple seconds and then—

Oh my god. Full, hot, burning in the best way. The banana got so much deeper than my fingers ever could. Nerves I hadn't known I had lit up like a brand-new light switch and blazed through my body, making everything tremble. I pulled it out to the tip, and the friction was fucking blissful. Then I pushed back in.

Sweet Jesus. Was this what Shane would feel if I fucked

him? My hand couldn't move fast enough, in and out, in and out, and I grabbed my cock with my other hand. Shane. Oh god, Shane.

Something inside me shot a blast of pleasure so intense it was almost pain, and everything exploded—my cock and balls all over my chest and my mind. For minutes, all I could do was lie there and tremble. Jesus H, I was gay. I was so, so gay, and I wanted to be gay. I wanted to be gay with Shane Bower.

Baby steps. Stop thinking about how stupid complicated that would be and just enjoy the afterglow for one damn minute.

By the time Donny pounded on my door and threw it open, I'd unlocked it, showered, dressed, and was just sitting on the bed pulling on my sneakers. He said, "Hey, dude, Ma's yelling for you. Come on. You're holding up dinner."

"Sorry. I'm coming." Yeah, but not as much as I'd come a half hour ago. I'd had to spray the place with the room deodorizer Ma kept in the bathroom trying to get rid of the smell of sex.

I stood and grabbed my jacket.

Donny held the door. "After all that running, you must be starved. Shit, you didn't even eat your banana."

I nodded and had trouble keeping a straight face. "Ma was right. It's too green."

ELEVEN

SHANE

"Nice of the Canalis to invite me again." Pops gave me a glance as I navigated the route to Resolute on a rainy Saturday. Jeez, Mable practically knew the way on her own I'd come so often.

"Yeah. Lucille says that Giuseppe really likes you and looks forward to your visits. I mean, they all like you, too, but anything that gets Nonno alert and interacting is especially important to them. After all, he's their patriarch, and getting him to care about things seems to reduce his symptoms, at least for a while. Is it hard to talk to him?"

"No, not at all. He sometimes forgets what he was going to say, but his memories of the past are still vivid. It's interesting to see time periods and events I remember from the perspective of an Italian who immigrated to America."

"It's nice of you to spend time with him."

"Hey, it's my pleasure." He looked toward me. "I'd never want him to see my visits as obligations or charity. I enjoy talking with him." He cleared his throat. "Not like I have so many friends I can afford to turn one down."

I raised my eyebrows at him. "You don't say. Maybe if you came to any of the fifty billion things I invite you to. Like the book club."

He harumphed. "Okay, I know I shut myself off and don't reach out to make friends. But I like Giuseppe, okay?"

"That's good, Pops. I'm glad."

"More than I like a couple of those other Canali bozos. Their attitudes are a little sketchy, if you ask me."

I sighed. "Yeah." Pops had honed right in on my constant mixed emotions whenever I was invited to the Canalis. I loved Lucille, Carlotta, Tessa, and even Nonna, despite her desire to fix me up with Tessa. Tony and Viv and their kids were great, and Angelo was polite, if distant. Then there was Mike—I couldn't seem to turn down an opportunity to be around him, even if I was now firmly stuck in the friend zone. My poor heart still held out hope, especially when he looked at me with that fire in his eyes. The other Canalis, however, were either unknown quantities, like their Uncle Ricky and cousin Tito, both quiet guys who slipped in and out of the house at whim, or full-on antagonists like Donny and Gabe. Admittedly, Gabe had come around a little after the résumé visit the previous week, but he might go right back to acting like a jerk now that my *favor* was over. Coming face to face with him and Donny took guts, and guts weren't what I loved spilling on my time off.

Pops said, "You haven't said much about Mike lately. Are these visits moving your relationship forward, whatever that looks like?" He snorted. Pops was generally a shit-or-get-off-the-pot kind of guy. He had a lot of compassion for Mike's situation, but I was his chief concern and I was doing neither.

"Uh… not really. Mike's been hanging out with me and my friends in Sac. Me coming to the Canali compound makes him antsy, honestly. He never knows what one of his family members is going to come up with next, like Nonna deciding I should date Tessa." I shook my head.

"What happened with that?"

I winced. "According to Mike, he and Tessa took the plunge and told Lucille and Nonna that I'm gay, so I wouldn't be interested in Tessa."

"That sounds like a big step for Mike." Pops frowned, and that made my stomach flip.

I blew out air. "Yeah, but he said they were just disappointed that I couldn't marry Tessa and didn't seem too put off by it. I guess we'll see today."

"You think that's the end of it? Surely the men are going to find out. Doesn't that worry Mike? He's been so touchy. That boy needs to stand up for himself and come clean, if you ask me."

I didn't disagree with Pops. But I could also see Mike's point of view, and I worried about him. *For* him. When I'd come out to my parents and brother, it had been horrible. They'd told me I was a sinner and perverted and kicked me out of the house that same day. I'd barely had time to grab a bag of clothes. That had been the worst day of my life. Devastating. If it hadn't been for Pops, who came right away to get me when I'd called, lavished me with unconditional love, and told me they were all idiots, I wasn't sure I would have survived. I didn't want anyone to go through that pain and certainly not Mike.

"I dunno. He sounded kind of jazzed that his mom invited me back to dinner."

Pops shrugged. "Maybe it takes some pressure off him that they know about you. That way, he doesn't have to second guess everything you say and do. You're not exactly Mr. Blend Into the Woodwork."

"Ya think?"

We both laughed, but the truth was, I'd toned down the Shane statement clothes when I visited the Canalis—fewer sparkles and in-your-face T-shirts—and I got the feeling Pops worried about that, even though he hadn't said anything.

Like maybe I was compromising for nothing except a few good meals.

A few good meals and a dreamboat who would never be mine. Le sigh.

Driving slowly through Resolute, we fell silent, each buried in our own thoughts.

When we drove into the compound, my eyes widened. Giuseppe was standing there with Lucille. After I'd parked and Pops climbed out of the passenger seat, carrying his cane but not using it much, Giuseppe approached the car with a smile.

He and Pops greeted each other with a wave, and Giuseppe said, "Thought you might like to come down to my place. Less noise."

"Sounds perfect." Pops fell in beside Giuseppe, and they walked slowly toward the small cottage where I'd been told Nonno and Nonna lived.

Lucille took my arm. "Nonno can focus better when all the boys aren't making noise."

Hell, I could focus better when the boys weren't making noise, but I didn't say that.

She drew me into a hug and lingered, holding me tight. I hadn't realized how nervous I was about Lucille knowing I was gay until that moment, when I felt myself relax. Was this hug her way of telling me it was okay? My eyes grew hot and my chest tight. If only my own mother had… damn. I was gonna lose it.

She squeezed me extra tight one last time before pulling back and looking at me with concern. "Aw, honey. You okay?"

"Yeah." I wiped my eyes and swallowed down emotion. "Yup. Good." I forced a smile.

She patted my hand. "Even better soon, I think." She wore an enigmatic smile as we walked into the house. What was up?

Inside, everything looked normal. The TV announcers blared, the fans cheered, and the beer flowed. A mob of Canali boys gathered in front of the TV while the women worked—even more testosterone in the room than usual, so maybe there was a big game. I noticed Uncle Ricky. Damn. The big guy was wearing a long-sleeved blue shirt over muscles that bulged. Total stud. He'd be mobbed if he ever walked into Friend of Dorothy. Farther down the couch, there was a shiny blond head I didn't recognize. Of course, my eyes latched on Mike like they were magnetized there. He glanced at me from the couch with a strange expression. Kind of halfway between deer-in-headlights and pissed off.

I cocked my head a little in a silent question, and his eyes shifted to his left. His dad sat beside him, then the unfamiliar blond, then Tony.

The blond turned his head and looked right at me. I took a little breath. He was stunning but in no way resembled a Canali. In addition to the slicked-back fair hair, he had very refined features, like some classical statue, unlike the rougher, more masculine looks of Angelo and the brothers. The guy smiled at me and surveyed me up and down. Um... okay.

I smiled back, feeling confused, and then walked after Lucille toward the kitchen, looking for my apron so I could help. It was a bit crowded since Tessa, Nonna, Viv, and Carlotta were all in there, whispering.

Lucille turned toward me. "Oh, no, Shane, you should go join the guys today." She glanced toward Tessa with a funny look, and Tessa smirked.

I glanced between them, but said, "I'd rather watch paint dry than watch sports on TV. I'm good." My apron was hanging on a hook inside the pantry where I'd left it last time I'd been there, and I tied it on. A big bowl of steaming potatoes that must have just come out of the boiling water stood on the counter. I opened a drawer where I was pretty sure I'd find the peeler and said, "Skins on or off?" I looked up just in time to see a silent, gesticulated conversation going on between all the women, which involved a lot of pointing toward the living room and back at me.

When Lucille saw me watching them, she giggled uneasily. What the hell? I planted my hands on my hips. "Okay, what's going on? You guys are about as subtle as a deer in pink flannel PJs."

A clipped voice from behind me said, "The real party appears to be in here."

I turned to see the blond guy.

He stuck out his hand. "Hello. I'm Mendelssohn Martin." He flashed the most perfect set of teeth I'd ever seen. They had to be caps. "My mother and Mrs. Canali are friends. And I'm very pleased to meet you."

Ah. The new guy was a family friend. I took his hand. "Hi. I'm Shane Bower." His skin was soft like velvet. Funny, I'd never thought about how callused Mike's hands were from all the axe wielding and hose handling. Whoa. That thought gave me a dirty shiver. "So, Mendelssohn? I've never heard the name before."

"You haven't?" His perfectly arched brows rose. "I was named for my mother's favorite composer. Surely you've heard of him?"

I gave a soft snort. "Sure. I've just never heard it used as a given name. So, what do people call you? Mendel? Sonny?"

"People call me Mendelssohn."

"Okay." Sort of pretentious, but I wasn't going to rush to judgment. He sure didn't seem like someone the Canalis would hang with.

He chuckled and flipped the ruffle on my apron. "I see you've been pressed into service. Perhaps I can be of use as well." He looked around questioningly.

"Not into football?" I asked with a grin.

"Decidedly not." He smiled back. Maybe Mendelssohn wasn't bad after all.

Tessa handed him an apron. Whatever the hell was going on, it sure seemed to be amusing her.

Mendelssohn looked at the red-and-black frilly apron like it might attack, but he took it and wrapped it on over his creased jeans and starched white shirt—uh, and tie.

I pointed to the potatoes. "We can cut those up and mash them."

His pale blue eyes widened, but he picked up the peeler I pointed at and held it up in his right hand with his left hand also raised.

I laughed. "Let me guess. You're a surgeon."

"How did you—" He glanced at his hands and grinned. "Oh. Indeed. Cardiovascular."

Nonna started to laugh. "Oh boy, that's too funny. Shane, you're so smart to have guessed that."

"Libras are very intuitive," Carlotta said knowingly.

Mendelssohn got pink in his cheeks. Maybe people didn't laugh at cardiovascular surgeons a lot.

I said, "Hey, Nonna, should we take off all the skins or leave some on?"

"Do what you want, dear. You always know the best thing."

I pointed to the bowl and said to Mendelssohn, "Since you're the expert, you peel some of them, and I'll start cutting up the others for mashing."

Sure enough, he was impressive at getting the skins off, and pretty soon I was adding butter, sour cream, cheese and a few chives to the potatoes as I mashed.

He said, "I'd hate to see the calories in this mixture."

I nudged him. "Just creating business for you."

For a second, he looked shocked and then laughed.

A yell went up from the TV viewers, and I looked over the

kitchen island just in time to come eye to eye with Mike, who glared at me from the couch.

I frowned back. WTF? What did I do?

I returned to potato mashing.

Five minutes later, I went in to zhuzh the table a bit, and Mendelssohn came along. I added some flowers and a set of candles Lucille had bought, and Mendelssohn walked around adjusting the napkins. I wasn't quite sure they needed adjusting, but what the hell. I didn't see any of the other guys keeping me company. It was nice of him.

Finally, the big old table groaned under the amount of food, and we all gathered to eat. Lucille explained that Pops and Giuseppe were having a great old time playing cards and were having their meal in the cottage, so I didn't worry about him.

I walked to the place between Lucille and Mike that I was usually assigned at the table, but when the chair pulled out next to me, I glanced over and saw Mendelssohn. Mike had been seated at the opposite end of the table, and I could have cooked s'mores on the fiery darts he was shooting from his eyes. Lucille, Carlotta, and Nonna, on the other hand, looked so full of themselves they should have popped, while Angelo, Gabe, and Donny shifted around on the spectrum from uncomfortable to creeped out. Uncle Ricky eyed the food like he might be planning to eat as quickly as possible and get out of there.

When everyone was seated, Lucille stared so hard at Angelo that he turned red. Then he cleared his throat and said, "So uh, Men—uh, Mendelssohn—" He put the emphasis on the second syllable, which definitely didn't sound like the composer. "Tell us more about yourself. I hear—" He glanced at Lucille. "—I hear you do medical research." Across from me, Tessa's eyes practically bugged from her head she was trying so hard not to laugh, which made me want to laugh too. I kept wondering where Lucille was hiding the flashcards that Angelo was reading from.

Mendelssohn replied very seriously, "Yes, I'm exploring evidence-guided treatment and risk stratification in improvement of outcomes."

Angelo just looked at him, then cleared his throat again. "Well, that's just great. Really great."

Tony burst in, "So what teams do you like for the NBA finals this year, Meldonson?"

Mendelssohn seemed stuck between planes of existence, not knowing whether to correct Tony's pronunciation, respond to the question, or accept some of the lasagna that had just been passed to him.

I took pity. "What do you think, Tony? Isn't that California team supposed to be really good?" Thus ended my total grasp of basketball.

"Oh yeah. I mean, Golden State? For sure."

By this time, Tessa was close to cardiac arrest and was going to need Mendelssohn's services soon. She had to be biting her tongue raw.

Lucille leaped in. "Mendelssohn, did you realize that Shane is not only a student of, uh, literature, but also an editor for people who write books and things like that? And he even does great résumés. You should see what beautiful work he did on Gabe's. Right, Gabe?"

Gabe looked up from his lasagna. "Yeah. Totally." He gave me a tight smile but looked like he'd prefer to be under the table.

Mendelssohn looked at me and nodded. "Valuable skill." He dished vegetables on his plate with exaggerated precision. "I'll have to ask him to do a résumé for me sometime."

"You know, that would be an excellent way to get to know someone," Tessa mused. "Maybe next time I meet a guy, I should offer to help him on his résumé. All sorts of biographical detail in there."

"Yes, what a fabulous idea!" beamed Lucille.

My gaze drifted from person to person, Lucille to Carlotta, to Angelo, and the others, all focused in one way or another on Mendelssohn—and me.

Well shit!

I wasn't generally dense, but somehow, I'd totally missed the fact that Mendelssohn Martin had been invited to dinner *for me*. As my blind date. As my fix-up.

Seriously? That kind of blew my mind. But apparently, it was actually happening. Lucille et al had apparently not only accepted the fact that I was gay, but decided to find me a boyfriend.

For a second, I felt my face flame and stomach churn. Then I took a breath.

Holy crap.

This family, especially these women, in some cases in contrast to their own personal beliefs, had searched through their acquaintances to find someone with an eligible gay son and had gone to huge amounts of trouble to stage a dinner party to show us off to each other.

Tears pushed behind my eyes again. Damn it. This had to rank with the kindest things ever done for me.

On the other hand, did that mean I had to date the guy?

Fortunately, my dense question about basketball had gotten the men talking, and things had settled into a more normal pattern. If I didn't count the glower of Mike who stared at me as if he had the magic power of killing with a glance.

What, precisely, did that mean?

Mike and I were friends, as defined by him. Every time we'd come close to renewing the kiss we'd shared in that canoe what felt like a century before, like on the dance floor at Friend of Dorothy, Mike had pulled away. So how the bloody hell had I offended him this time?

"Care for more salad? This is excellent." I looked up at

Mendelssohn, who was smiling at me and holding the salad bowl. Hey, this dude was nice, and he was making an effort.

"Thank you. I'd *love* some," I said loudly.

For the rest of the dinner, Mendelssohn and I chatted, the rest of the family stopped trying to talk us up to each other, and Tessa pulled back from a complete meltdown of hilarity.

Pops came in after Giuseppe had fallen asleep and sat watching yet another sports program with all the guys. Mendelssohn helped me and the women clear the table and then said he had to go. "Would you walk me out?" he asked.

"Sure."

He said his goodbyes to everyone, and Lucille, Carlotta, and Nonna all gave us significant looks as I pulled on my jacket to accompany Mendelssohn to his car.

It turned out he drove a Tesla. A new one. I didn't know much more about cars than I did about sports, but I kept up on electric vehicles. "Nice ride."

"Yes." He smiled. "Musk may be an asshole, but he does know his batteries."

I snorted since this was one of the few things he'd said all evening that I heartily agreed with.

He said, "I believe all the Canalis are very anxious for me to ask you out."

Not *all* the Canalis, but I kept that to myself. "I'd say you're correct. Honestly, I'm touched at how much trouble they went to setting up this totally random, chance meeting."

He smiled. "So, would you like to make their dreams come true? You're obviously young, but I find you quite attractive."

I gazed into the near perfection of his face and found it—boring. "Thank you, Mendelssohn, but the truth is I'm not as available as the Canalis believe." There. In some strange way, that was the truth.

He blinked, and a look of mild disappointment crossed his

face. "Oh, I see. I think Mrs. Canali will be very disheartened."

I nodded. "Yeah. I'll talk to her."

"Well, should you ever change your mind." He slid a card out of his pocket and handed it to me. I wanted to giggle. No asking for my phone to put in his digits. Mendelssohn Martin handed out business cards to potential dates. Then he took me totally by surprise and leaned in to kiss me right beside my mouth. His lips weren't as soft as his hands. "Maybe I'll see you again."

He slid into the Tesla and drove away in a crunching of gravel.

I stared after his car, all the mix of gratitude, embarrassment, and a dash of formless pissed-offedness roiling in my brain and gut.

"So after all your sparkly unicorns and fine words about finding your tribe, what you really want is a beautiful, rich doctor with a Tesla." Mike's voice dripped acid as he walked from behind the truck behind me.

My pissed-off took shape and form. The shape was Mike Canali. Planting my hands on my hips, I snarled, "What the living fuck is your problem? You haven't done one thing this entire night except glower and glare like the fucking Kraken. I'm the one who should be pissed. You saw that your family was trying to set me up, and you don't even bother to warn me?" I slammed a finger into his chest, ready to chew up Michael Canali and spit him out. "Fortunately, he turned out to be a nice guy, but thanks a whole hell of a lot for nothing."

We stared at each other. It was disgusting that the stupid Italian could stand there with his mouth opening and closing like a fish and still look so gorgeous. And he still made my heart ache. I shook my head. "Never mind. This whole thing is pointless." I turned, took two steps, and a hand like steel gripped my upper arm.

"Shane, wait."

Through my teeth, I gritted, "Let go of me."

His grip softened, and he reached down and took my hand instead. Then he pulled me toward him as he walked backward toward the line of trees and bushes beyond the parking area.

And, of course, I went.

TWELVE

MIKE

This whole thing is pointless.

Shane's bitter words stabbed me in the gut as I dragged him away from the house, away from prying eyes and ears.

I knew what he meant. This awkward dance we'd been doing—trying to be pals and living a double life. Me acting like we were just casual friends in front of my family, who were taking off with ideas of their own about Shane. And then there was me hanging out with Shane and his friends in Sac and having to fend off all the guys at the clubs.

And the stupid thing was, neither one of those schizo realities was what I wanted at all.

Apparently, Shane was over it. The thought that he might just give up on me entirely had me tied up in even bigger knots than I'd already been in.

We reached the woods. A few steps in, Shane stopped, turning into a lead anchor. Impressive, really. "What the hell are you—" he began.

I grabbed his face in both hands and crushed my mouth to his. I guess I expected him to just melt. I imagined that everything I had in my head, all the ways in which I yearned for him, would be the way he felt too.

But that didn't happen. He pushed me away, surprisingly strong. He stood there, breathing hard and glaring at me. "You don't get to do that!"

I didn't? Oh fuck. Oh man. Suddenly, nothing was more important in the world than convincing Shane to let me kiss him again. "I'm sorry," I blurted.

He crossed his arms over his chest. "Oh yeah? For what, exactly, are you sorry?"

I had to think about it. My brain was a muddle, colored with frustration and desire and, yes, wild, crazy jealousy. But I knew it was important to say the right thing. "Um… sorry I freaked out about that Mendelssohn guy?"

Shane narrowed his eyes. "Surely you knew they were fixing me up." He sounded hurt.

"I didn't. I swear." I held up a hand like *Scout's honor*. "Even Tessa didn't warn me. I didn't have any idea they would do something like that until the guy showed up tonight."

Shane looked doubtful. He raised his chin. "If you'd known, would you have tried to stop it? Or would you have stood by and watched me being set up just to make sure no one in your family would think you gave one flying fuck about me?" His tone was defiant, but his eyes teared up.

Oh fuck. I'd hurt Shane. Really hurt him. "I'm sorry. I'm sorry I'm such a fucking closet case with my family. I'm sorry I've tried to hide what you mean to me. It's been a shitty thing to do." It was finally hitting me how shitty. Yes, I'd been nice to Shane when he came over, but in a distant way, not even like we were *good* friends, and I hadn't told anyone we were hanging out in Sac either. "If I'd known what Ma was up to, yes, I absolutely would have stopped her. I would have found a way."

I knew that for certain. When Ma had introduced me to

Mendelssohn tonight—*Don't you think he and Shane would be perfect together?*—she'd been so proud! Beaming, like she was the most with-it mother on Earth for fixing up a gay family friend.

All I'd felt in that moment was stone-cold dread. Mendelssohn was so good-looking. And smart. And, more importantly, out. It was like watching the train you were supposed to catch taking off without you, and you'd be forever lost in a foreign country. I had to face it—if it wasn't Mendelssohn, it would be someone else. Shane was too appealing to be single for long.

"Why would you have stopped them?" Shane asked, still looking defiant. "You keep telling me we're just friends, so why shouldn't I go out with someone else? Someone who actually wants me?"

"You don't think I want you?" I gaped at him.

He raised his eyebrows at me as if to say *are you stupid or what?*

And yes, I was. Those big clear eyes of his were telling me exactly how much I'd damaged his faith in me. And it had to stop now.

"I never stopped wanting you," I said fervently. "I think about that kiss in the canoe all the time."

"You do?"

I took a step closer. He still wasn't exactly giving out *jump me* vibes, so I reached out slowly and stroked his cheek with one finger.

"I do. I'm tired of fighting it. I thought it would be less complicated trying to be friends, but it's more complicated, and I can't take it anymore. I just want you. I don't know how it will all work, but I—please let me kiss you."

He started to say something, stopped. He stared at me as if trying to make up his mind.

God, don't let it be too late.

Then he threw himself at me. He wasn't that heavy, but he

struck me like an arrow, hard and sharp and deep. I felt it all the way to my bones. His mouth was on mine, greedy and warm, and my head spun into outer space.

This. Shane pressed against me, wiry and strong and hard, his mouth hot and hungry, sucking at mine. This was everything in the world. This *was* my whole world right then.

I fumbled for the back of his shirt and blissed out when I got my hand under it to feel bare skin. The dip of his spine was so sexy. I spread my palm against it while the other hand gripped his ass and pulled him tight. Against the softness of his belly, I felt my own hardness. He was hard, too, like a bar against my hipbone. *This. This is who I am. This is what I want, just like I imagined when I was wielding that stupid banana. God, yes.*

For the moment, I cared about nothing else in this world. I couldn't get enough of him, and I couldn't get it fast enough. I was shaking and probably choking him with my tongue.

Shane pulled away from the kiss. His eyes were blazing. "Is there somewhere we can go?"

I blinked at him helplessly. Where? At my place, there'd be the possibility of Donny walking in at any moment. Or anyone really. Canalis didn't respect boundaries. There was no safe place in the main house. But I needed this so badly.

"Never mind." Shane looked around, then grabbed my hand and led me deeper into the woods.

I couldn't even think of a nice spot in here. But it definitely had to be out of sight. We picked our way over some brush and logs, not talking. When we found a large tree a ways off the path, Shane stopped and put his back to it, pulling me against him.

We kissed and kissed, his hands all over me and mine all over him. He reached between us to cup my dick, and I about lost my mind.

"Shane," I breathed into his neck. "Fuck, I need you." I'd

never felt so out of control, so teetering on the edge of lust and, I don't know, totally breaking down.

He unbuttoned my jeans. When his hand wrapped around me, I'd swear it was electrified. A spark went through me that made me jolt. I groaned.

"You're so beautiful," he whispered as he tried to sink to his knees.

I stopped him with a grip on his elbow. I wanted him to suck me—so damn much. But not here. And not now. I dunno, I felt like I didn't deserve that from him with the way I'd acted. And I wanted to touch him, show him how much I desired him, more than I wanted to be taken care of.

So I pressed him against the tree and got my hand down his pants. "Together," I said, heart pounding.

He nodded. "O-okay. Together."

His hand wrapped around me again, and I had to close my eyes and kiss him. I had to hide there, let my mind go and focus on the way it felt. His hand was long-fingered and strong, and he rubbed and played exquisitely until my eyes wanted to roll back in my head. I could only return short jerks, too shaky to do anything fancy. But the noises in his throat were appreciative anyway.

And just about the time I was gonna beg for more, his thighs trembled. He was close. He increased the pace of his strokes—hard and fast.

I came, warm waves of pleasure that made me gasp into his mouth. His dick hardened and jerked in my hand, and hell, that was the sexiest thing I'd ever felt.

We collapsed against the tree as I blissed out. My heartbeat pounded in my ears.

"Ow," Shane said.

"Oh, sorry." I stood up.

He rubbed his back sheepishly. "There was a knot or something."

"You okay?"

"I'm fucking great. You?"

I smiled big. "Perfect."

We cleaned ourselves as best we could using leaves and our underwear and zipped up.

"Wanna take a walk?" I asked, though my limbs were jelly.

"Sure."

Shane met my eyes only briefly, as if feeling awkward now. I didn't blame him. I'd sure been blowing hot and cold. I took his hand, and we returned to the path, then took it toward the road. The wind was sharp, and it reminded me it was a chilly November day, and I wasn't wearing a coat. I laughed.

"What's so funny?" Shane asked.

"It's cold out, and I didn't even feel it until just now."

"It's cold out?" he joked, deadpan. "Must be the hot cannoli in you that's keeping me warm."

"Yeah, yeah." I squeezed his hand.

We came out at the edge of the country road we lived on. There was no traffic, but I let go of his hand. Anyone might drive by, and chances were good they'd be a Canali. Which made me have to say what I was thinking.

"So… I want to see you. If you want to see me. But I'm not ready to come out to my family yet."

Shane gave me a sympathetic look. He didn't tell me what an idiot I was, which I appreciated.

"Soon," I said. "I think? Maybe. But not, like, right now."

"Your mom's been pretty good about it with me," Shane said softly. "Surprisingly good."

"Yeah, but you're not her son." I winced at how that sounded. "I mean, she likes you a lot. And she still wants you to come over. So that's good. That's… a lot. Better than I'd hoped for. But still… maybe we could give her time to get used to that? Time for you to be around the house as, you know, a gay guy and let them see you're just a normal person. Let that sink in a little before I'm all, like, *surprise!*"

"I guess I can see that." Shane had a little frown between his brows.

I wished I could take that frown away, but I couldn't promise him what he really wanted to hear.

"Anyway, Ma and Tessa and Nonna aren't the problem. It's Donny and Gabe and… and my dad."

Pa hadn't been rude to Shane. He wouldn't be, not after the Medal of Valor and how Ma had taken to him. But I'd seen the way he looked at Shane when he thought no one was watching—part bewilderment, part disdain. He didn't get men like Shane. He never would.

The thought that he'd look at me like that… it made me want to hurl.

I glanced at Shane, who walked quietly beside me, brow furrowed. The idea of disappointing my father was not enough, however, to make me give up Shane.

I took his hand again. "I want to be with you. I can come to Sacramento. Just… please give me a little more time in terms of us, here, at the house."

"Mike," he said, his blue eyes soft. "I'd never push you to come out to your family. That's your journey, not mine." He started to say more and stopped.

I heard it all the same—*but I'll only wait so long.*

I swore, some days, fighting fires seemed like the easiest part of my life.

"Are you busy tomorrow? It's my last day off before a five-day shift. I could drive down, and we could do some-thing, Like, during the day."

Shane smiled. "I have a paper due, but I can finish tonight, if I'm motivated. And you provide a lot of motivation."

That evening after Shane and Pops had gone home, no one seemingly the wiser about what earth-shifting change had occurred between me and Shane that day, and Mama and

Nonna still babbling on about Mendelssohn, I felt exhausted. I left the main house, intending to go back to my place and crawl into bed, even though the sun was barely down.

Tessa caught up with me on the back lawn. "Hey, Mike!"

"Hey." I couldn't manage much of a smile. I was glad when she walked with me instead of making me stop. I was still aimed at my bed.

"About today..." she began.

"Yeah, thanks for warning me," I snapped, remembering how blindsided I'd been when Mama introduced Mendelssohn.

Tessa grimaced. "Sorry. This wasn't my idea. It was all Ma and Carlotta. But still, I knew about their plans." She shrugged. "I honestly didn't think you'd care. You always act like you're not that close to Shane."

My feet stopped on the grass of their own accord. I rubbed my forehead. Being in the closet was so fucked.

"Hey." Tessa touched my arm. "You don't have to say anything. I saw it today. You looked like you'd lost way more than your best friend. That's why I wanted to say sorry. Sorry I participated in any of that. This. I...."

I looked at her, feeling helpless.

She put her arms around me and hugged me tight. "Why didn't you tell me?" she whispered.

Oh my God. Tessa knows. I let that sink in, waiting for the panic. But it wasn't as much terrifying as it was... a relief.

"Don't tell anyone else. Please?" I wasn't above begging.

"I won't, Mike. I promise. But God! You sure fooled us all. There was Rose in high school. And I just thought you were picky, I guess."

Tessa let me go, and we continued on toward my place. "I am picky."

She smiled. "Yeah. Shane's amazing."

"We're not...." I began. But, hell. "It's new. Like, today new. That we're a thing. But yeah, he's awesome."

She put her arm around my shoulders and hugged me as we walked. "Aw. That's great news! So Ma's plan worked after all? Only not the way she thought. Not surprised. You were about to rip that poor guy's head off." She laughed, a happy bright sound.

I stared at her narrow-eyed. "Right, you mean that poor, gorgeous, rich cardiovascular surgeon who drives a Tesla? Oh poor baby."

She laughed. "At least Ma and Carlotta figure Shane deserves the best." She shook her head. "But I thought *that poor guy* was about to bite the big one tonight."

I grinned. "Right, Dinner and Death at the Canalis."

She chuckled and squeezed me tight. "How about you and me get shitfaced and talk? Donny went off with Gabe to do some lamebrain thing or another, so we have time. Seems like we have a lot of years to catch up on, baby bro."

"I'd like that," I said, meaning it so, so much. If I had Tessa on my side... well, that was step one, wasn't it? "Thank you," I said.

She snorted. "You kidding? I'm about to grill you 'til you scream for mercy."

Only no grilling was necessary. We talked until midnight, and I told her things I'd never told anyone.

Turned out the first baby step out of the closet was pretty great.

THIRTEEN

SHANE

"Shane, what *are* you doing? I haven't seen you fuss this much since you went to the medal awards."

Poor Pops was just trying to get to the bathroom to pee and wash his hands, and I was hogging the mirror, thereby blocking the toilet and sink. "Sorry, Pops." I took one last glance and hurried back into the bedroom for an additional layer of clothing. It was chilly outside. I closed the bathroom door behind me so Pops could at least do his business in peace.

By the time Pops walked out rubbing his still damp hands together, I'd pulled on one of my nicer sweaters, in a teal blue-green to match my eyes, over my long-sleeved shirt.

Pops raised his bushy eyebrows. "You look nice. Is there something momentous going on I'm unaware of? A Hanukkah party I wasn't invited to?"

"Yeah, I'm pretty sure Hanukkah isn't in November this year, Pops. I'm going out with Mike today." Jeez, I even sounded breathless to me.

He frowned. "Haven't you gone out with Mike at least once a week for over a month?"

"Yeah." I swallowed, and he just cocked his head. I rushed on. "But this time, it's, like, a date?"

A slow smile spread across his face. "Ah ha. I thought the two of you might have changed your relationship status. So, Lucille's strategy backfired, huh?" He chuckled.

After my confrontation with Mike had turned into the best kind of reconciliation yesterday, I'd floated home on a dreamy cloud but hadn't said anything to Pops. It was too new, and I'd wanted to hold it close to my heart. But when Mike had confirmed over text that he wanted me to spend the day with him today, I'd gone into total first-date syndrome.

I gave Pops a side-eyed look. "What do you know about Lucille's strategy?" Mendelssohn hadn't been there very long after Pops came back from Giuseppe's.

He gave a little canary-consuming smile. "Carlotta told me that she and Lucille had cooked up the perfect date for you, and she was fit to burst with excitement about it. I had a feeling when you didn't mention it, that something had gone awry in meet-cute-land. So what happened? Mike get jealous?"

I snorted and felt my cheeks warm. "Yeah. Very. Much to my surprise."

"Well good. It's about time he understood that keeping you at arm's length was playing with fire. And with his training, he should know better."

"Oh, Pops." But damn, it was nice to think he believed that.

"I figured you were gonna run out of patience eventually." He sat on the edge of the bed. "So what romantic events did you two plan for your first big date?"

I clutched my hands to my chest. "He told me to choose."

"Smart man. What's on deck?"

"We're going to the zoo!"

For a second, he just stared at me and then started to laugh. "Oh good. Slobbery giraffes and smelly orangutans. You hopeless romantic, you."

———

"Jesus, look at that tongue. It's longer than my arm!" Mike shied from the probing quest of the giant giraffe for more food, stepping back on the platform that let us meet the huge animals almost face to face.

I leaned in and whispered against his ear, "Umm. What I couldn't do with an appendage like that."

Mike's cheeks turned pink, and he laughed. "Bring it on."

I grinned. It was fun being the more experienced gay guy.

I took his hand and waited while he tensed and glanced around. Gradually, he relaxed, and we wandered away from the giraffe encounter toward the meerkat enclosure. The little critters raced around from one hole to another, but they always had their sentries, standing on their haunches, noses to the sky, watching for predators.

Mike pointed and grinned. "I'm like them. Hypervigilant. Sorry about that."

"It's okay. Trust me, it takes nerve to hold a guy's hand in public, even when you're out. I know it's not easy for you, and if you'd rather not, I understand." Actually, I wasn't pushing Mike's boundaries too much. The day was cool and threatened rain, so not a lot of people were visiting the zoo.

He smiled at me gratefully, but said, "Your hands are cold." He slid my left hand into the deep pocket of his puffer jacket, which definitely made me swoon.

Was this really happening? Was Mike Canali, gorgeous fireman and star of my licentious dreams since the Crest Lake fire, actually on a date with me? I didn't entirely trust it. But I was sure as shit gonna go with it.

I led us toward my fave animal enclosures, the cheetahs

and the red pandas, and we walked along in warm, companionable silence, but my hand in his pocket was an intriguing distraction. He slid a finger between mine, slow and sinuous, and it brought up all kinds of zoological ideas.

As we gazed at a mama cheetah with two half-grown cubs looking all fuzzy and ferocious, I let my hand explore the depths of the jacket pocket. Interesting. Apparently, our finger-play had brought some other appendages into prominence, and through the puffy nylon, I could feel a definite half-mast condition.

I explored.

Mike gasped.

I chuckled and continued outlining his protuberance.

When a flock of children ran up to the cheetah display, I gave a gentle tug in the best places, and we walked farther down the pathway to the red pandas.

I murmured, "These are my nominees for the cutest creatures on earth." Of course, I hadn't stopped my in-pocket massage.

Mike's breath came fast and raspy. "Cutest after you." He stepped closer to me so my hand could plunge deeper and get a better grip. At the same time, he pressed his erection against my thigh.

My own penis was pushing so hard against my fly, I had to have teeth marks on the head. I waved my unoccupied hand toward one of the pandas draped luxuriously over a branch. "Look at that tail."

"Oh yeah, I can hardly see anything else." He slid a hand under the bottom of my jacket and over my butt cheek until he was tracing the crack in my ass, up and down and up and down.

When the horde of children ran to the pandas, we were both half-giggling and half-gasping. Succumbing to the better part of valor, we removed our hands from their more-than-desirable locations and started walking toward the front of the zoo.

After a couple minutes moving at speed, Mike cleared his throat. "Are you cold?"

"A little, but I'm going to take you inside, so you'll warm up."

"Oh, where?"

"You'll see." I tried not to look too calculating.

When we got to the large house near the front entrance, Mike looked up at the sign and stopped dead. "Uh, no. Nope. No way."

"Oh come on," I laughed, "They're beautiful."

"You didn't grow up in Resolute. We get rattlers up there. In the garage sometimes. Once in Nonna and Nonno's house. If you ever want to see ten grown-ass tough guys act like teenaged girls, bring a snake around our house."

I laughed. "Good to know the family's Achilles heel." I leaned in and spoke softly. "Didn't I ever tell you that I have a deep and abiding preference for snakes?" I grabbed his hand and pulled him toward the Sacramento Zoo Reptile House.

While Mike did spend the next few minutes cringing, he was a good sport and let me pull him from anaconda to cobra to pit viper as I gazed in fascination.

"So, Slytherin, huh?" Mike gave me a look.

I frowned. "No, Gryffindor forever, but I remember as a little kid thinking I must have parseltongue." I snorted. "My loving snakes was just one more reason my family thought I was of the devil." I pulled on Mike's hand. "Come on. Let me show you my favorite king cobra and then your suffering will be over."

"Hey, mister, are you holding that guy's hand?"

I blinked and looked down at a little boy, maybe eight or nine, staring at Mike's and my linked hands. Mike tensed, his hand pulling away fast, and I glanced around for the potential irate mother about to spring on us and accuse us of corrupting her darling, but no one else was around.

"Uh, hi. Are you lost?"

"Heck no." He pointed through the archway that led out of the reptile house. "My church group is here. But I saw you and wanted to ask you. Is he your boyfriend?"

I glanced at Mike. Okay, kind of his call. Not like a little kid would out him, but still.

Mike looked at the boy with his cute curly hair and missing teeth. "Right. You guessed it. We're boyfriends."

I had to smile because damn.

The kid smiled too. "I thought so." He crossed his arms. "I already told my mom that when I grow up, I'm going to have a boyfriend."

"Oh really?" Mike nodded with great seriousness. "It's fun to have a boyfriend." He gave me a quick, hot glance that went straight to my cock.

"I know." The kid smiled. "I really like boys."

I couldn't resist. "What did your mom say?"

He shrugged. "She said I could have any kind of boyfriend I want. I told her I know." He took a step back. "Thank you. There are a lot of girlfriends out there." He waved his hand vaguely toward the world in general. "I like to see boyfriends sometimes. Bye." He ran out of the reptile house and dissolved into the pack of children moving by.

Mike stared after him, lips parted. "What just happened?"

"Representation matters."

"Wow. That kid's young."

I shrugged. "I knew I was different when I was his age or even younger. And today, kids see gay people a lot more, so they're more aware of it as a possibility than we were." I glanced at Mike. "What about you?"

He sighed. "Nope. I didn't see gay men around town growing up in Resolute. And it's not like you'd ever find *Queer Eye* on our TV, or even *Will and Grace*. So I fought it all the way." He gave a little sigh. "Hell, I guess I haven't stopped fighting yet."

I took his hand again, and this time, he accepted it willingly. I said, "It's nice to see that the boy's mom is accepting."

Both of us fell silent for a minute, basking in the idea so fervently to be wished.

Mike said, "Before we leave, let's go in here." He pulled me toward the gift shop. "I want to get you something to remember our first official date."

"Oh, wow." I blinked hard. "Thank you."

Inside the store, the shelves were crammed with every variety of stuffed animal toy. Mike grabbed an alligator and nuzzled it against my neck, making attack noises. There were lots of mugs and water bottles with glitter, but Mike zeroed in on a glass case against the back wall that was filled with commemorative jewelry. He peered in, seeming to stare at everything. Then his eyes lit up, and he said to the salesman, "May I see that, please?" He turned to me. "Close your eyes."

"Why?"

"Uh, is the concept of a surprise unfamiliar to you?"

I closed my eyes, but oddly, what he said was true. As a child, my family hadn't believed in frivolity like surprise parties or special gifts told to Santa in secret. In fact, Santa Claus had been considered anathema, a distraction from the true meaning of the season.

I felt something slide onto my wrist, and the salesman said, "Looks like an excellent fit."

"Can I look now?" Clearly, surprises were torture.

"Okay. You can look."

I opened my eyes and blinked down at a slim silver band that clasped my left wrist, and from it dangled a small, detailed charm. I felt my smile spreading across my face. The charm was a little coiled snake. I laughed as the first tear fell on my cheek. "Thank you. This means more to me than any present I've ever received."

He looked at me questioningly, and then, as I wiped my eyes, he seemed to get that this had more significance than he'd realized. Without even glancing around, he folded me into his arms and hugged me silly.

My phone buzzed in my pocket. I was happy to ignore it, but Mike let me go, looking at me expectantly, so I took it out. I smiled.

"Something good?" Mike asked.

"It's Ro. He's sending me info on the Thanksgiving parade next weekend."

"Thanksgiving Parade?"

"Yeah. Ro and I are members of the Pride Center. It's the LGBTQ group at Sac State. We're marching in the Sacramento Thanksgiving parade, which is actually on the Saturday after Thanksgiving. He was just telling me we're up to thirty people signed up to march now. So that's cool."

Mike's face did something complicated. Had he been contemplating other plans for us for Thanksgiving weekend? A boy could dream, though Ro would kill me if I dropped out of the parade now.

"Do you have to be a student to march in that?" Mike asked.

"No. Anyone can walk with us. Last year, we had some parents and other allies. Why?" But my increased heart rate and hopeful lilt to the end of my question said I knew.

Mike shrugged, but his face was glowing. "I dunno. I always thought it would be amazing to walk in a Pride parade. To be that open and proud about it. I've seen pictures online, and they made me feel envious, I guess."

"Why don't you come! It's not an actual Pride parade, since those are in June, so it's pretty lowkey. But walking with the Pride Center, we all show our rainbow colors, and it's obviously an LGBTQ group. It's fun! It'd be a perfect baby step."

"You think?" Mike chewed his lip, looking torn. He'd

come so far since I met him. He was like a new man when we went out to the clubs now. I was suddenly convinced this was exactly what he needed as a next step. Besides, the idea of having my gorgeous boyfriend with me in front of the entire Pride Center was pretty damn sweet.

"Yes, Mike. It'd be great! We all dress up in crazy gear and wave Pride flags. You'll love it! Ro will be there, and everyone is nice. Plus, some of the people in the group aren't gay, so it's not really a proclamation. Just support. Allyship. Say you'll come!"

His hesitant expression cleared, and he broke into a smile. "Okay. I'll do it."

My fingers hesitated over my phone. "Are you sure? 'Cause if we put you on the list, it's kind of crappy to back out. We have to tell the parade organizers how many we have and all that."

I saw Mike swallow, but his smile didn't falter. "Yeah. Totally. I'm in."

Whoa. This was my day for wonderful surprise gifts. I refused to let myself tear up again, though, as I typed the message to Ro. He replied with an emoji of an excited puppy jumping up and down. And then probably with tons of questions, but I turned off the text alerts and stuck the phone back in my pocket.

As we walked to the car, Mike said, "I got us another, uh, surprise. But it's cool if you want to beg off."

I clapped my hands. "What is it? What is it?"

"I sort of rented a room. A hotel room. Just in case you might want to, you know, have some privacy. But now that sounds presumptuous. I don't want you to think I only care about one thing."

I stared at him with my mouth open. "Are you freaking kidding me? I sleep on the couch so my grandfather can have the bed, and you share a house with your homophobic brother, and you'd think there's a universe in which I wouldn't give my firstborn for a hotel room?"

"Shhh." My voice had risen, and he glanced around, laughing. "Yeah, that's about where my head was at when I made the reservation." He grasped my hand, and we started walking faster. "The hotel is only two blocks away. I haven't checked in yet, and I'm not, uh, I mean, I'm not sure—"

I chuckled. "Not up to checking into a hotel with no luggage holding another guy's hand? I get it. That's brass-balls material. I'll stay outside until you register. Call me when you get to the room, and I'll come in." I chewed the inside of my lip. "But are you sure you can afford this?"

"Yeah, no worries. I don't make all that much yet, although California pays firefighters better than almost any state. My folks don't charge rent, and between Ma and the fire station, a lot of my food's covered. Cal Fire even pays for me to get my EMT. So I've been socking money away."

I frowned at him even though I wanted to run, not walk, to this hotel. "I don't want you wasting your money on frivolity." The second the words left my mouth, I slapped a hand over my lips.

He looked startled. "What?"

"Oh my God. I just sounded like my father. Heaven help me." A muscle jumped in my jaw. "Mike, let's go invest some of your hard-earned money in our own happiness."

He grinned like a loon.

So did I.

FOURTEEN

MIKE

I hadn't been this nervous since the first day of my Cal Fire training intensive. I was going to be alone with Shane. I'd wanted it so badly that day of the Crest Lake fire when we'd kissed in the canoe. I would have given anything to be somewhere safe, alone with him in a bed, so I could do all the things I needed in that moment. And I'd imagined it a hundred times since. Shane had no idea the starring role he'd had in my fantasies for months. If he did, he'd probably run screaming. Now it was finally happening.

I felt like a sleaze for dragging him to a hotel room on what was really our first actual date. But if there was one thing I'd learned growing up in my family of first responders, it was to make the most of the time you had. Fortunately, Shane seemed as enthusiastic as me.

The hotel was nothing fancy, just a Days Inn. But it was the best I could justify spending money on. I checked in while Shane hung out in the car, then texted him the room number. I waited in the hallway until he emerged from the elevator. His blue eyes sparkled with mischief, and he had a sexy smile as he walked up. I used the key card to open the door, smothering a nervous laugh. Then we were inside, away from anyone or anything that could judge us.

We stood there for a moment, just looking at each other. Anticipation crackled in the air—along with nerves. I was gonna say something pathetic like, *well here we are*, when Shane pushed off the wall, his eyes hungry.

"Let's go. I want to see it. All of it." He waved a hand up and down my body.

I laughed nervously. "Pushy much?"

His smile was wicked. "I can be as pushy—or submissive —as you want me to be. Or we can take turns."

Holy shit. A spike of heat rushed through my body. I dumped my jacket on the floor and whipped my long-sleeved T-shirt over my head, letting it drop.

He stared at my chest, eyes wide. And, damn, all those hours in the gym had been worth it. "Jesus, Mike." He ghosted his fingertips over my pecs and down to my abs, which had a six-pack if you squinted in the right light. My mom was too good a cook for it to be pronounced.

I shivered. His fingertips felt so hot in the air-conditioned room.

"Now you," I said, my dick throbbing at the mere idea of seeing Shane naked.

He bit his lip, his hand dropping away from my stomach. "I'm not ripped."

"Don't care." I reached out to grab the front of his purple T-shirt. He raised his arms, and I tugged it over his head and tossed it.

He seemed to make a conscious effort not to cross his arms over his chest, but his eyes were worried.

"You're just how I imagined you." I ran both palms over the caps of his shoulders and down his chest, his skin warm under my hands. He was thin with only a little definition in his chest. His stomach was flat. It was clear he didn't work out, but he had a naturally lean frame. His skin was pale and lightly freckled. He had rosy pink nipples that pouted out in a way I'd never seen on a guy. The sight of them made me want to fall to my knees. I wanted to suck them, they were so sexy. And I wanted to suck other parts of him too—badly. I'd given up trying to figure out why Shane did it for me like this. I was just glad I'd found him.

"Um… I don't have any stuff with me," Shane said.

I left off staring at his nipples and blinked at him. "Stuff?"

"Condom and lube." Shane raised a *duh* eyebrow.

Oh. For some reason when he'd said *stuff*, I'd thought of an overnight bag. My cheeks heated, though I didn't know why. It's not like I hadn't seen lots of porn with men fucking each other or imagined it with Shane. But it was different when he said it out loud.

"Do we need it? I mean. I was thinking…." I hesitated.

"What were you thinking?" Shane took a step closer to me and put his arms around my neck. "What do you want? Use your big boy words," he teased.

I huffed. "Shut up."

He smiled but raised a brow in query.

I took a deep breath. "I've been thinking a lot about sucking you. I picture that. And vice versa. Are you into that? Blowjobs?"

Shane chuckled and then melted against me, kissing me hungrily. He coaxed my tongue more deeply into his mouth and sucked on it, moaning. I took that for a *yes*. My dick took that for a promise, throbbing in my pants. And damn, the feel of his bare chest on mine was exquisite. I got pretty sensitive when I was horny, and currently, just the brush of his nipples against mine was enough to make me come, which I so didn't want to do yet.

I shuffled us backward toward the bed, my mouth still fused to his. The back of my knees hit the mattress hard, and I sat with an *oof*, unfortunately disconnecting from his mouth.

I moaned unhappily and was about to drag Shane down to me when I realized—hmmm. The bed put me at exactly the height of his zipper.

Oh God. This was about to happen.

I stared for a heartbeat, then fumbled for his button. "Get these off." I didn't recognize my own voice. "I want to touch you while I do it."

"Now who's being pushy?" Shane asked. But his voice quivered, and he hurried to kick off his shoes and shove down his jeans, tossing them aside.

When he stood up, his dick was long and pink and sticking straight at his chin. It was the hottest thing I'd ever seen. He gripped my shoulders as if he needed the support. Wow. I ran my hands down his thighs, just taking it all in.

"I can go first," Shane said. "If you want."

"Anxious, are we?" I grinned and gave him a look through my lashes. "I have done this before." It was practically the only thing I had done with guys, and not nearly often enough. But still, I thought I was decent at it.

His Adam's apple bobbed as he swallowed. "Well then. Let's go, Canali." He took hold of his shaft and guided it to my lips, painting them lightly with the warm liquid on the tip. Fuck, that was sexy.

I opened my mouth, just a little, staring up at his eyes as he rolled the head around the opening of my lips. I tickled his hole with my tongue, which got me a soft, grunting sound, and his eyelids fluttered. He tapped my bottom lip. I opened a tiny bit more, and he pushed the tip inside, not even the whole head. I suckled on that inch of skin, watching his brilliant blue eyes go dark and intense.

"Fuck," he breathed.

I opened a little more. Inch by inch, we drove each other mad with teasing—me with how much I wanted him choking my throat and him wanting to be buried inside me. Finally, he couldn't take anymore and pushed in all the way. His cockhead slicked over my palate and into the back of my throat. I started to gag but remembered fast and relaxed my muscles. As a gay, closeted teen, I'd practiced on the zucchini Ma always had overflowing in her garden, and I could do this. I dug my fingers into his hips and held him there, loving the feel of him, hard as a rod, filling my mouth.

"Gotta… Oh God. Mike." Shane gripped my shoulders tight and pulled back. Then he was fucking my mouth. I slid my hands back to hold the round globes of his ass, encouraging him to move, to fuck me. My dick pulsed against my fly, I was so turned on. It was perfect bliss to have him moving in and out of me like this, every noise he made, every slide of his hard dick so sexy, I thought my head would explode—and my balls too. Since my mouth was busy, I let my eyes beg him to keep going, to take what he wanted and use me.

He stared back at me, face grimacing with pleasure, his eyes going sharp and muzzy at the same time somehow. His upper lip trembled, then his thighs.

"Gonna… want me to stop?" he panted.

In answer, I sucked harder and stuffed him inside by pushing my hands on his ass. He groaned out loud, and three strokes later, he pushed in hard and came down my throat, both of us whimpering and moaning. Yes. God, yes. I'd only ever tried swallowing once before with minimal success, but this was Shane, and I wanted it all.

When he pulled away, I flopped onto my back and scrambled for my zipper. I was so close. He batted my hands away, fell to his knees like a collapsing building, and managed to get my pants undone. I looked down to watch as he stuffed my dick in his mouth and sucked hard.

I nearly screamed, it felt so perfect. "Oh, fuck. Oh, fuck. Already close," I breathed as he sucked, and hot pleasure swirled in my balls. "Oh, fuck. Oh."

I came, eyes squeezed shut against the intensity. He

nursed me through it, pulling hard and then gently as my climax peaked, until I had to push him away, I was so sensitive.

He crawled onto the bed and tugged on my arm until I wormed my way up to the pillows. We lay there, panting. I still had my jeans on, though they were open and my deflating dick was exposed. Looking down at the oh-so-sexy sight, I had to laugh.

"What?" Shane asked.

"I didn't even get undressed."

He made a thoughtful sound. "Kind of hot like that. Like a secret blowjob." He found my hand and threaded his fingers through mine.

But the word *secret* bugged me a little. I had too many secrets, and I didn't like them. Not that I'd ever want anyone in my family clued in as to where and when I got blowjobs.

I let go of his hand, turning onto my side so I could look at him. Smiling, he faced me. God, I could stare into those magical eyes all day.

He held up his wrist. "Thank you for my beautiful bracelet." The corner of his lips tugged up. "And for getting this room."

"Abso-fucking-lutely. But we'll have to figure out something else. I can't afford one every time."

Shane thought about that. "Roland's roommate is always traveling for work. I might be able to borrow his place sometime."

That sounded iffy, but hey, beggars couldn't be choosers. "That'd be good."

"There's no place on that big old Canali compound that's private enough?" he asked, tucking his hands up under his chin, a move which made him seem so young.

"Not really." Yeah there were a few outbuildings and the garage. But none of them were safe *enough* in a family like mine. I was too paranoid to risk even a one percent chance of getting caught. And yeah, sometimes Donny stayed over with his current girlfriend—which changed almost weekly. But with my luck, he'd come home early. Donny catching us was a nightmare on a scale surpassed only by the idea of my dad walking in on Shane fucking me or something. I shuddered.

Shane must have felt my shiver because he reached out to rub my arm. "It's okay. Baby steps."

I didn't want to think about it—about where those baby steps would lead. Not here, not now, when I had Shane naked in front of me. I just wanted to *be* for an hour. Be my true self. Be with Shane. And if that was wrong, then mea culpa.

I sat up enough to shuck off my jeans, then rolled on top of him. I'd just come, but all that bare skin against me, the sensation of his limp dick, still moist and hot, against mine…. Heaven.

"I have this room all night. You could stay."

His eyebrows went up, and he looked at me. "I can do that. Can you?"

I shrugged. "I'll tell the family I spent the night at a friend's."

"Cool. Your mom will probably get all excited and think you've got a new girlfriend." He was smiling, but there was sadness behind it.

I took a breath. "I just want to be with you, Shane."

For a second, he gazed at me and then said, "And I want to be with you. So yes, Mike Canali, I will sleep with you."

My heart soared. "I doubt we'll do much of that." I kissed his throat, and it was so yummy, I started to suck a hickey there.

He squirmed and laughed. "Hell yeah, I'm all in. Just don't stop."

———

Monday morning when I drove up to the main house, Pa's truck was in the driveway. He was home. That meant Ma would have made a bigger breakfast than usual—bacon, eggs, maybe even pancakes. I was *starving*.

I whistled a happy tune as I skipped up the porch steps. I wanted a yummy breakfast, and then I had to get ready to go on shift. Shane and I had gotten maybe two hours of sleep last night. We'd done sixty-nine, took a long shower together complete with soapy handjobs, and rubbed against each other until we were both raw. It had been the best night of my life, but I was gonna pay for it today at work. Hopefully it'd be quiet, and I could nap at the station.

I let myself in the front door, shutting it quietly in case Nonno was in the living room sleeping like he often was in the mornings.

"I don't like it, Lucille. I don't want it in my house!" My father's voice, firm. He sounded upset.

I froze, listening. What was going on?

"Don't say *it*. This is not an *it*, Angie. It's a *him*. Are you saying you don't want Shane in our home? The nice boy who saved our Mike's life? Who won a Medal of Valor and has been so helpful to our family?" Ma's voice, angry.

"I don't want that influence on our grandchildren! So, no. I don't want a gay person hanging around this house. I'd feel the same way if he was the damn pope!"

Icy dread slicked through my veins. I leaned against the wall by the front door because my knees threatened to collapse.

"Being around a gay person does not make children gay," my mother said firmly.

"It's an influence! Children are sponges. You know that."

"About some things, yes, but sexual orientation doesn't work that way," my mom insisted adamantly. "Tessa says—"

"Never mind Tessa. What does Father O'Brien say? Have you spoken to him about it? If you haven't, you should!"

Father O'Brien was the priest at Saint Thomas, where our family had gone to church since well before I was born. My heart sank. He was a nice man but traditional to the core. I held my breath.

Ma was quiet for a moment. "Father says *hate the sin, love the sinner*. What's he gonna to say? All our other children have their issues. It's not our place to judge."

"Shane is not one of our children! We don't have that in our family. Thank God." My dad's tone was disgusted, and something deep inside me cracked. My throat got tight, and I couldn't breathe.

"This is my home, too, Angie. And I'm not going to abandon Shane," my mother said. "I'm not gonna reject that boy. That's not the way this family operates. Heck, that's not the way I'd treat a dog."

"I'm not saying you have to reject him. Once in a great while, he can come. But no more of this crap with trying to fix him up. If he steps foot in this house, he doesn't bring the gay thing up! Or have men around. That's too far, Lucy. That's too damn far!"

Too damn far. I didn't hear the rest of the argument. I couldn't bear to. I let myself out the front door and ran into the woods. Funny how much you can puke, even on an empty stomach.

FIFTEEN

SHANE

"You had that man all to yourself yesterday and you took him to the zoo?" Ro swatted my arm. "You might have to turn in your official gay boy credentials, my friend. I mean seriously. I knew you were looking for a little tail, but this is ridiculous!" He chugged his caramel macchiato in mock outrage.

I leaned in so he could hear me over the surrounding conversations of the Get Perky customers. Being Monday morning, it was still busy at ten o'clock. Everyone needed their caffeine fix to face another week. "It wasn't as PG as it sounds. Let's just say we created enough animal magnetism to end up in positions worthy of the bonobos." I grinned.

He frowned. "What positions?"

I raised my eyebrows and widened my eyes.

"Seriously?" I loved his stunned expression.

I looked coy. "We might have gotten a hotel room after."

He slapped a hand to his chest and bucked back in his chair, making it scrape the floor. "Oh my Gawd. You're killing me." A few people stared, and he lowered his voice. "Did you have to drag him kicking and screaming? Gods and fishes, tell me everything."

I glanced around at the crowded room to see if anyone was listening and almost laughed at catching myself acting like Mike. "No, I didn't drag him anywhere. *He* got the hotel room."

"Are you sure this wasn't just a vivid dream you had?" Ro appeared both delighted and doubtful.

"Nope. He had it all set up and was so cute about it, like he didn't want me to think he was only interested in one thing." I snorted. "How adorable is that? As if I hadn't been dreaming of that one thing since the Crest Lake fire."

Ro clasped his face with his hands. "Awww." He leaned closer. "But, uh, what *one thing* did you do?"

I gave him a look and nodded toward the other customers. "Not really the place to get into the deets."

"Crap." He sat back in his chair, looking disappointed. "But it was good, right? Is he that gorgeous all over? Please tell me he is."

I beamed. I'd felt so good, sometimes I swore my heart was going to lift right out of my chest on the tail end of a helium balloon. "It was. The best."

Ro sighed. "God. He's so hot. But what brought this on? How did the boy loosen up so much?"

"You won't believe this…." I told him how Lucille and Nonna had wanted to fix me up with Tessa and then learned the *horrible truth* about me. "But they didn't take it badly. In fact, they set up a dinner to fix me up with another guy and guess what? Mike got pissed and decided to finally make a move."

Ro sighed. "That's so romantic. That's awesome news, right? Is Mike going to come out to them, since his family is so accepting?"

I shrugged. "Soon, I think. He's still nervous about taking that step, and I understand why. I mean, his whole world revolves around that family. They're not just his blood. They're his friends, his teachers, the backbone of his profession. Hell, they even provide the place he lives and most of his food." I raised my brows. "I've tasted that food. A guy could stay in the closet for less." I laughed. "But I think he's encouraged. I mean, who'd have believed his mom would go so far as to try to find me the perfect boyfriend? It was such a kind thing to do. And OMG, was it ever effective, jealousy-wise."

Ro smiled and put a warm hand on my arm. "I'm so happy for you. I know I've been a be-atch about Mike sometimes, but you know it's because I love you, right? I'm just trying to be sure nobody hurts my BFF."

I leaned over and hugged him. "Love you too."

"I can hardly believe Mike agreed to march in the Thanksgiving Parade with the Pride Center. He must have had a whole epiphany at once. The parade's only, like, thirteen days away. There's still lots to finish."

"I'll do all I can to help."

"Good." He gave me a significant look. "I hope Mike doesn't chicken out."

"He seemed really sincere and excited about it." My shrug was full of hope.

He leaned back. "What's next for the Shane and Mike show?"

"We're going clubbing next Saturday, and he's coming to my apartment to pick me up."

"Dayum. So he's not worried about Pops knowing his big secret?"

I shook my head. "Pops has known Mike was gay since the fire, but he's been pretty damned disappointed about Mike's waffling and ignoring me in front of his family." I smiled and wrapped my arms around myself. "The fact that Mike's willing to come to my place suggests he's more positive about our relationship. Like maybe he feels worthy of Pops's good opinion."

Ro spread his palms and stuck out his lip. "I hope you're right, my friend. But yeah, meeting the folks is a good sign." He grinned. "Glam it up, boyfriend." He waggled his fingers as he pushed back from the table and returned to his barista station.

———

"Shane, if you polish that wineglass one more time, I'm taking it away from you."

"Sorry, Pops." I set the wineglass down on the counter in my tiny kitchen and walked into the living room, short stroll that it was. Pops was lounging in his favorite chair, staring at his tablet on which he read his news.

He said, "Sit. He's not due for another fifteen minutes." He set his tablet aside.

I sat.

For a moment, neither of us said anything. Then I asked, "Are you going to see Giuseppe anytime soon?"

"Haven't been invited."

"Oh. I guess that's not unusual. They probably wouldn't think about guests for Nonno separate from the rest of the family." I chewed my lip. I'd noticed that Lucille hadn't invited me or Pops to Thanksgiving yet. Neither had Mike. Every time I got a text, I half expected it to be an invite from one of them and got to swallow my sadness when it wasn't.

"Where does the family think Mike is when he's out with you?"

"Oh, uh, I don't know exactly. I suppose he's got other friends." In truth, I never asked Mike exactly what he told his parents or brothers about his social life. I didn't want to hear about lies he'd told. Lying in general made me antsy. I disliked it so much that I'd ended up getting tossed out of my home rather than do it. Even lies of omission made me uncomfortable, which was one of the reasons I was so pushy about my gay boy style. I didn't want people thinking I tried to trick them in some way. I respected Mike's situation, but the less I knew about the specifics, the better. "He's a grownup. He doesn't have to report everything to his parents."

"Have you met Lucille?" Pops snarked. "But I'm happy to hear things are thawing a bit at the Canalis. I'd sure like to see that man come into his own and live his life." He smiled softly. "Whether that life includes my grandson or not."

"Thanks, Pops. It's going good. Like Mike says, baby steps. But, yeah. I'm feeling pretty positive about it." I fingered the bracelet Mike had bought me at the zoo.

The knock on the door rocketed me out of my chair.

Pops snorted. "Take a breath."

I gave him a quick hug as I walked by his chair, then inhaled and opened the door. Oh wow. "Hi."

"Hi." Mike smiled reflexively, but then it spread to his eyes—and my heart.

"Come on in for a bit before we go."

"Uh, okay." Mike walked past me and straight to Pops. "Good evening, sir." They shook hands, and Mike sat on the couch opposite Pops. He set a small gym bag on the floor beside him. Did he come from working out?

Like always, Mike looked amazing, but he wasn't dressed to go clubbing. He'd been getting more and more daring over the weeks of going out with me and my friends. He'd started that first night we'd gone to Friend of Dorothy in black jeans and a tight black T-shirt, but he'd showed up the next week in a net shirt with low-rise Levis, and I'd thought I'd pass out. Tonight, though, he was in plain jeans and a navy-blue Henley under his black leather jacket. A Henley to go to a gay club? Dear god, any club worth its glitter would take away my gold sneakers and spangled jockstrap if I tried to get him in. Still, subtlety, thy name was Shane Bower. I needed to chill until the right moment. "Can I get you some wine, Mike?"

"Sure, that'd be great." Funny, his eyes were a little glassy already, like he'd been drinking. That shouldn't have been the case, though. He worked what they called the California swing shift where he was on twenty-four hours and then off twenty-four hours for five days. Then he got four days in a row off. This was his time for off days, so I was pretty sure he had gotten off his last shift recently.

"Pops? Want some wine?"

"Sure, why not?"

I slipped into the kitchen and poured three glasses of white wine, all the while plotting how to get Mike into something that wouldn't get him accused of being straight. I'd bought him a pair of firefighter bikini underwear on a whim, but somehow I doubted he'd wear just that.

When I came back into the living room and distributed the glasses, Pops and Mike were just sitting, both of them trying hard not to look uncomfortable. Odd, I thought they were past that stage. Still, seeing them in the same room together made me believe that the whole Shane and Mike thing could really happen, and god, it made me happy. I was so gone for the guy it was ridiculous.

We all sipped wine, and the two of them talked about football for a few minutes. I sometimes forgot that Pops had interests outside the ones he shared with me. Man, we did take parents—and grandparents—for granted.

After a few more minutes, with the wine mostly consumed, I cleared my throat. "So Mike, we should think about going."

"Oh, right." He stood. "I need to change first." He picked up the gym bag. "Can I use the bathroom?"

Whew. I almost wiped my forehead. "Come on into the bedroom."

Pops picked up his tablet and made a show of looking at it as Mike and I walked into the bedroom.

The minute the door closed behind me, I grabbed him, and he came willingly into my arms. The smell of beer on his breath made me blink, but hell. Who needed to relax more than firefighters? I whispered, "It feels like I haven't seen you in forever." It had been six whole days with Mike on his intense shift and me in school. I hadn't seen him since the night we'd spent at the hotel and made our giant leap into a more-than-friend relationship. My body craved his.

"Yeah, not even a whole week." He grinned when he said it, but still. Maybe it hadn't seemed long to him, what with fires and such.

I stretched onto tiptoe and fit my mouth to his. Oh. Perfect, perfect. I caressed his lips with my tongue and then ran along the seam until he opened with a soft moan. Thank you very much. I dove in and let the heat of his mouth spread to my brain because who wanted to think when they could kiss Mike Canali?

We clung there, exploring each other's mouths for several minutes, but finally, he said, "I'll change so we can go dance."

"Oh, looking forward to dancing, are we?" I grinned. "Since when?"

"What I'm looking forward to is having you in as few clothes as possible as close to me as possible, so if that's looking forward to dancing, then hell yeah." He kissed my hair and pulled that ridiculous Henley over his head.

I propped my butt on the bed. "What's with the shirt?"

A crease flashed between his eyebrows. "Nothing. Just an old shirt I had. I was, you know, at home, so I couldn't exactly doll up for Donny's appreciation."

I snorted, but Mike didn't laugh. He looked a little intense. Still, I forgot about the shirt fast as he pulled the baggy jeans down his legs revealing—ta-da—a miniscule pair of black bikini briefs. The briefs cupped that delicious bubble butt and those powerful thighs so lovingly, I had to suck saliva into my mouth in place of the other things I'd rather be sucking. "That's pretty fabu, but—" I held up a finger and retrieved the briefs I'd bought for him from the drawer.

Mike gaped at the scrap of fabric with the bright red-and-gold Cal Fire insignia and laughed. "You're kidding me."

"Only for the hottest of the Hot Cannolis."

"Fuck. Why not?" His eyes glistened as he dragged the bikinis down his legs, revealing his long, thick, beautifully shaped cock, now at half-mast. When he pulled the bikinis up, his dick kind of danced around before he finally got it corralled in the pouch.

I laughed. "It's trying to escape." I was so tempted to give it someplace warm and wet to go, but Pops was in the living room. That just wasn't happening. Instead, I made a turn motion with my finger, and Mike spun around, showing off his bare buttocks outlined by the red bikinis. "Oh yes, a total Hot Cannoli."

He struck a pose with an arm behind his head. "Oh, yeah, baby, that's me. Pure cream in a crispy shell. The only cannoli to ever be served hot. Yeah, baby. Yeah, baby." He danced around with his butt bobbing, and it was such an un-Mike thing to do that I laughed.

After taking a low bow, he pulled his tight, black jeans from his gym bag and dragged them on over the bikinis. The jeans rode low on his narrow hips, and I leaned forward and pulled the straps of the bikinis over his hipbones so they showed. Oh man, sex-y.

He pulled his black net shirt out of the bag next, but then he paused in front of my floor-length mirror. He made a face that, if I captioned it, would have said, *Not bad*. He flexed one way and then the other, then shoved the shirt back into his bag and pulled his leather jacket on over his bare chest.

I giggled. "Who are you and what—"

"Yeah, yeah." He waved a hand at me and laughed, a little

too loud. He spun around. "Ready for action, baby. Where are we going?"

"A new place."

"Oh, where?"

"You'll see." I chuckled and pulled my fluffy pink coat on over my jeans, but I planned to leave my shirt at the door as well. I'd been waffling on where to take Mike that night, but his comment about getting me in as few clothes as possible had sealed the deal. That and his daring choice in clothes. Timmy's it was. Sometimes you just had to say *fuck baby steps*.

———

"Where the hell are we?" Mike stared out the window as I parked Mable next to a jacked-up truck more fitting of a redneck bar than a gay club. But as we watched, two guys in bikinis, leather harnesses, and high heels climbed out and strutted across the parking lot to the sprawling warehouse building. There was a light over the door, but not so much as a sign.

I made a sweeping motion. "This is Timmy's, another stage of your gay education."

His eyes widened. "Shit, I've plunged down the rabbit hole."

I squeezed his arm. "Don't worry. If you don't like it, we'll leave."

"Fuck that. I'm up for anything."

Oh really? He sounded a little overly jacked. But hey, enthusiasm was good, right?

I ditched my shirt in the car, we pulled on our jackets against the chill, and walked to the door, where I showed my membership card to the bouncer, who was the size of a small state. Timmy's was a private club, although the membership fee was very minimal or I never could have afforded it.

Winston had introduced me and Ro to it, and I hoped maybe we'd see him and Chas there tonight.

Mike looked at me quizzically as we stepped into the reception area and yet another host inspected my card. As we walked into the flashing lights of the club, I said, "Since Timmy's is private, they can do a few things that the public clubs aren't allowed to do." I swept a hand toward the small stage where two buff guys danced, wearing body paint and nothing else.

"Wow."

The dance floor was fairly crowded with men in every kind of outfit and costume from fancy dress to almost totally nude. Everyone was grinding and rubbing indiscriminately. Timmy's redefined wild.

I found a small, round table that two guys were just leaving, and Mike and I sat, hanging our jackets on the backs of the chairs to claim the territory and leaving our chests bare.

Mike looked around anxiously. "Where's the waiter? I need a drink."

Alrighty then. I waved toward the server, and he hurried over. I ordered my usual Cosmo, but Mike said, "Give me a double shot of scotch on the rocks."

I must have looked shocked because he grinned at me with a lot of teeth. "You don't know everything about me."

"Never said I did."

Mike glanced around with wide eyes, but he didn't seem freaked—yet. Timmy's was a big step, but I wanted him to know what was out there, even if he didn't choose to partake. Plus, Timmy's was fun as long as you didn't get too crazy. The people-watching was priceless.

When the waiter brought the drinks, Mike chugged the scotch, only coughed once, and waggled his finger for another. WTF. I sure must not have known everything.

Just to make conversation, I said, "So how'd your mom take my refusal of Mendelssohn? Do you know? Was she disappointed?" I chuckled. "Am I going to find myself with another blind date next weekend?"

It was like somebody pulled a plug. All of Mike's lightness dimmed, and that crease popped between his brows. "Uh no. I don't think she'll be setting up any more dates." He grabbed my hand. "C'mon, let's dance."

He pulled me to the dance floor, yanked me almost impossibly tight, and started swaying. Not that I minded, but he seemed a little off. I pulled back and looked at Mike's tense face. "Is something wrong? Was your mom really offended because I didn't like Mendelssohn?"

"No. I mean, I have no fucking idea. Whatever." He pulled me in closer, and I danced with the tension for several minutes.

It took a bit, but finally the press of chest to chest and the friction of our thighs rubbing together squelched whatever was going on in Mike's brain. His breathing rasped and hands explored. Our cocks met in a scrape of denim that was both titillating and frustrating.

He clasped me under the butt and pulled me so close we barely pretended to dance.

We kept that up for a few minutes, and then he pulled me back to the table, where he chugged the second double scotch. Thank god I was driving. I'd have to get him to crash on the couch while I shared the bed with Pops. There was no way he was driving back to Resolute tonight.

He stared around, licking the last of the scotch from his lips. "So I didn't even know there was a place like this."

I nodded. "Yeah, places like Timmy's with no dress code and a back room used to exist a lot. Now they're less frequent and are usually private."

"What's a back room? Gambling?"

I chuckled. "No. Sex. It's sometimes called a darkroom."

"No shit?" He stared at me with his mouth agape. "People go in and—"

I waggled my eyebrows. "Right. Have sex. It's dark-ish and mostly about sex with strangers or in groups. People pretend it's all anonymous, but you can actually see who you're hooking up with." I held up my hands. "I've been in there, but anonymous sex ain't my bag, baby."

"So if you walk in there, are you automatically agreeing to sex with strangers?"

I shrugged. "No, although you're likely to get hit on if you're not already attached. And I mean physically." I laughed.

Mike leaned in, breathing hard, his breath smelling of alcohol. "So if two desperate guys who don't have a place to have sex were to go in there and get it on, that wouldn't be breaking any rules, am I right?"

I had to admit that sounded damned good. "I like the way you think. But… it's pretty wild. There are other people in there."

"Where's the room?"

He's not serious. I pointed to the back wall of the club. "Back there."

"Show me."

"Seriously? Are you sure you're ready for this?"

"Sure, baby, what do you think? I don't want to win my gay stripes?" He laughed at himself.

I stared at him to be sure he was in his right mind because he'd had a lot to drink. But he seemed lucid even if a bit manic. And, hey, I wasn't turning down sex with Mike Canali.

"Oookay. Just stick close to me."

Still breathing hard, he followed me to the back wall of the club and stopped for one more shot of what he casually called *liquid courage,* and we walked down a dimly lit hall. At a door in the back, another one of those mountain men stood guard. This time, my membership card was showing him the condoms in my pocket. He growled, "Use them," then opened the door, and I pulled Mike into a barely lit room in which soft music was drowned out by the grunts, moans, and screams of sex. Jesus, the smell of the room was enough to make me come by itself. I visited Timmy's occasionally for the wild atmosphere, but I'd only been in the playroom once, and that had been a bit much for me.

Beside me, Mike whispered, "Jesus H."

I laughed softly and said in Mike's manic voice, "Welcome to the back room, baby." I stretched out a hand and made my way through the crowd of bodies toward a side wall where I could make out an empty space. I maneuvered Mike's back against that wall and fell on him, devouring. Hellfire, just being in this room with Mike was porn times ten, and my cock was screaming to get out of my jeans.

Mike had to feel the same way because he pulled me in tight and was ripping my fly down. In seconds, he had our cocks out and rubbed together in his hand as he gasped and moaned. Oh yeah, the power of the back room was working on Mike in a very big—and long way. Me too. I'd always keyed in to audio during sex. It was hot to hear the sounds of other people's pleasure. It made me empathize with what they were feeling and ramped up my own sensations. And it was so much hotter to hear them in person than in porn.

Wildly, we rode against each other, Mike squeezing and pumping, both gasping toward completion. Yes, I wanted it to last forever, but with these smells and sounds, I needed to come immediately, and my body screamed for completion.

Mike's big hand tightened and pumped faster until my brain went totally offline and my balls took over. I moaned, "Oh shit. Wanna come so bad. Just do it. Do it."

"Oh, oh. Fuck yeah!" Mike sure hadn't screamed like that at the hotel. I wanted to laugh, but wanted to come way more. He yelled, "Oh, shit, Shane, yes. Fuck!"

Feeling his hot spunk bathing my cock did the last trick, and my balls gave up their load, adding to the warm, sticky mess in Mike's hand that I loved. I chuckled and shivered.

Like someone yanked a train emergency cord, Mike froze. "Oh my god, oh, shit, no." And instead of working to get at me, he was clawing to get away.

"What? Mike, what's wrong? What the hell?" But by the time I got the words out, Mike was thrashing his way through the bodies toward the door.

Tucking my cock in, I floundered after him, getting snarls and complaints from the people I stepped on.

Out in the hall, Mike was practically running, and I took off after him. He plowed through the crowd, grabbed his coat from the chair, and was out the front entrance in the parking lot before I even got to the door.

Finally, I got my jacket on and went out into the chill of the night in more ways than one. I found Mike leaning against Mable, gasping for breath, his eyes wide and staring.

"Mike?" I grabbed his arm and shook. "Mike, what's going on?"

He blinked and seemed to focus on me. "I saw someone. Someone I know."

"Okay."

"Don't you get it? I saw someone I know from Cal Fire! From the Butte fire station. Shit, Shane, he could tell Donny or Gabe. God, he could tell my father!"

I grabbed both his arms. "Mike, anyone in the back room at Timmy's, first, isn't watching you and, second, isn't advertising the fact that they were there to their employer, even if they're out. The chances they'd say something to anyone in the fire department are zero."

He stared at me for a long moment. His breathing slowed. "Yeah." He nodded. "Yeah, you're right. Sorry. I had too much to drink. I kind of freaked for a minute."

He sure as shit had. I had to forcibly smooth the crease between my brows. What was up with Mike? "It's okay. Hop in and we'll go back to my place."

"Okay. Yeah. Fine. You don't want to get another drink, though?"

"No, we've had enough. Right?"

He reluctantly nodded, but he still looked haunted.

As we drove past the entrance to the club on our way out of the lot, Mike started to laugh.

Okay what now? I smiled. "What?"

"That guy I saw in the back room?"

"Yeah."

"He just walked out." His laugh turned to a cackle. "Not who I thought it was. This dude is a complete stranger." He laughed hysterically and kept it up for a full minute.

As I drove back to my apartment, my stomach was unsettled, and my hands gripped the wheel. It was nothing. Everyone had bad days. Maybe Mike had had a rough week at the station. Maybe something had happened that had nothing to do with me or with coming out, like a tragedy during a fire or something. That would put him on edge. As the boyfriend of a firefighter, I'd have to be understanding about that sort of thing.

I would have asked him what was wrong. But Mike Canali had passed out, face smushed against my passenger door window.

SIXTEEN

MIKE

Even the rocking couldn't soothe me. First time it failed since I was a little kid. I kept pushing with my foot, and the bench swing kept moving, but all it did was upset my stomach. Ma's snarky retort to Pa asking about when dinner would be ready rang in my head. Jesus, they'd barely exchanged a loving word in days, and all I could think was it was my fault.

"What are you doing out here?" Tessa wrapped her cardigan sweater tighter around herself and sat next to me on the swing. The bench swing would normally be filled with Tony's kids or our younger cousins, but the Thanksgiving Day was cold, and there was some video game tournament going on inside.

"Nothing." I kept pushing with my foot, though it was heavier with Tessa on it.

"You don't wanna watch football? The guys are really into the game."

I shrugged. "Not in the mood."

"Hmmm." I could feel her looking at me. "You could help us in the kitchen."

I gave her an *are you crazy*? look. "There are so many female Canalis in there, I'd be lucky to be able to breathe, much less help."

Tessa laughed. "True. Why do you think I'm out here?"

I attempted to smile, but it was halfhearted at best.

Tessa snuggled closer to me and put her head on my shoulder. "You didn't want to invite Shane?"

She had her friend Natalia here, and there were a dozen other plus-ones, so inviting Shane shouldn't have been a big deal. Except it was.

I hesitated. "I don't need drama with Pa today."

"Do you know what's going on?" She took my hand. "Ma and Pa are fighting. He came into the kitchen to get more dip, and they wouldn't even look at each other. It's seriously weird. I haven't seen them not on speaking terms since Cousin Jessy got pregnant."

She sounded worried. She wasn't the fucking Lone Ranger.

"Pa put his foot down after the whole Shane fix-up thing. He doesn't want the gay in the house," I said bitterly.

"He said that? Oh, Mike. I'm so sorry."

I didn't say anything. There was nothing to say.

"You need to talk to him—and Ma too. It's one thing when it's a stranger. But if he knew about you...."

"I don't want to talk about it right now. Okay? And don't tell anyone!" Just thinking about it made me feel sick.

"I won't! But you know I have your back. Ma and Nonna too."

"Yeah, well, if it comes down to Pa versus Ma, guess who's going to win?"

She sat up to give me a funny look. "If you think it's Pa, you seriously underestimate our mother."

I shook my head. "He lays down the law in the house, Tessa. Come on."

"Maybe. But if Momma ain't happy, *nobody's* happy."

I didn't answer. Just thinking about it made my head ache. I couldn't even see a world in which this ended well. It was seriously fucked.

"It'll be different when it's you, Mike. It has to be different." She said it stubbornly, as if she could make it so.

But the hole in my chest was so big and dark, there wasn't much room in there for hope. Not anymore. Not after overhearing Pa that day. Those words he'd said were like poison. They'd hurt at the time, yeah, but they seemed to hurt worse every day, like I was undergoing a slow death. Making my pa proud had always been everything. Now I knew for a fact he despised me for who I was, even if he didn't know it yet.

Hell, even the idea that Tessa knew about me was scary now. I trusted her, but she wasn't secretive by nature. Still, too late. I couldn't take back coming out to her, and it felt like one more giant cliff for me to fall over.

We rocked in silence for a few minutes.

"It's weird not having Shane here," Tessa said. "It's like he's already part of the family, like we ghosted him or something. Feels shitty."

"Yeah." It totally did. But the fact that Ma *hadn't* invited him told me I was right about how Pa made the rules.

"You know Ma loves Shane, right?" Tessa said. "She's been digging into PFLAG and reading books…. Oh man, I'll bet she feels so bad about not inviting him for Thanksgiving that tomorrow she wants to—"

"Hey."

I'd been looking at Tessa, so Donny's voice made me jump. And goddamn it, we couldn't even talk out here without being in danger of being overheard. He was just stalking up, though, hands in his pockets, so it didn't seem like he'd overheard anything.

"Hey, Donny," Tessa said lightly. "Is it time to eat?"

"I dunno." Donny shrugged. "I, uh, just wanted to talk to Mike."

Tessa stood up. "Cool. I'll go check on dinner."

She walked away as if it was all no big deal. Either she was a great actor, or it wasn't to her. Must be nice. Donny sat down heavily on the bench swing. I gripped the edge of the seat and stopped the movement of the swing by putting both feet hard on the ground, ready to bolt.

"Jesus, will you fucking relax?" Donny said. "What's with you?"

"Nothing." I stared down at the ground. The grass was worn away right below the swing, it was used so much. I toed the dirt.

I heard him sigh. "You've been avoiding me, and now I can't even fucking sit by you? What the hell did I do?"

He sounded so genuinely bewildered. I glanced at him. He had on a rust turtleneck sweater today, probably something Ma or one of the aunts bought him for Christmas some year. Like all my brothers, Donny was stupid handsome. Maybe he was the best-looking Canali—barring Uncle Ricky. He was almost three years older than me, and growing up, I'd idolized him so hard. Everything Donny did, I had to do. Sports. Games. Going for a run. What Donny wanted was the coolest, just because he wanted it. Toys. Albums. Vehicles. When he'd driven his first used white Chevy pickup truck home at seventeen, I'd thought it was the greatest truck in the whole wide world, and now I drove one. And when he'd invited me to move into the little house with him, I couldn't imagine a better setup. It had been great. Or as great as it could be with a slob who left wet towels and underwear lying around and spent a lot of time in his room watching porn.

But now? These days, I couldn't even look at Donny without feeling pissed off. I hated that but had no idea how to fix it.

"Seriously, what's goin' on, Mike?" Donny asked, his dark brows furrowed. "You're always gone, and you won't tell me where. You hardly talk to me, even at work. And now the family's fighting over this stupid Shane shit. This fucking sucks, man."

"What has this got to do with Shane? It has nothing to do with Shane!" I said, too loudly and too forcefully.

He blinked at me and held up a hand. "Okay. Fine. I'm just sayin'…. Ma and Pa are fighting about Shane, and he's your friend. I guess."

"He's not—!" I started to deny it but shut my mouth. Fuck Donny. "Yeah, he's my friend. But I've got nothing to do with Ma and Pa fighting. And he's not here anyway, so fuck off."

Donny looked at me like I was crazy. "Okay. Okay. Forget Shane, all right? Jesus. What the hell, bro. What are you so pissed about?"

"I'm not pissed. I'm… I'm hungry. Starving in fact. Let's go before I start eating the grass." I stood up.

"Mike. Come on," Donny said, exasperated. But I walked away toward the house.

———

By the time I found a parking space in downtown Sacramento, I was frazzled. The Saturday after Thanksgiving meant streets packed with shoppers and parade-goers. About the time I lost the second parking space to an asswipe in a souped-up Porsche, I considered turning around and going home.

But home wasn't a place I wanted to be these days. Getting away from there suited me just fine.

I finally got my truck squared away and texted him. He told me where to go to meet up with the group we were supposed to be marching with. The Sac State Pride Center was near the back of the parade, and they were lined up at the staging area on Clarendon Street.

Before I left the car, I opened my backpack. *Festive*, Shane had said. Like, festive how? I didn't know how to dress festive for Thanksgiving and wasn't sure they'd be doing Christmas yet, but they had Christmas stuff in the Macy's Thanksgiving Day parade on TV, so I'd taken a chance with a skintight long-sleeved red T-shirt, green suspenders, and a large, flashing candy cane pin that was Tessa's.

The key element, though—the stupid, cowardly element— was a red plaid lumberjack's wool beanie with a big bushy black beard attached. I'd been a lumberjack for Halloween in high school and had saved the costume. I sat there in my truck, holding the cap and beard and combing the knots out of the fake hair. The beard and hat would hide my face. And yes, that was chickenshit. Even I could see the irony of coming to march with a Pride group and wearing a disguise. But if I didn't wear it, I'd be paranoid all day about being seen. Resolute was not Sacramento, but it wasn't so far away that someone from the fire department might not be in the crowd today. And I couldn't be seen and have to deal with a lot of bullshit about why I was walking with a Pride group. Yes, Shane insisted that all kinds of people walked in Pride parades, not just LGBT folk, but this wasn't Pride. It was Thanksgiving. And somebody could make a deal out of me marching, and I'd get pissed and make a scene, like at the club the other night. I just… I was too on edge. Everything inside me felt raw. I couldn't deal with it.

I'd almost not come at all. But I'd told Shane and Roland that I would. And after me and my family had ghosted Shane and Pops over Thanksgiving, I just couldn't bail on today too. Besides, part of me wanted this. Like I'd told Shane, I'd always dreamed about marching in a Pride parade someday. Of course, I hadn't planned on coming disguised as a chickenshit. I sighed.

As usual, everything I wanted was in direct conflict with my real life. But fuck it. Baby steps. I tilted the mirror and put on the cap and beard, took off my coat and added the suspenders, too, just to make it look like a real costume.

I found the staging area. It was a total scene. There were floats and marching bands in spangly uniforms, a brigade of older veterans, various business groups, and even a women's quilting society. Their quilted turkey banner was great. I gave one of the older ladies carrying it a thumbs-up and a grin, though maybe she didn't see it under the beard.

I continued on, texting with Shane about what to look for until I finally spotted the Sac State Pride Center banner and then… Shane. I paused to look at him for a moment. It was funny how literally just seeing him made my stomach go all warm, sent tingles throughout my body, and set my heart racing.

He was so cute, so perfect to me. And he was genuinely a good person as well. I liked him so much. I wouldn't give him up. I *wouldn't*. And I wasn't going to think about Pa today, or Donny, or the fire station, or anything. I shut it all off like a tap. I was here, and I was with my gay peeps, and fuck the rest.

"Hey." I touched Shane's shoulder, and he turned to look at me, startled.

He blinked, drawing back. Then his eyes widened, and he got a huge smile. "Mike!" He threw his arms around me, and I held him tight.

"I hope you're into beards," I teased.

He drew back so he could get a good look. He tugged on the fake hair. "You forget to shave this morning? You Canalis are always rocking the five-o'clock-shadow thing, but this is impressive even for your hairy ass."

"I was hoping you might like the sexy lumberjack look."

"Oh, baby, do I." He kissed me—on the mouth.

I froze for a moment, then remembered that no one here

knew me. Or could know me. Wasn't that the whole fucking point of the beard? So I kissed him back.

"Hey, you. Did you bring some for everyone?" Someone poked my back with a finger.

I turned to see Roland. I gave him a smile. "Hey, you. How's it going?"

"Couldn't be better. Sac State, baby!" He was totally jazzed.

"It's pretty cool," I agreed.

And now I got a good look at what other people were wearing. There was a lot of red and green, some elf-like costumes, mostly paired with rainbow knee socks, rainbow pins, and rainbow hats. So rainbow-Christmas as the theme. I wasn't too far off, thank God.

"Nice of you to show up," Roland said.

"Yeah. Why not? Gotta support my... my guy."

Shane took my hand and squeezed. "How was your Thanksgiving?"

I felt a fresh pang of guilt. "Oh, it was a total Canali madhouse. So many people. You didn't miss much." I tried to sound casual.

Shane nodded, but I could see the disappointment in his eyes. And yeah, it sucked not being invited to your boyfriend's holiday meal, especially when you'd been there for many other meals. If that's what we were—boyfriends. My stomach got tight to the point of pain. I wasn't gonna think about that now.

"So when do we start?" I asked brightly.

"These things always take forever," Roland complained.

Shane checked his phone. "Should be soon. The parade was supposed to start a half—oh, look! The line's moving."

"Oh, shit. Wait." I scrambled for my backpack and brought out the candy cane. I turned it on so the candy cane flashed. "Yes or no?" I held it in front of my crotch.

Shane laughed. "Definitely yes. Please, Santa." He batted his eyes.

I waggled my eyebrows. "I'll take a raincheck for later." I pinned it just below the button on my jeans.

And then we were moving. It was slow going at first as we got out of the staging area. But then we were marching down streets lined with people. A girl and a guy carried the long Pride Center banner in front of our group, both of them dressed in Santa hats, rainbow tights, green felt skirts, and Sac State T-shirts. I'd stuffed my coat in my bag, and it was cold out in my long-sleeved T-shirt, but exhilarating too.

My first Pride event! It really was awesome, seeing so many in the crowd cheer and clap for us, from teens to old people. There were only a few sour faces. My heart swelled with joy and nerves. I was marching, proudly, with a group of my fellow queers, and I was holding hands with my boyfriend. And yes, I was wearing the beard, but fuck it, I was here, wasn't I? I was doing this!

I waved at people on the sidelines and grabbed mini candy canes from the buckets of them Roland and another guy carried, tossing treats to the crowd.

"Aren't we supposed to chant slogans or something?" I asked Shane, feeling a burning need to scream something rebellious like *We're here, we're queer, get used to it!*

He shook his head. "Not in this parade. This is just, you know, holiday cheer. Showing our presence."

"Oh." I was a little disappointed. "So we're not going to burn City Hall or anything?"

He laughed. "Uh… no. That wouldn't be very festive. Ask yourself: What would Santa do?"

"Lick my candy cane?" I waggled my hips.

"No, that's what Shane would do." He smiled warmly at me. "Hey, I really appreciate your being here. I'm sorry we're not more militant today, but we can play a game of War later."

"Strip War? Sounds good. Where's the French Revolution when you need it, huh?" I parried. I saw a big bald guy giving us two thumbs-up on the sidelines, and I raised both arms high, bringing Shane's hand up with mine. "Whoot!" I hollered. The guy grinned.

"You feeling okay?" Shane asked me when I lowered our arms.

I glanced at him. "Yeah, why?"

"You seem a bit... hyped."

"Hey, it's my first Pride parade!"

Shane grinned. "True. I forget these things. Let's do it up then." Shane grabbed Roland's entire bucket and handed it to me, and we moved to the side of the group, throwing mini candy canes to the onlookers and waving.

We'd just passed the capitol park when I heard someone yelling, "Shane! Shane! Yoo-hoo! Shane!"

It wafted to me over the sound of the high school band in front of us, currently playing "Jingle Bell Rock." I scanned the crowd, but Shane got there first. He waved enthusiastically. "Hello! Hey, Mike, it's your mom. And Tessa. And Nonna and Carlotta!"

I spotted them as the words left his mouth. There they were, in the front of the crowd on the street. Ma had on her gold wool coat and a rainbow scarf, and she was holding up a hand-lettered sign that read "PFLAG." Tessa was beside her in a teal fleece jacket that set off her black curly hair, and Nonna and Carlotta waved cheerfully.

"Hi, Shane!" Ma screamed, face all bright and cheerful.

No. Fucking no. The world fell out from under my feet. It was like a big sign came up in front of my face—*You want to be out and proud? Well, this is what that looks like, asshole.* I was going to throw up. I stumbled, already turning, and fought my way through the Sac State group.

"Mike? What's—" Roland's face, concerned, swam into view. He blocked me, and I pushed him, hard. I had to get away. My heart pounded a warning beat in my ears, and I felt cold all over. Couldn't breathe. Had to get some space.

What the fuck were they doing here? Why? *Why?*

Had they recognized me? My hand went up to feel my wool cap and beard even as I dove on, into the crowd on the opposite side of the street, past families and couples. My disguise was still there. And I hadn't seen recognition in their eyes. They'd been focused on Shane.

They hadn't seen me. Or recognized me. Please, God, let them not have recognized me. But oh shit, what if someone said something? What if Shane said, "You just missed Mike."

"Mike! Mike!" Shane's voice from behind me.

But I just ran.

SEVENTEEN

SHANE

I stared after Mike, my heart hammering, and then at Lucille, Carlotta, Nonna, and Tessa all rushing up to me with huge smiles. My brain flew in a million directions. What the hell were they doing here carrying Pride signs and wearing rainbow scarves? I mean, my heart swelled at the idea that they'd come to see me, but I wanted, needed to go after Mike. Jesus he must not have known they were coming and been blindsided. But he could have said that he was here supporting Pride the same way they were. No big deal.

I waved. "Hi, guys. What a wonderful surprise, but I have to—" I pointed vaguely in the direction of the parade that was moving away from us.

Lucille waggled the ends of her scarf. "We know you're busy, and we don't want to interrupt. We just came to support you. And, real quick, next Sunday, we're celebrating Tito's birthday, and I'd love it if you would come. Maybe you'd like to help decorate, so come early?"

I must have beamed like a lighthouse. They still liked me and wanted to have me around! After Thanksgiving and no invitation, it had been stupid and entitled, but I'd been really hurt. I'd worked like crazy to have a fabulous Thanksgiving for Pops, Ro, Hissy, Chas, and Winston, but it was hard to get over my own feelings of having somehow done something wrong with the Canalis. Like maybe they were mad that I brushed off their blind date, like I was too full of myself or unappreciative. But obviously, all of that had been in my head. "I'd love to come. Thanks."

Lucille clapped her hands together. "Oh good. I'll remind Mike to remind you." She gave me a huge hug. "Now go on and do your thing. Yayyy Pride."

I felt lit from the inside. They all smiled at me except for Tessa, whose gaze seemed a little worried. Maybe she'd seen Mike? Saw him run? Jesus, I needed to find him. He'd been so jumpy and manic lately. I had to calm him down. "Thank you all so much. Love you!" I ran off, tacitly in the direction of the parade, but then I doubled back toward the alley I'd seen Mike run down. God, I hoped he was still there. I also hoped I hadn't been rude to Lucille and the others. It would have been fun to spend a few minutes with them, me and Mike both, but that was probably more than I could expect from him.

I sighed. I was completely gone over Mike, but I sure didn't love being in a relationship with a closeted man. It was compromising and felt even shittier than I'd imagined it would.

Weaving through the crowd, I spied the alley ahead of me and followed the smell of Chinese food from the restaurant that backed onto it. A quick glance down the narrow space showed Mike leaning against the side of the building, his hands on his knees and that silly beard brushing his chest. We'd made cute jokes about it, but I knew he wore it to hide, and I had to accept that he was trying. Hell, he'd shown up, which, after how squirrelly he'd been last week, I'd doubted.

I approached him like one of the frightened horses they showed in cowboy movies, my hand extended.

He didn't acknowledge that I was there. He was still breathing hard, and his olive complexion had gone ghostly pale. Jeez, was he sick? This reaction couldn't be just because he saw his mom, could it? I gently touched his arm. "Mike? What's wrong?"

He reeled back like I'd slapped him. "My mother—Nonna, why did you do it? Why did you invite them when you knew I was coming?"

I frowned. "I didn't invite them. I had no idea they were coming. I guess they just came to support the Pride Center and to support me. It was a kind thing to do."

"You didn't tell them?" He snarled it, which I just didn't get.

"Of course not. Why would I do that?"

He took a step toward me, and I actually fell back a little. "To nudge me along? Put me in a situation where I have to come out whether I want to or not?"

I saw red and planted my fists on my hips. "Fuck, Mike. I've suffered being ignored by you, being insulted by others in front of you, and you not even caring, being fixed up with random strangers.... If I haven't forced you to come out by now, why would I do it today?" I sucked in air and calmed myself. *He's got reasons. Good reasons. So much to lose.* I forced a smile. "Don't you see this is a *good* thing? Your family went to all this trouble to show me they support me." Mike was staring at me with wide, crazy eyes. My gut clenched, and I raced on. "Your mom even invited me to come to Tito's birthday party on Sunday and help with the decorations. I love your family. I mean, most of them. Your mom and Carlotta and Nonna and even Tessa are like family I never had." I blinked at the truth of that and pushed my excitement toward him, wanting him to get it, but his lips had parted in what looked like disbelief. My voice rose in forced enthusiasm. "She said she'd remind you to remind me about the party, and I thought Tito's always so quiet and shy, I bet I can coax him out of his shell and—"

"Nooo!" His voice echoed off the walls of the narrow alley.

I blinked at him, confused. "What? What do you mean *no*?"

He looked at me like he didn't know me. "Jesus, Shane, don't you get it? You can't come to Tito's birthday. Or anything else." He started pacing back and forth like an insane tiger in a cage. "Pa told my ma he doesn't want you in the house. And if she does invite you over, *rarely*, you can't bring a guy along. And for sure no more blind dates because you'll corrupt the children with the gay, and we Canalis are not like that! We aren't gay. We're never gay." His voice was shaking like he might scream or cry.

I wanted to do both. I was stunned. "He… your dad really said that?"

Mike ran a frustrated hand over his head. "Yeah, I'm sorry. I never meant to tell you. I didn't want to hurt your feelings. But you've got to understand that you can't come over anymore. It just won't work." He started pacing again, but I couldn't move. I felt like I'd been slapped.

"Your father really said that. Out loud. Was it in front of everyone?" I barely got the words out. Angelo had never been warm toward me, but I thought he and I were okay. I thought the Medal of Valor meant something to a man like him, my having worked with Mike to save all those people the day of the Crest Lake fire. But apparently, it didn't mean shit.

My skin felt icy cold, but my cheeks burned in humiliation.

"He said it when he was arguing with my ma. It's insane. They're at each other's throats, and I've never seen my family like that. I mean they bicker and nag, sure, but this is really bitter. The fact that Ma came here today…. Shit. I don't know what's up with that. Is she *trying* to defy my dad?" He waved his arms wildly. "Shit, Shane, don't you see? I haven't even come out, and you're tearing my family apart all by yourself." I took a step back, and his eyes widened. "No, I didn't mean that exactly. I mean—"

I nodded, my whole body slowly chilling. *I'm tearing his family apart? I am? It's all my fault?* A little voice in my head told me to try to understand, to be cool. But fuck that! The words tumbled out. "Yes, I do see. I see that your father essentially called me a pervert in your hearing, and you didn't say anything. Didn't defend me or tell him that you're gay too." I narrowed my eyes. "I see that you're blaming me for tearing your family apart rather than blaming their homophobic prejudices or that uber-macho Canali culture." This time, I took the step forward. "And I see that you're a chickenshit who uses every excuse you can get your hands on to keep yourself chained to other people's bullshit ideas." I yanked on the idiot beard.

He had the fucking nerve to look at me pleadingly. "I can't lose my family, Shane. I mean, you walked away from yours, but I really care about my family. They're all I have."

I held up my hands and backed up. "Right. I wanted to get thrown out at sixteen for simply being who I am. I did it to make a point that I didn't need a family. That's why gay kids hang out on the streets and in foster homes. Because they don't really care about their families. You fucking idiot."

"I… I didn't mean that." This time, he looked guilty.

"Yes, you did." I sighed. "But realize that if I'm no longer welcome in your home, Mike, then neither are you. Whether or not your family knows you're queer—you are. And the only way it's ever going to get better with those macho brothers and father that you call role models is if you give them a chance to be more than they have been. But you won't require even a baseline of respect and understanding from them." I shook my head. "You'll never come out. And I'm furious at myself for not demanding a baseline of respect from you either." My heart cracked so hard I was sure I must be bleeding through my rainbow sweater. "So I guess that's it, Mike. We're done here."

I registered the shock on his face for just a second before I turned and walked down the alley toward the crowds. It was disgusting that my shoulders tingled with the desire to feel Mike's hand pulling me back. Stopping me from walking away. Stupid.

All I could think of was getting to Mable and driving home, but where was she? My brain was like a black hole. I couldn't remember, so I just staggered toward the parade. A float full of dogs, some kind of doggy daycare probably, stood stopped ahead of me with dogs and their owners milling around the float. I plopped my butt on the curb next to it, too tired to walk anymore. A wet kiss on my cheek gave me a moment's heart leap until I looked up into the soft-eyed face of a golden retriever. My lips turned up as I petted him. "You love everybody, don't you? You don't care if I'm weird."

"Jesus, man, where have you been? I've been searching everywhere." Ro gripped my arm.

"Bye, guy." I kissed the dog on his head and stood, only a moment before the dog group started moving. Ro pulled me, and I walked beside him.

He frowned. "You look like a fucking zombie."

Leave it to Ro to come up with the definitive description. The walking dead. Accurate.

He glanced around. "Where's Mr. Sexy Lumberjack?"

I shook my head.

Ro, bless him, just kept blabbing, the words bouncing off me like a tin roof. Ping. Ping. "So that was Mike's family? Jeez, I thought he wouldn't come out because his family was all up in their religion and shit, but they sure looked supportive. I mean, after you left, they came over and put money in the collection can and took the literature from the center. They were great." I didn't reply, and he turned and looked at me. "Wait. What's wrong?"

I stared at the ground.

He grabbed my arms. "Okay, this is bad. This is not my Shane. What the fuck? Did somebody hurt you?" He glanced at the hordes of people still milling around the parade ground. "We need to get you out of here. Where's Mable?"

"I—I can't remember."

"We'll pick it up later then. Come on. I'll drive." He slid an arm around my shoulders and guided me to his car that was parked behind the staging area. I crawled in and didn't really care where we were going. As he drove, he talked on his cell phone—about me, I was pretty sure. And then he was guiding me to his apartment, and I didn't remember how we got there. Hissy was sitting inside.

She bounded up and hurried toward me with her arms open. "Oh, honey, you look terrible."

For a second, I wanted to shy away. One nice touch and I'd fly into a million pieces. But Hissy knew no boundaries and gathered me into her arms, pulling me down on the couch with her. As I buried my face in her shoulder, she said, "Ro, dear, I made hot chocolate. Will you pour us all a cup?"

For a few minutes, she just rocked me, but then I smelled the warm, comforting chocolate coming closer, and she said, "Okay, cutie, sit up, drink your chocolate, and start talking."

I managed the first two, sipping from my cup as Ro and Hissy drank theirs and looked at me. The chocolate really did taste good, but my throat was so tight, I didn't trust myself to speak.

Finally, Hissy said, "Let me start. You and Mike broke up."

Ro's head snapped up. "No. I mean, they've been doing so well. Mike even came to the parade today, and he's been hanging out with us at clubs. Hell, Shane's got Mike's relatives wearing rainbow gear and cheering for the Pride Club. They're solid. Aren't you, Shane?"

Hissy gazed at me. "Shane?"

I was afraid to say the words because they'd make it so final, so I just nodded. "Hissy's right."

"What happened?" she asked softly.

I sighed so deeply my ribs should have cracked and told them about some of Mike's growing anxiety for the past few weeks.

Ro scowled. "He wore that fake beard today, and I thought it was to be cute."

"Nope. He just didn't want to be seen with me. Or us. Or whatever."

"But jeez, four members of his family were there cheering for you."

My heart throbbed with a painful ache. "Maybe you noticed that all the people at the parade were female. Apparently, I've caused a huge rift in his family between the pro-Shane and anti-Shane factions. The men don't want me there, and his father's declared I'm no longer welcome in their house." I inhaled and felt my spine straighten. Amazingly, the telling was making me more angry than sad.

Ro slammed his mug on the brick-and-board coffee table. "Fuck that! I knew that guy was gonna break your heart."

Hissy put a hand on my arm. "And Mike is siding with the Y chromosomes?"

I shrugged. "Well, he's not siding *against* them. He thinks he'll lose his family. And, of course, as I know so well, he might." I drained my cup. "I'm done. I love him, but..." I blinked hard. It was the first time I'd said the word out loud. *Love.* But it was true. My first real love... and it was already over.

Hissy rubbed my arm comfortingly. "Love is a gift, but it can't have too many strings, or you compromise yourself. If you have to change who you are to be loved, then it's not really love, is it?"

Ro said, "Can I carve that on my bedroom wall, please?"

I nodded, trying hard not to fall over the precipice of hopelessness that loomed in front of me. It would be so easy to fall in. But if I did that, I might never find my way out.

"Truth?" Ro spread his hands. "I was surprised you put up with his being in the closet for as long as you did. I figured he must be making big strides toward coming out, or you'd have given him his walking papers by now."

Hissy hugged me one-armed. "No one understands better than Shane how hard it is to be estranged from family."

I nodded. Oh shit, every day I battled against remembering the horror, betrayal, and heartbreak of the day my parents had thrown me out like a piece of trash. The heat behind my eyes finally won and splashed on my cheeks.

"That's true," Ro agreed sadly. "Hell, my dad still treats me like an alien. But I'll tell you one thing. Being estranged from family is a fuckload better than being estranged from yourself."

And that's what I should carve on my bedroom wall.

EIGHTEEN

MIKE

I managed to make it back to Resolute in one piece, which was remarkable considering I didn't remember the trip at all. I drove through the little town, passing the general store and ice cream shop. My home town. Ma and Pa had come from the Bronx, and my oldest sibs remembered it, but I'd been born here. Today, driving through, it felt less like home and more like a prison, and I had a life sentence.

I drove past the main driveway to the house. It didn't look like Ma and the rest had gotten back yet. Good. I drove around the side and parked in front of the small cottage Donny and I shared. His truck was there. I sat in the driver's seat of mine and stared at nothing for a while.

So I guess that's it, Mike. We're done here.

We're done.

Shane had finally kicked me to the curb. Which meant my secret life was over. It should have been a relief. No more lying about where I was going. No more split reality, Jekyll and Hyde. For weeks, I'd felt like I was being ripped in two. Now the tearing was done—and half of me was gone.

Instead of relief, all I felt was shock and the promise of pain. It was as if someone had opened my chest and landed one sharp, quick blow on my heart that shattered it. And I was in the moment where you felt the blow, and you could see all the cracks, but it hadn't yet fallen to the floor in a million pieces.

Shane.

I could go on without him, sure. But what would be the fucking *point*?

Shane was the only person I'd ever met in my whole stupid twenty-two years that I could see spending the rest of my life with, being a couple, maybe even getting married, growing old together. When he was Pops's age, he'd still be adorable. And real. And honest. And curious and smart AF.

He was beautiful, inside and out. Only now he was gone because I was a coward. Medal of Valor? What a joke. Shane had proven he was a thousand times braver and more courageous than me. Some fucking hero, I couldn't even save myself.

I sat there for a long time until someone rapped on the window. I blinked and looked out. Donny.

Donny, my one-time role model and now chief torturer. Welp, I had no place else to go. No, I'd torched that option. I opened the door and got out, not looking at him.

"What're you doing?" he asked as I pushed past him for the house.

"Not feeling good." I kept walking.

"Bummer. What's the matter?" He jogged to keep up with me. "Stomach or something?"

"Yeah." I opened the front door so hard it banged into the wall. "I'm going to bed to sleep. Just leave me alone, okay?"

"Want me to get Ma? Or some tea or something?"

I shook my head and went into my room. I locked the door.

———

"You don't come out of your room for two days straight. Now you won't even talk to me in the car?"

Donny and I were driving in for the start of another shift at the fire station. We always drove in together when we had the same shift hours. I couldn't think of a good reason to avoid it today, and, frankly, I didn't care enough to try. "Good summary, yeah," I said dryly.

Donny huffed. "You're being a dick. You know that, right? And I'm getting fucking sick of it."

"I'm sick of a lot of things. That's life," I snapped.

"Now you're a fucking philosopher," Donny muttered.

We didn't speak again until we got to the station.

Our shifts began with a briefing of fires in our area. There was good-sized wildfire up north and some small ones in SoCal, but nothing serious in our jurisdiction, so it looked like it'd be a quiet shift. I silently cursed. My skin itched with a need for action, something to distract my mind. But apparently, I wasn't gonna get it.

Instead of actually *being* a fucking firefighter, I started on a long list of chores reserved for the rookie—me. I made a pot of coffee, cleaned the bathrooms, and then looked over a bunch of boxes that'd been donated to the station. There were lots of canned and dry goods. I hauled the boxes up to the kitchen and started unpacking them, fitting them into the large wall of pantry cabinets.

I'd hoped being back at work would help me stop chewing my own paw off—mentally speaking. But my brain refused to leave its well-worn groove. For the past two days, I'd clung to my phone like it was my own personal battery pack, hoping Shane would text or call. I'd wanted to reach out to him, but couldn't think of a single goddamn thing I could say to him that would make a difference other than *I just came out*, and that option made me want to barf.

I never heard from him, which just confirmed that we really were done.

Ma had stopped by the cottage with some soup 'cause Donny blabbed that I wasn't feeling good. We'd sat at the table while I ate, and she'd chatted about Shane and the parade, oblivious to the fact that I'd been there. She went on about PFLAG and how much she liked the website for the Pride Center at Sac State, where Shane went.

I finally looked at her and said, "Why are you doing all this when you know that Pa will never accept Shane, or anyone *like* Shane, ever again? Are you a glutton for punishment, or what?"

She stopped talking abruptly and stared at me. "Did your father tell you that?"

"I heard him talking about it." I stared down into my soup.

She sniffed. "Your father's very traditional, which is one of the things I love about him. But it can be a real pain. Sometimes he can be…" She paused as if choosing her words. "Stubborn. And not open to new things. But that doesn't mean we all have to follow his lead, Mikey. He'll come around eventually."

I smiled bitterly. "Yeah, no. He won't."

"Who's known him longer, you or me?" she asked firmly.

"Who's more like him?" I challenged back, putting down my spoon.

She frowned. "What? Because you're a boy?"

"I can't have this conversation." I'd gone back to bed.

I replayed it now as I shoved bags of rice and dried beans onto a lower shelf. I could still see the sad look on my mother's face. But she'd get over it. She hadn't lost the person who was probably the love of her life. No, that was me.

Brian came into the kitchen and grabbed a mug to get coffee. "Hey, Mike! How's it hanging?"

"Fine." I moved on to unboxing the canned soup.

"Who's cookin' today?" Brian asked, pouring milk into his cup, fridge door open.

"Roster's right there," I said. *Duh.*

He closed the fridge door and looked down. "Shit. It's me. Motherfucker."

I rolled my eyes. Brian was a good guy but not the most attentive. Which meant we'd probably be getting this canned soup and dried cheese sandwiches for dinner.

"Joanne's gonna kill me," he groaned. "Don't tell her I had dinner duty and forgot."

"Sure," I said. I didn't think I'd see Brian's wife anytime soon.

Donny walked in. I stiffened but continued to unpack cans.

"What's up?" Donny asked Brian.

"Just figured out I have dinner duty tonight," Brian groaned. He brightened. "Hey, if I make spaghetti, can you do a salad?"

Donny snorted. "Don't see my name on the roster. Sorry, bro."

"Oh come on. I'll help you next time it's your turn."

"Nope." Donny sipped his coffee. "You're on your own, buddy. Besides, salads suck."

I snorted. Typical Donny. He sat down at the table. Just one more box to unload, and I could get out of here.

"Oh, yeah, that reminds me. Joanne wanted me to invite everybody over to our place on Saturday for Jack's fifth birthday. There'll be kids there but lots of grown-ups too. Pizza. Beer. And whatever good shit Joanne makes. So you guys wanna come?"

"Nah, man," Donny said regretfully. "Tell Joanne thanks, but we've got Tito's birthday party on Saturday."

"Tito?" Brian sounded confused. "You've got a Tito? I thought I knew all your brothers."

"He's our cousin from New York. He's been living with us for, what, like a year now, Mikey?"

I nodded, keeping my eyes on the cans of tomatoes I was putting away.

"Yeah. Something happened to him in New York," Donny went on. "A mugging or something. So his folks shipped him out to us to recuperate, and he stayed." He laughed. "Like anyone would want to go back to New York after experiencing California weather. Am I right?"

"Is he in fire like the rest of you knobs?" Brian asked.

"Nah. He does something on computers. You know what it is, Mike?"

I knew Tito had invented some database system for collectors, but I didn't know the details and didn't care to explain what I did know to Donny. "Nope."

"Well. Shit. Joanne's gonna be bummed," Brian said.

"Sorry, man. Another time. Or you guys could come over to ours. You know Ma. The more the merrier."

"Nah, Joanne's got a whole thing planned. Bought decorations and everything."

"Cool," Donny said.

"Hey, so at this birthday party, will that super-gay guy be there?" Brian's tone was teasing.

I dropped a can back into the box and turned my head sharply to look at Donny. The way Brian said it made me think Donny had been bitching about Shane to him. Maybe to all the guys. Hot rage sparked inside me—the first thing other than grief that I'd felt in days.

"Are you talking about Shane?" I asked Brian very carefully.

"Is that your little gay friend that comes to visit and decorates the house? Honestly, I have a hard time picturing it. You and Donny and Tony and Gabe and your dad... and then *that*." He laughed some more. "Sounds like a reality show or something."

Donny laughed too, but there was a cruel edge to it. "Tell me about it. But you'll have to take it up with Ma. She loves the guy. But I guess she always did want another girl."

I was only partially aware of flying across the room, grabbing Donny's T-shirt, and yanking him to his feet. Somewhere in my brain, his shocked face registered, but my arm was already cocked back. I punched that stupidly handsome face as hard as I could.

Donny went down like a sack of bricks, and I fell on top of him, still punching. I hit his shoulders, arms… I was enraged, but there was still enough sanity left to avoid hitting him in the face again.

Donny rolled me over and got on top of me. He punched me in the chest once, twice, three times. "What's your fucking problem?" he screamed.

In the distance, I heard the word spread—*Fight! Fight!*

I shoved Donny off. We both scrambled to our feet and circled each other, fists raised. People spilled into the room, but it barely registered, my tunnel vision locked on Donny and the cold anger on his face.

We skirted the table, counters, each other. He threw a punch. I ducked out of the way and landed one to his gut, but he was ready, and my hand bounced off hard muscle. Fuck, that hurt. I'd really busted my knuckles up when I'd hit his jaw. Hard-headed bastard. But I ignored the pain, not caring. No, I wanted *more* pain. I deserved it.

I threw a punch, but Donny knocked it aside and plowed into me. Then we were in a clinch, both of us punching each other's sides, backs. Donny was swearing, but it was as if my voice had left me. I couldn't say a word. I was disappearing bit by bit.

"Hey! Hey! Knock it off!" someone said.

Somebody grabbed my shirt from behind, and then Donny and I were pulled apart. We glared at each other.

"I said knock it the fuck off, you two!" Chief Reiger's

hardass tone snapped me out of it enough to look at him. His hands were on his hips, face red and eyes snapping with anger as Brian and Henry held Donny, and Luke and Jordy held me. "There's no goddamn fighting in my station. I don't care if you're brothers. I'll fire both your asses right now!"

That took the rest of the heat out of me—and Donny, too, apparently. I slumped and they let me go. Donny rubbed his jaw. "He started it," he said like we were twelve.

"Because *he's* a fucking moron!" I shouted. My mouth filled with copper, and I spat a wad of blood into the sink.

"I don't give a shit!" Chief said. "You're both—"

A shrill wail. The alarm.

"Shit," Chief said, as everyone else scrambled for the door. He paused enough to point at both of us. "You two are on duty. You've got a job to do. I don't want any more of this horseshit today. Clear?"

"I'm cool," Donny said, giving me a disgusted look.

"Clear," I said.

"Now go. Go, go, go!" Chief shouted.

We ran for the pole and slid down to where our gear stood ready. Sliding into our boots and pants as a unit, we pulled our suspenders onto our shoulders and shrugged into the heavy coats. With helmets in hand, we ran to the trucks.

————

The fire was a warehouse blaze in progress, and a gnarly one. When our truck pulled up, there were already a couple of cop cars there and a few dozen civvies walking around. Maybe they worked here. The warehouse was huge, a long-ass rectangle, almost as wide as a city block, four stories high, and it looked old. The brick was pockmarked in places, and some of the windows were broken out or boarded up on the north end, like they'd given up main-taining that section. Black smoke poured from the south of the building, and flames licked the bricks that surrounded the windows.

We jumped out. I scanned the GIS map for a fire hydrant or outdoor spigot until a cop ran up to me and pointed to his left. "Hydrant's on that end."

I thanked him and hopped back on the truck to tell Henry, who was driving. He steered the truck that way, slowly as the crowd parted. We stopped at the hydrant, an old yellow one, and jumped out. Luke and Jordy ran over to the hydrant with the tools to open it while Brian and Wes pulled out the hoses.

A few minutes in, Chief called us over for a huddle. He stood with an older man who had mousy brown hair and a moustache.

"Guys, this is Mr. Brooker, plant manager. Mr. Brooker says there's a hazmat containment room in the warehouse."

"Yeah, far north end." Mr. Brooker pointed to the end of the building that looked disused and wasn't on fire.

"What's in there?" Chief asked. "Explosives? Flammables?"

"Mostly flammables. Acetone. Ethanol. Maybe some sulfide."

"*Maybe* some sulfide," Chief repeated harshly. Dipicryl sulfide was an explosive.

"Well… uh…" Mr. Brooker's eyes darted to the building nervously. "…we're not supposed to store that here, but it can be a few months between pickups."

"How much stuff is in there? Can we get it out?"

Mr. Brooker shook his head. "There's a lot. Some is decades old. It'd take at least a full day, trucks, and hazmat to move it."

"Shit." Chief stared at the guy. "You do have sprinklers in the containment room, right?"

Mr. Brooker chewed on his moustache. "Um. Yes. But I'm not sure they're working."

Chief cursed. The state had all kinds of regulations about

how businesses were supposed to store hazardous materials, but it was clear this guy had let a lot of it slide.

"But all the hazardous chemicals are in that room," Mr. Brooker said adamantly. "And the fire's not down there. That's good, right? All you have to do is keep the fire from getting to that end of the building. You guys can do that, can't you?"

Chief ignored him and made a call asking for hazmat support. Then he clicked off and looked at us. "It'll take some time for hazmat to arrive, and you heard Mr. Brooker. We can't let the fire get to that room. Luke, Jordy, Henry, Donny —you stay here and get the hoses on the main fire. Someone needs to go check out the north end of the building. Start at the last entrance and walk towards this end. See how far the fire's—"

"I'll go," I said, interrupting him.

Chief Reiger looked at me dubiously. "After today, I don't know that I trust you to do much of anything, Mike."

"No, I can do it, I swear, Chief."

Chief hesitated for a second. "Okay, fine. Go get me a sit report. And take some of the extinguishers. Brian, you go with Mike."

"I'll go," Donny said firmly. "Sorry about the fight, Chief, but we're brothers. Besides, someone has to keep an eye on me." He smiled like he was being charming. I inwardly rolled my eyes.

"Fine. Brian, you work on the main fire. Donny's going with Mike. Load up on extinguishers and go in on the far end. I want a report on where the fire is inside ASAP. When you find it, call in and we'll send a team to you. If it's too close to the hazardous material, get the hell out of there."

"Got it," Donny said.

We grabbed fire extinguishers from inside the truck. The ones Cal Fire used were ammonium-phosphate-based, and they were big, heavy, and bright red. I swung two onto my back, and Donny did the same. We grabbed our breathing apparatus and headed for the far end of the building, double-time.

The door was open, and inside, the building was dark thanks to the boarded-up windows. As I penetrated in a few steps, dirt crunching under my boots and big, weird machines rising up beside me in the gloom, it felt like I'd fallen down a huge rabbit hole. We turned on our headlamps and made our way through a large room cluttered with leftover junk that somebody must have paid a mint for back in the day. The air was full of visible smoke but no flames. We moved on, passing through room after room. The smoke crept up on us like ghosts, and it seemed to grow hotter, as if we were getting closer to hell.

The speaker piped up in my SCBA helmet, and Chief came on. "We're seeing flames moving towards you on the fourth floor. Seems like it's spreading fastest up there. You guys go check it out, but abort if it's too close. Got it? Over."

Donny's voice replied. "Roger that. Yeah, nothing spotted so far here on the first. Mike and I'll head up. Canali out."

The next hall we moved into, Donny headed for the stair-case, and I followed. By the time we got to the fourth floor, I was breathing hard from the effort of carrying the gear and heavy extinguishers. Plus, we hit thicker smoke. The fire was definitely worse here.

Donny slipped one of the fire extinguishers off his back and motioned to me. "Let's go." Carrying the extinguishers like weapons in a war against an unseen monster, we walked into the next room.

It was lighter because, unlike the first floor, the windows weren't boarded up, but they were dirty, and some were missing entirely. That might have been why the fire was spreading faster—circulating fresh air meant more oxygen to fuel the flames like some evil coconspirator. We swept the room with our headlamps. No fire in sight. Extinguishers in hand, we moved ahead.

"Stay close!" Donny said, his voice loud over the speaker.

I heard him, but the order only made me want to move farther away. A strange feeling that had crept over me when I entered the building grew moment by moment. A numbness, an unreality. I wasn't afraid. I didn't care. Not just about this fire, but about anything. About Donny, about my family, about being a goddamn firefighter. About everything that I once wanted. Nothing seemed important. Hell, it didn't even seem *real*. I might as well be reading about the fire or watching a movie instead of living it as I wandered deeper into the smoke, eyes peeled for flames. I was a zombie, the walking dead.

Donny called my name, told me to stay close, but I kept going. What was the point anyway? Was I going to spend the rest of my life hiding who I really was? Maybe I should just leave. Leave the family. Leave home. Leave everything.

Shane.

I missed him so much. I loved him. Was *in love* with him. But he was right to dump me. I hated myself for not being fucking worthy of him. For being too cowardly to stand up to my family for him. He should have left me. Hell, *I* wanted to leave me.

And then I found the fire.

The room was vast, but it was empty, abandoned, and brightly lit by the flames that crawled up the walls like a living animal. There was nothing on the floor except for a bit of trash. Even the boards were soft and squished and wobbled under my feet as if no one had walked up here in a very long time, like the whole thing was rotten and ready to crumble, the wood dry and soft—perfect fucking fire fodder. Food for the monster.

Whoever owned this building should have torn it down years ago. Now they were gonna pay the price.

I walked forward with my extinguisher, spraying the walls, but a fire extinguisher was a pitiful match for this blaze. Its hissing sound was barely audible over the crackle of the fire.

A lick of flame raced across the floor toward me like a long-lost friend coming to say hello. I sprayed that fucker and then moved ahead a step at a time, spraying here, there. The foam doused everything it touched, but it didn't touch enough.

If only it could be quick. Dying, that is.

At that moment, I couldn't see myself walking out of this building, couldn't see myself returning to the station, couldn't see myself going home where Donny was in my damn house watching my every move. Where Pa would be at every meal saying how much he hated gays. I hurt so fucking much. I just wanted it to end. If only it could be quick. But fire, man. Fire's not quick.

I moved forward, the boards creaking under the weight of me and all my heavy gear. I sprayed the flames.

"Mike! Mike!" Donny sounded frantic in my headset. I didn't care.

I stepped forward and sprayed some more. I was supposed to put the fire out, right? That was my job. All the things I'd heard in my training, warnings about unsafe structures, the signs, they were all there. I should turn around.

I didn't care.

"Mike! Come back! The floor's gonna go!"

I stepped forward, spraying the flames. The ceiling was so far up there, I couldn't reach it with the spray, but orange flames were having a dance party up there too. I stepped forward, angling the nozzle at the floor.

And I suddenly had to laugh. Fuck, wasn't this me all over? Here I was, moving ahead into danger, but spraying an extinguisher to put out the fire. As if, even here, even now, I couldn't make up my mind what I wanted.

Good old Mike. Too fucking afraid to reach out and take what he really wanted.

Jesus.

Beneath my feet, the floor cracked loud enough to be heard over the roar of the fire. I froze, extinguisher in my hand.

"Mike!" Donny's voice, begging. "Turn around, bro. Please!"

The wood cracked again, and I went down an inch.

Shit. Shit. Was this happening? Nothing seemed solid. Inside, I felt nothing.

"Mike! The floor! Come back toward me, slowly!"

I shuffled in a turn far enough to see him. Donny in his mask, reaching out his hand from the door to the room, his eyes wild behind his goggles. "Mike! Come on! Get back here. I can't get closer, or I'll add to the weight on the floor."

I just looked at him. Should I keep going? Was this dangerous enough, or did I need to punish myself some more?

Shit! The floor dropped away until all I felt under my feet was space. But I only fell three or four feet. The extra fire extinguisher on my back caught on the edge of the planks and brought me up short with a jerk and a grunt. The fire extinguisher I'd had in my hands rolled away.

I was stuck there, in the hole up to my chest, most of my body dangling over thin air. The fire extinguisher on my back ground into my head where it was caught against the boards by the single strap and bearing my full weight.

Donny tossed his fire extinguisher aside and dropped to his stomach on the floor. He crawled toward me and stuck out his hand. "Mike! Grab my hand! Hurry!" He reached out, reached out.

I stared at his open palm. I could take it. He could pull me to safety. But then what? What was the point? I looked up into his eyes. He looked so scared. My brother, Donny Canali.

Hot Cannolis. My idol growing up. All us men walking around like we owned the joint. I'd been so proud to be one, once upon a time. But Donny had abandoned me, insulted me, even if he didn't know it. I couldn't take Donny's hand.

The extinguisher strap snapped.

"No!" Donny screamed.

And then I fell.

NINETEEN

SHANE

"Talk to him, Shane." Pops leaned forward in his chair, pleading. Not for the first time in the last few days.

"I did." I flopped back on the couch and gritted my teeth, feeling my jaw muscle jump. It was harder to scream through gritted teeth.

Also not for the first time, he said, "Angry words spoken in an alley don't count. You've both had some time to think. Clearly, you're miserable. I'll bet he is too."

"Not fucking likely." The words spit out on their own, and I sighed. "I'm sorry, Pops. But honestly, he was very clear about how he can't lose his family."

"Of course he doesn't want to lose his family. Few of us do. But I doubt he realized he was about to lose you."

My lips compressed in a good imitation of a sulky child, but I couldn't help it. "I don't mean that much to him."

"Come on, kid, you know that's not true." He spread his hands. "Yes, he's done some asshole moves, but the guy's in a whirlwind. Things you take for granted are brand new to Mike. The sneer of someone on the street is water off a duck's back to you. To him, it's a punch in the gut. He's used to being admired, prized, and loved by everybody, including his family. Come on, Shane, he's an exceptionally handsome, tall, macho, white male and a firefighter, for crap's sake. He's the All-American Hero. Coming out means people won't see him like that anymore. That's a lot to give up."

I stared at Pops as his words sank in and goosebumps sprang up on my arms. Whoa. I hadn't thought about it from that perspective. I'd always been femme. People knew I was gay when I was six. Ro too. Winston was black, so he'd been discriminated against for a million reasons. The closest to Mike's situation I knew personally was Chas, and he hadn't come out until later, after college and the NFL. I knew it meant a lot to Mike to be considered a hero. He'd grown up with that mythos. But it hadn't occurred to me that he might think coming out would kill that as well. Of course, I didn't believe that, but I could see that Mike might. "I guess the fact that he even considered coming out to be with me is a big deal."

Pops sighed. Definitely losing patience. "Do you honestly want Mike to come out *to be with you*?" I frowned at him. "Don't you want him to come out to be himself?"

"Well sure, but—" But what? Again, Pops was right. This was about Mike, not me. I'd told myself I wouldn't push him, and I'd tried hard not to. But in the end, I had. I said I didn't expect Mike to come out to be with me, but secretly, I did. I'd believed that he'd be so enthralled with the community and my friends and, of course, me, that he'd throw over all his objections and loss and open that damned closet door. And it had been all of, what, three months since we'd met? Shit, what a two-face I was.

The phone in my pocket rang. Mike! I grabbed for it so fast I fumbled it and had to leap to catch it.

Pops chuckled, and it reduced the tension. But when I looked at the display, it said, "Tessa."

I blinked at it for a moment, then answered. "Hello?"

"Shane, this is Tessa." Her voice reeked of tension.

"Yeah, hi." I couldn't hide my disappointment. "How are you?"

"Not good. Listen, Mike was hurt in a fire. He's been admitted to the hospital."

Pure fear shot through me. "No!" I slapped a hand to my mouth, then pulled it away. "What hospital? Where is he?"

"Oroville Hospital."

"How badly is he hurt? What happened?"

"Bad, but not too bad." She was still talking, and I heard something about, "I'll call you as soon as—"

Fuck that! "Tessa? I'm on my way." I clicked off.

Pops was standing. "What happened? Mike?"

I nodded frantically as I ran for my coat. "That was Tessa. He's in the Oroville Hospital. He was injured during a fire."

"Shit!" He frowned. "Please keep me in the loop."

All I wanted was to be driving. "I will."

Zoom, out that door and into Mable so fast my gold sneakers should have scorched. Trying not to break every speed law in California since I did not want to get pulled over, I still managed to make it into the Oroville Hospital parking lot in an hour.

I made another run into the lobby. The Oroville Hospital was a smaller one, much less crowded than the big city hospitals I was used to. Still all hospitals had rules, right?

Jeez, I should have asked if he was in the ICU. They'd never let me in there. Worse, it would mean that Mike was in critical condition. But Tessa had said bad, but not too bad. What the fuck did that even mean? Good job getting basic info, Bower.

Putting on my best, concerned, polite member-of-the-family face, I walked up to the information desk in the lobby. "I'm here to see Mike Canali."

The dark-haired woman at the desk looked up at me with

an expression I could only call longsuffering. "You're a second cousin once removed, I have no doubt." She sighed.

I nodded and showed all my teeth. "How did you know?"

She waved a hand. "Second floor. He's in room 221, but go to the waiting room and—wait. He's only allowed two visitors at a time, and I imagine someone is directing traffic up there. There are so many of you." She waved again, this time toward a bank of elevators behind her and then looked back at her computer screen.

Once again, I took off at a run and toggled the elevator button seven times. Didn't come any faster.

Finally on the second floor—felt like twenty— I hurried off, glanced at the signage, identified the direction of 221, and took off running again. Several vending machines lined the walls with a man kneeling in front of one of them, stretching his arm up into the product area. I ignored him and focused toward the break in the hall ahead that suggested it was the waiting room. The sound of voices echoed from that area. I ran faster.

As I passed the vending machine, the guy stood up and back really fast and Bam! Total collision. The man was much bigger than me, and I pinwheeled toward the wall, staggering. A powerful arm grasped me and pulled me toward— Holy shit, it was Donny.

He frowned at me, and his grip tightened. "Shane! Good. I need to speak to you."

Okay, he was twice my size, the biggest of the Canali brothers, and the meanest, but damn, no one told me what to do, except occasionally Pops. My heart hammered, but I yanked my arm to no effect and gritted out, "Let the fuck go of me."

I could barely believe it, but his eyes widened, and he released me instantly. "Oh, I'm so sorry. See I'm kind of upset and—" He inhaled. "Would you mind talking to me a minute? Please?"

Right off the top, I could think of fifty reasons why I minded talking to Donny, but the only one I said was, "I really want to see Mike."

"Ma and Pa are in there right now, so they won't let you in anyway and, well, this may be my only chance to speak to you, and it's really important."

He looked so sincere, I couldn't say anything but okay.

He gestured to a bench on the other side of the hall and guided me to it.

I was practically jumping out of my skin, but I stuck my hands under my thighs to keep from fiddling and looked up at him. Wow. A scene from the movie *Twilight* popped into my head, when Edward the vampire—le sigh—says he's the apex predator because everything about him, the way he looks, smells, sounds, sucks in his prey. Donny was gorgeous. One of the few men more beautiful than Mike. But Donny was scary. The words rushed out of my mouth. "How's Mike? Is he going to be okay?" A deep crease popped between Donny's dark, arched brows, and I panicked. I grabbed his arm. "What?"

For a second, he stared at my hand, and I quickly removed it. Then he sighed, "Physically, he's pretty banged up. He fell fourteen feet through a burned-out floor and crashed to the story below. He hit his head hard, but, of course, he was in full gear. It protected him somewhat. By the time I got to him and rescue came, he was conscious, but they're checking him for a concussion. He sprained his wrist and wrenched his shoulder, but he didn't break anything." Donny shook his head. "Us dumb, tough Canalis. They're treating a laceration on his leg where a board penetrated his fire suit. Various cuts and bruises. But that's it."

I exhaled a breath I wasn't aware I'd been holding. That sounded terrifying, but at least he'd be okay. I almost laughed with relief.

Donny said, "But there's a bigger problem."

My head snapped up.

Donny looked around, as if to make sure we were alone, and lowered his voice. "He... he did it on purpose, Shane. He went into a situation that he knew was stupid dangerous and unsafe." He gritted his teeth. "And he did it for no reason. He can say he thought there was someone in there, but fuck, it was obvious to a kindergartner that the end of the building was deserted. He... fuck. He fell partway through the floor, and I tried to get to him, but he wouldn't even take my hand!" His voice shook, and he blew out a pained breath. "I haven't told anyone except you, but you know him, Shane. You're his friend. Why would he pull a stupid-ass stunt like this? I mean, it was like—" He leaned in close to my ear and whispered, "—like he wanted to hurt himself. He could have died." The anguish that idea caused him shivered in his voice. He wiped a hand over his face.

I stared at Donny in horror. Oh God, Mike. I knew he'd been under so much pressure and manic and not quite right. But this? I desperately wanted to scream at Donny, *Because you're all a bunch of frigging, homophobic idiots* as I beat on him.

Take. A. Breath.

I was as much responsible for Mike's hopelessness as Donny or Angelo or any of them. When he'd needed support, I'd been too busy protecting myself.

I stared at my hands. "I... I can't say for certain, Donny. That's not my story to tell. But I know he's been very conflicted lately."

"Conflicted? Shit, I'm conflicted every day. That doesn't mean I'm going to off myself."

I stared into those midnight eyes. "Look, just talk to Mike. Really talk to him. Find out who he is instead of who you want him to be."

Donny blinked. "Is it the firefighter thing? I mean, I know there's a lot of pressure from Pa and the family to join the fire corps. And he's the youngest, Pa's last chance for another hot shot, so Mike's always the one on the hot seat. Maybe he wanted to be an artist or something?" Donny truly looked mystified. "But shit, he's so good at firefighting. He already won the Medal of Valor. And he's a fucking hero and—"

"Listen to me, Donny!" I grabbed his arm, and this time, I didn't let go. "Talk to your brother and really listen to what he says. Yes, he's the youngest, so he's got piles and layers of family tradition and expectations on top of him. He's got five of you to look up to, plus your dad. It's a lot when you're... when you've got your own issues. Just talk to him."

He looked at me sharply, and for the first time, there was some kind of understanding, of knowing, behind those eyes. He opened his mouth to reply when Tessa trotted up. "There you are. Donny, it's your turn." She smiled at me, tight and worried. "Hi, Shane. Thanks for coming."

"Hi, Tessa." I stood, and we hugged.

Donny stood beside me and gave me one last look, then hurried down the hall.

Tessa slipped an arm around my waist. "What was that about?"

If Donny hadn't told the others what Mike did, it wasn't my place to. "I ran into him, literally, when I came in. He's really worried about Mike." That was one way of saying it.

She frowned. "We're all worried about Mike. Come on. The rest of the family is in the waiting room."

She led me that way, her arm still around my waist. When we turned the corner, I gasped and stopped so fast I yanked her back. *Canali, to the max.* Every chair was filled with a dark-haired, good-looking Canali or related humanoid. Some even leaned against the wall. I recognized many of the faces, but there were a good half dozen I didn't know. Wow. I'd never seen them in force out of their natural habitat.

As I stood there gaping, Carlotta and Nonna came rushing across the room, with Carlotta cooing, "Oh, Shane, thank you for coming to see our poor, fallen hero. He'll be so happy to know you're here."

Nonna gazed at me, holding my arms. "I knew you'd come. I saw it."

I let them both hug me, but over their shoulders, I saw the glares from Gabe and the neutral stares of Tito and Uncle Ricky. Only Tony and his wife gave me welcoming smiles, while still looking worried.

There wasn't an open seat, so I just stepped to a corner and stood there, feeling eyes crawling all over me. Of course, I was in Shane gear, pink and gold to the max. Jeez, even my damned jacket was pink. Tessa stood beside me while Carlotta and Nonna went back to their chairs.

Mostly to have something to say, I asked Tessa for an update on his condition. She was just reiterating what Donny had already told me, when an older nurse called, "Is Shane Bower here?"

I raised my hand a little, wondering if I had to check in or something.

She said, "Come with me, please. He's asking for you."

Donny must have told Mike I was there. My heart leaped and fell at the same time. Was he going to be happy to see me, or was he just going to tell me to go the fuck home—that we'd broken up and I'd already screwed with his head enough?

What the fuck did I care? At this point, I'd give anything just to lay eyes on him. To know he was okay.

As I walked beside the nurse in her soundless shoes, Donny strode past us the other way and gave me an intense look. The nurse was saying, "You must be a very good friend. He's such a hero, isn't he?"

"Yes. Yes, he is." I didn't tell her that for a little while, he'd been my hero.

We got to the door, I heard Angelo's voice murmuring inside, and I almost turned and ran. But the nurse had pushed the door open and gone ahead. She was saying,

"Look who I brought. Your friend, Shane." She kind of pulled me, and I ended up at the foot of Mike's bed with Angelo glaring. Lucille jumped up to give me a hug.

All I could see was Mike.

He lay in the bed, pale, with red splotches on his face and a painful-looking red scrape on his neck. There was a bandage on his head and his thigh, his wrist was in a small cast on the coverlet, and both hands were covered with cuts and bandages. But his gaze could have started a whole new fire. Just seeing him was like breathing for the first time in days.

Lucille looked up at me. "Thank you for coming, honey."

"I thought only family was allowed in here." Angelo glared daggers at me.

Before I could reply, Lucille said, "You know perfectly well that they're making exceptions for our Mike."

"He's got enough people hanging around here as it is."

"Mike asked to see Shane. So just stop, Angie." Lucille planted her fists on her hips, ready to fight.

Angelo opened his mouth, and Mike held up a hand and then winced. "I not only asked to see Shane—I'd like to speak to him *alone*. Please." Angelo scowled, and Mike repeated, "Alone."

As Angelo stood from his chair, grumbling, and Lucille waited to be sure he left, I tried to hear over the pounding of my own heart. *Don't blow this. Don't blow this.*

The door clicked behind me, and Mike looked toward it as I made a quick peek over my shoulder to be sure they were gone. Then our eyes met.

"I'm sorry," we both said simultaneously.

He frowned, which looked painful. "What are you sorry for?"

I stepped closer. "Walking away from you. Protecting myself instead of helping you through the hardest time of your life. Donny said—" I swallowed hard. "—he told me that you walked into that fire on purpose. I hope that's not true, Mike, but if it is, oh god, please don't do that ever again. Even if you want a different life that doesn't include me, there are so many people who love you and always will. You're important to your family and to the world. I shouldn't have walked away when you needed to hear that."

He shook his head. "No way. You thought I was the world's wussiest coward who'd never live up to his commitments to you or myself. And you were right. I'm just surprised you didn't walk away sooner."

I made another step to the side of his bed. "Who am I to call you a coward? It's your life. Even if all I can ever be is your friend, I am that. I don't want you to do something that isn't right for you just because of me. Hell, that's not love, and it's certainly not friendship. I just want you to be okay."

He stared at me with a little crease between his brows. "Does that mean you *only* want to be friends?"

I chewed my lip as I stared into those dark, dark eyes. *Don't blow this.* "I want you to be happy. I don't think you'd be any happier making me your dirty little secret than I'd be. So I guess I want to be whatever lets both of us be ourselves. And you get to decide what that is for you." He looked so vulnerable and beautiful against those white sheets. I wanted him so desperately. To hold him against the gaping wound in my chest and protect him from everything, but I already saw what happened when I tried to force him to fit my pictures— like everybody else did. I smiled softly. Time to let go.

"No, dammit!" The shout made me jump back as he half sat up and grimaced in pain.

I rushed to grab him and lowered him to the pillows. "What do you mean, no? No what?"

He thrashed his head back and forth. "I don't want that."

"Want what, Mike?" I sat on the edge of the bed.

"I don't want you all reasonable and noble and bullshit, with this *it's my life and I get to decide every fucking thing about it.* I want you calling me on my crap and expecting me to do the right thing. Claim some of my life, please, Shane. I want you to. I want you to love me."

When the words were out, he froze, and so did I, only inches from his face.

He whispered, "I... I need you. Don't let me do stupid, cowardly, dumbass shit like I pulled in that building. I'm scared, Shane. I can't go on hiding, or I'm afraid of what I'll do. And I can't face this without you. Just tell me you'll be on the other side waiting for me after I talk to my family. I don't want to lose you—not over being in the closet, not for anything. Not ever."

Oh. My. God. Fireworks went off in my heart and exploded into my brain, and all I could do was lower my lips to his.

I kissed him—gently out of respect for his many bruises. But, damn, it was sweet. I loved him so much it hurt. *Loved.* Absolutely, yes. I pulled back. "I do love you, Mike."

"I love you, Shane. So much." His warm gaze ran over my face, and he smiled.

My heart throbbed at the words. Mike loved me! I'd thought I'd lost him, my beautiful, sweet, sensitive, brave fire-fighter. My dream guy. Now he was looking at me like he felt for me the way I felt for him. But I was still scared, worried about him. "Did you really try to hurt yourself?"

He took a deep breath, his eyes going sad. He hesitated, then nodded. "I think it was more that I just... couldn't see a way forward. I was reckless. I made the stupidest possible decisions in that building, and I don't ever want to feel that way again. It's been pulling me apart, living like this. I can't lie anymore."

I understood that feeling. Knew it intimately. "So it's time then?" I asked, a lump in my throat.

"It's time," he agreed. "Would you... would you ask them

to come in? Just Ma and Pa and my sibs. That's enough people to come out to at once."

"Are you sure you want to do it now, while you're hurt? I know you have a head injury. Maybe you should wait until you get home." I gently squeezed his arm.

"No, now," he said, determined. "Please. Please help me do this. Go get them."

"Okay. If you're sure." My heart was pounding. "Do you want me to stay? Or I'm happy to wait in the waiting room with the others."

He reached up and touched my cheek. "No. I want you here, with me. In the room. Everywhere." He frowned. "If that's okay. I know it's asking a lot. It won't be pretty."

Okay? I'd walk over coals for this man. "I'll be right here then. You know I'll be here for you, no matter what happens, right? I told you before—you can come home with me if you need to. Live with me and Pops. You'll have friends and a community. I won't leave you again."

This got me a genuine smile. "Thank you for that. It helps."

I nodded. "Okay then. I'll go get them."

TWENTY

MIKE

I looked around the room at the faces of my family—Pa, Ma, Tessa, Donny, Gabe, Tony, and Viv. It sucked that Ace and Paul weren't here. They were cooler and had been around a lot more than the rest of my brothers and might be on my side. Plus, if I was gonna jump off the ledge, I might as well do it to everyone at once. But they weren't here, and it was time. The fingernails I'd been hanging on by were about shot. It was time to fall.

And I had Shane. I glanced at him. He'd moved to a corner of the room to be unobtrusive, and a frown of concentration lurked on his brow, but he gave me a little smile. He'd said he loved me. If I had Shane, I'd be okay, no matter what. It had taken way too long, but I knew that now.

Tessa must have figured out what was going on because she gave me an encouraging smile and nod, even though she was biting her lip. I wasn't the only one who was nervous.

"Mike?" Pa asked, face concerned. "You wanted a family meeting. What's up?" He glanced warily over at Shane, then back at me.

My pulse throbbed in my neck, and a wave of nausea swamped me, leaving me hot and cold at the same time. I'd dreaded this moment for as long as I could remember—pretty much always. But I was lying here in a hospital having royally fucked myself up. If I kept this secret any longer, it was going to kill me.

"Mike?" Ma took a step toward me but stopped, wringing her hands. "Go ahead and tell us whatever you need to tell us, Mimmo."

I looked down at my scratched-up hands with the bandaged wrist because I couldn't look at their faces while I made my confession.

"I'm gay," I said. My voice sounded funny because my ears were ringing. I always figured I'd say more, when the time came. But really, what else was there to say? Those two words were everything.

The room was silent for a long moment. I finally looked up and saw shocked faces. Ma was crying quietly, dabbing her eyes with a Kleenex. My dad…. Jesus. His face was red and slack. I'd never seen him look so bleak, not even when Gabe had that motorcycle accident. A stab of pain shot through my chest at the sight of him, and I wished I could disappear. I wished I could be someone else—for him.

But then he opened his mouth.

"What, because you've been hanging out with him?" He waved toward Shane, his lip curled in disgust. "You don't need to be like him, Michael. That's the last thing you need."

Okay, not happening. I expected it for myself. But goddamn it, he didn't need to hurt Shane. "It has nothing to do with Shane," I said firmly. "I've known since I was seven. Nothing *makes* you gay. I was just born that way."

"You were born a Canali!" Pa shouted, shaking his head.

"No, he's right, Angie," Ma spoke up. "I've been reading all about it. People are born that way, and that's just the way it is. Oh, Mimmo." She crossed to me and hugged me gingerly. "I'm so sorry you've been carrying this burden for so long. But I love you. *We* love you. It's gonna be okay."

Tessa came up on the other side of my bed and squeezed my arm. "I'm proud of you, Mike. Love you, baby bro."

I attempted to give her a smile, but the look on my dad's face had struck pretty deep. I'd expected Tessa and Ma's support, and while I was grateful to have it, it was the rest that truly terrified me.

"Well it's not okay with me," Gabe said loudly. My gaze snapped to him. His arms were crossed over his chest, and he was glaring at Shane. "Sorry, Shane. You're smart, and I appreciate what you did for me. I get that you are who you are and... whatever. But my brother isn't like you." He looked back at me. "You're not like that, Mike. I don't know why you've gotten this into your head, but if you don't want to fuck up your entire life, you'd better get it out right now."

"Not all gay people are the same, Gabe," Tessa snapped. "Mike grew up with you bozos. Of course he's gonna act like you. That doesn't mean he's not gay."

"It sure as shit does!" Gabe yelled.

"Gabe's right," Pa said. "You'd better listen to him, Mike, if you won't listen to me. You wanna throw away everything you've worked so hard for? Your career? Your family too? Then keep talking, buddy."

"Angie! Don't say that," Ma cried. "Don't you ever say that! You don't speak for this entire family. Not if you're gonna be like that."

"You don't speak for me!" Tessa agreed. "I absolutely support Mike." She looked around. "Tony?"

Tony and Viv had been quiet. I put a hand over Tessa's and looked at them. Tony's eyes were sad. "You're gonna rip this family apart, bro."

"Anthony," Pa warned. "Tell your brother what a mistake he's making."

Tony held up his hands. "I'm not on anyone's side. It sucks, but Mike's gonna do what he's gonna do."

"Well I support you, Mike," Viv said stubbornly. "There's nothing wrong with being different."

"Different?" Gabe countered in disbelief.

An argument broke out—Pa and Gabe yelling with Tessa and Ma and Viv and Tony trying to calm everyone down. If I could have slunk away, I would have. But I was in a hospital bed hooked up to an IV, so I was stuck there. Maybe Shane had been right. Maybe I should have waited.

I looked over at Shane. His face was full of sympathy and worry. He gave me a look, something like *stay strong, you've got this*. And it struck me that he'd been through this scene before and that having to watch my family fight about it was probably bringing back a lot of painful memories. I hated to put Shane through this. It'd been unfair to ask him to stay.

I closed my eyes as my family's angry words bounced around the room like shards of glass. This was the worst-case scenario, as bad as I'd feared. And, sure, lately Tessa and Ma's support had become clear. But that almost made it worse because now it wasn't just me that my Pa and brothers were rejecting. Tony was right. Now it was ripping my whole family apart.

I needed to go away and leave them all alone.

"It's really very simple!" Shane shouted.

I opened my eyes to see he'd moved closer to my bed and stood next to Tessa. His eyes were glassy with tears but also snapping with anger. Everyone shut up and looked at him.

"You can accept Mike the way he is, the *reality* of him instead of the version he's tried so hard to be for you all… or you can say goodbye. I haven't seen my parents and brother for five years because they couldn't accept me. So that's your choice. Simple." He looked right at my dad.

Pa grimaced and shook his head. "He's been fine all these years! Nothing has to change. *You* put that into his head."

Shane frowned. "If you think he's been fine, you don't know your son at all."

Pa's face got that expression that would send us all scurrying when we were kids. That *you're in big trouble now* face. "You're not part of this family, son. You don't know what you're talking about. Why are you even here?"

"Angie! Don't be so rude," Ma said.

"I'm the one being rude?" Pa shouted.

"Pa, I asked Shane to be here!" I reached out for Shane's hand, and he took mine, careful due to the bandages. "He's my friend, and, yes, he is part of this family." Maybe that was chickenshit again, saying *friend* instead of *boyfriend.* But I honestly didn't want my dad to lay into Shane any more.

"He's part of the family as far as I'm concerned," Ma said stubbornly.

"Me too," said Tessa.

"What, we're voting now?" Pa said. "I'm talking about blood!"

"And marriage—" Tony put in.

"Fine. And marriage," Pa conceded. "The point is—"

A loud whistle pierced the room.

We all looked at Donny as he lowered his fingers from his mouth. "I have something to say." His face was red, and he took a deep breath. "Pa, Mike hasn't been okay. He hasn't been okay for a while. Shane's right." He looked at me, his eyes wrecked. "What you guys don't know is that... is that what happened to Mike today wasn't an accident. I'm sorry, Mike, but they need to know. He walked into that fire on purpose today. And just before he fell through that floor... God. I'll never forget the look on his face... so much pain. Like he'd just given up." His voice shook, and a tear ran down his cheek. Fuck. I'd never seen Donny cry. He took a choked breath and wiped his face on the crook of his sleeve. "Shane's wrong about one thing, though. The choice isn't to accept Mike or say goodbye. The choice is to accept Mike or go to his funeral."

Ma gasped.

"Mike," Donny said, straightening his spine. "You do what you gotta do to be happy, man. You can be gay as fuck, if you need to be. I love you, one hundred percent, and you'll always be my brother." The last few words were barely audible, and Donny walked out of the room, overcome.

Everyone looked stunned. Tessa wrapped her arm around my shoulders and drew Shane closer, and the two of them, me, and Ma huddled together. Ma was crying again.

"Oh, Mike," she said. "I'm so sorry, Mimmo. Why didn't you talk to me? Don't you ever do anything like that again!"

"It's gonna be okay, Mike," Tessa agreed tearfully. "I promise it will."

"I'm gonna check on Donny," Gabe mumbled. He gave me one last look, but the fight had clearly gone out of him. He left the room.

Viv and Tony had been whispering. Tony put his arm around Viv and faced me. "You have our support, Mike. Whatever you need. I mean it."

"Thanks, guys," I said weakly. I was still in shock about Donny. He was the last person I expected to support me. Holy shit.

Everyone stared at Pa, who wiped his face. He just looked sad now. "If what Donny said is true, we need to talk, son. And you're off duty, as of now."

I swallowed and nodded. I couldn't blame him. Mental fitness in firefighters was a big deal, and I'd been anything but mentally fit during that fire today. If I wanted to get back into action, I'd have to earn it.

"Angie," Ma prompted, her tone pleading.

Pa held up his hands in surrender. "I don't understand this. But I guess the world moves on whether I understand it or not. You'll always be my son, Michael. That's all I know how to say right now." And he, too, left the room.

Viv and Tony came over and hugged me.

"Thanks, Viv. Tony," I said.

"I mean it, whatever you need," said Tony. "I'm sorry if I've ever been dickish or said crap about gays." He looked at Shane apologetically and back at me.

"If you ever said anything like that, it was to agree with Gabe and Donny," I said. "The same way that I did. Probably *less* than I did. You and me are good."

Viv poked him in the ribs with an elbow. "You see? That shit always comes back to bite you. Anyway, love you, Mike."

"Love you too."

Another hug, then Tony and Viv left. Only Ma and Tessa stayed—and Shane.

I lay back in bed, my head swimming. It was done. And whatever the fallout, at least I didn't have to live with that secret anymore.

"You okay?" Shane asked.

Ma felt my forehead. "Are you in pain? Want me to buzz for the nurse? You should sleep now. You've been through so much. My poor baby. And did you really walk into that fire today? What were you thinking? It was because of this? Why didn't you talk to me sooner, Mimmo? You know I would have understood." Ma was an emotional wreck, tears still streaming down her cheeks.

Tessa said, "Ma. You're right that Mike needs to rest. Let's talk to him later, okay?" She walked to Ma and put her arm over Ma's shoulder, trying to lead her from the room.

"Yes, yes. But …you're going to be all right?" She held back, studying my face.

"I'm sorry I scared you, Ma. I'm okay now," I said and realized it was true. This had been hard, and it wasn't all puppies and rainbows. There was more work ahead—with Pa, with Gabe, probably with Donny. But even so, the sense of weight on my chest was gone. I wouldn't drown in my own self-deception. I looked up at Shane and held out my hand again. He took it carefully with a puzzled little smile. This time I pulled him close, tugged him down to sit on the bed next to me. "Ma, Tessa, I also want you to know… Shane's my boyfriend."

"Oh my God!" Tessa grinned. "I'm so happy for you guys!" She left Ma and ran over to hug Shane. He hugged her back.

"Thanks, Tessa. That means a lot," Shane said.

"Are you kidding? You're already my favorite brother. Sorry, Mike." She gave me a wink. "How long has this been going on?"

"Not long," Shane glanced at me.

"About a month," I said at the same time.

But Ma was still standing near the door, her mouth open. I felt a sudden ache. Was being with Shane a bridge too far? "Ma?" I asked.

"I'm just… I'm shocked," she said, eyes wide.

Shane and I shared a glance.

"But you said you love Shane," I pointed out.

"I do love Shane," she said. "But don't you realize… Nonna's second sight told her Shane would join our family. For once, she was actually right!"

TWENTY-ONE

SHANE

I pulled into the parking lot of the hotel, basking in the warmth of Mike sitting in the seat next to me. I could swear even Mable was running smoother than normal, she was so happy.

I turned off the ignition and gazed at the man I loved. Yes, loved, proclaimed out loud and sealed in Mike's blood. It had been two weeks since Mike's big revelation. For one week, he recovered in bed at home, doted on by his mother, aunt, sister, and of course, grandma who was very proud to have predicted my rise in family position. His brothers and cousins had tiptoed around him, but Donny's semi-conversion to the dark side had gone a long way to smoothing the path. Mike's dad was avoiding him, but I hoped he'd come around. Happily, that worry felt far away tonight.

At the moment, Mike's resemblance to a deer in head-lights was only slight, and, besides, he was such a well-dressed deer in his slim dark-brown pants and teal—yes, I said teal—blazer. His shirt, unbuttoned at the neck, was freaking copper-colored. I shook my head. "Who are you and what gay man's closet have you been raiding? You look fabulous, darling!"

His eyes widened. "Too much?"

"Not even. Honest. You look wonderful."

He grinned. "I have to confess, I consulted Ro."

I laughed. "Cheater!"

"Hey, Queer Eye for the queer guy. The outfit was a present from Ma."

I smiled. It felt good to hear words like that fall comfortably from Mike's lips. Tonight, however, was a big test. His first-ever serious date with a man in a restaurant that wasn't even in Lavender Heights, so no guaranteed warm reception, followed by a stay at a hotel with elevators and everything. He only looked a little nervous.

He glanced out Mable's window toward the door of the very nice hotel. "It sure was great of Pops to do this."

I smiled. "Yeah. The best." Pops had given me an early Christmas present in the form of gift certificates I was to spend on a special night with Mike.

Mike said, "You look great too."

I gave a half-bow complete with a sweep of my arm, which had to look funny sitting behind the wheel. "Thank you, kind sir." Still, my chosen outfit for the night wouldn't do much to tone down the impact of a male/male couple out on the town, with its gray wide-legged trousers and cinched-waist jacket. "I found it in one of the little discount shops in Lavender. It's real designer. Christian Siriano, in fact. Ta-da!"

"It looks nice." The chances that he knew who Christian Siriano was were slim, and he glanced distractedly toward the hotel entrance again.

"Let's check in and then eat dinner. I'm starved."

"Okay." He gave me a brave smile.

We grabbed our overnight bags from the back and walked toward the entrance, me slipping my arm through his. Come on, this was a date.

In the well-appointed lobby—ooh, I had to remember how they'd used the flowers on the chandeliers—I crossed confidently to the desk, carefully picked the female clerk versus the male, and smiled as I said, "Good evening. Shane Bower checking in."

She smiled. "Yes, Mr. Bower." Her fingers clicked the computer keys. "We have a room for two with a king bed, correct?"

"Yes." I did not clear my throat, though I wanted to. Hotels played a very small role in the Shane Bower story, so it took concentration to be cool.

She looked up at me. Her gaze slid past, and her lips parted. She didn't say, *Oh my*, but boy, I bet she wanted to. I didn't have to look back to know her eyes had connected with the perfection of Mike Canali.

She noticeably swallowed, and her fingers clicked keys. "I was able to secure you a room on a higher floor, Mr. Bower, with an excellent view of the skyline." She flicked a glance at Mike, as if for approval.

Trying not to grin, I looked back. "Mike, guess what? This lovely person has gotten us a room with a view. Isn't that wonderful?"

For an instant, he looked confused, but then he smiled, flashing Canali razzle-dazzle all over the lobby. Would the desk clerk survive? "Thank you so much. That's so kind of you."

"Uh, two keys?" She couldn't take her eyes off Mike. Hell, I knew just how she felt.

I replied, "Yes, please."

"Help with your bags?"

"Nope. We have them, thanks."

On a sigh, she pushed the key packet across the desk and said, "I hope you have a wonderful stay."

"I'm sure we will." She never even looked my way. If I

could have captured the movie going on in her brain, I'm pretty sure I could have replaced E.L. James.

As Mike and I walked to the elevator, he gave me a look. "What was that about?"

"She rewarded your gorgeousness with a better room. I have to remember that when I'm doing future negotiations."

He snorted and pushed the up button, then looked down at himself. "These clothes really work, huh?" He looked so proud of himself.

"Darling, you have been hiding your light under a very boring bushel. But I'm not sure the world is ready for a gorgeous Canali man who knows how to dress." Our room, that had been changed from the fourth to the fifteenth floor, was at the end of the hall, meaning we'd only have one set of other guests to bother and held the possibility of two window walls rather than one.

It took a while to notice that, however, since the minute we got inside the door, we fell on each other like drag queens at a Victoria's Secret sale and didn't come up for air until a good four minutes of kissing had been accomplished. When Mike pulled away, he moaned, "I don't need dinner."

I stepped back and planted fists on my hips. "But I need my date. I didn't comb the thrift shops for this outfit for nothing, bucko."

He nodded, still breathing hard. "You're right. This is important. My first date. At least, my first official date now that I'm out."

I blinked hard and wrapped my arms around him. "I love you."

His eyes went all soft. "I'm so glad, Shane. Thanks for being patient with me. You've been such an inspiration. And not just because I'm too selfish to ever let you go."

Whew. I hugged him tight and stepped away, wiping at my eyes. "I don't want to go to dinner with a puffy red face, so how about we leave our bags here, resist the temptation of a king-size mattress, and you escort your date to the Top of the Scene?"

He stuck out an arm. "I'm honored."

When we got off the elevator on the top floor and walked to the host desk at the restaurant known for its gorgeous view, Mike's arm tensed a bit. I was tempted to drop my hold but didn't.

The maître d', a distinguished gentleman in a tuxedo, looked up at us, his cool gaze connecting with our linked arms. "Good evening. May I help you?"

I smiled. "Yes, reservation for Bower."

He glanced at his computer and then back at me. "Our best view table." His lips turned up slightly. "A special occasion?"

I took a breath and said, "Yes. Our first formal date. And my grandfather's holiday present."

His lips turned up ever so slightly more. He waggled a finger behind him. "James, please take this beautiful couple to table sixteen and serve them each a glass of champagne with my compliments. A first date is momentous. Here's to many more."

"Thank you. Thank you so much."

Mike stuck out his hand. "Thank you for helping to make our evening special."

The man shook Mike's hand with a smile, his gaze very likely assessing who was the gay newbie in our pair.

When we got to the table, the waiter looked a bit confused for a second, and Mike quickly stepped forward and held out my chair. I gave him a huge smile. A few people at tables nearby stared, but I was so used to it. Well, not at five-star restaurants, but still—Mike had his back turned so he didn't see.

Our waiter glided over with two tall flutes of bubbly, compliments of the maître d'. As soon as he'd walked away, Mike picked up his glass, held it out, and then said, "Anything I do with you is special, but this is amazing. Thank you for thinking of everything and making my first date one I'll remember forever."

I knew my eyes must be sparkling as I clinked his glass and said, "You ain't seen nothing yet."

He looked half-excited and half-scared.

The bubbly went down real easily as we perused the menu. Mike whispered, "Just how big a gift did Pops give you?"

I chuckled. "Enough. He wanted us to have a great time."

"Did you mention that I'd be happy with a Motel 6, a hot dog, and you?"

I laughed and tried not to sniffle as the waiter came to take our order. Mike asked for a steak, and I ordered salmon, plus another glass of champagne for both of us since Pops had specified we should have a toast on him.

When we were alone, sipping the last of our first glass of bubbly, Mike said, "For some reason, I've never asked you if you ever thought you liked girls?" He grinned. "I'll bet you're one of those—what's that word I heard in the club—gold-star gays, right?"

I cocked my head. "Actually, that's a pretty silly term some TV host made up. Even if you've been married twice and have six kids, if you're gay, you're gay, and there's no gold stars and bluebirds for having a simpler journey." I rotated my glass. "But in answer to your question, no, I never thought I liked girls, but I gave it a chance. When I was about nine, I knew I was really different from my family and that I thought boys were pretty. I said that out loud one day, and my mother shushed me so hard, I thought she'd shove a dishrag in my mouth." I sighed. "That was the moment I knew that being different was not okay in our community. So I watched the other boys and mimicked what they did. I couldn't get good at baseball, so I ran track, which meant I didn't have to set foot in Little League. I was no Usain Bolt, but was pretty fast, so my father left me alone. Meanwhile, I noticed that the boys all liked girls. They said they didn't. Called them names and stuff, but they secretly did. I kept waiting for it to happen to me. I prayed for the moment it would. But I'd be nice to a girl and end up her best friend." I shook my head. "Then when I was twelve, I went to a track meet, and a boy from another school pushed me into a storage closet and kissed me. I quit waiting to like girls." I looked up at him. "What about you? With the reputation of the Canalis to live up to, I'll bet you dated a lot of girls. Before you knew you were gay, I mean."

"You'd lose that bet. I dated a lot of girls *after* I knew I was gay." His smile looked bitter. "I so desperately didn't want to be queer. I even tried having sex with a girl once and failed epically. Blamed it on too much to drink. Total crock. Meanwhile, I was getting sucked off by every gay guy I could find. And I learned how much I enjoyed returning the favor." His eyes went all dark and suggestive.

"And you do so brilliantly," I purred.

"With you, I was inspired."

Be still, my heart. "Stop that, or we'll never make it through dinner."

They served our meals, and we ate, chatted, and laughed for a good hour of total indulgence. As we were finishing our entrees, a man's voice called, "Mike? Is that you?"

Mike turned fast in his seat to see a tall, good-looking guy who appeared to be in his forties with a pretty woman next to him. Mike's Adam's apple bounced. "Uh, hi, Leon."

My stomach flipped. Damn. Things had been going so well.

Leon said, "I thought that was you. Hey, your station must be paying rookies better than mine." He laughed and waved a hand at the elegant surroundings.

"Actually, the meal was a holiday gift."

"Wow. Good gift." He turned to the woman. "Have you

met my wife, Marge? Marge, this is Mike Canali, one of Angie's boys."

Displaying his Canali manners, Mike stood and shook her hand. "Delighted to meet you." And the moment of truth arrived. He turned to me. "This is Shane Bower, my—"

I hopped to my feet and stuck out my hand. "Mike and I met in a fire and have been good friends ever since."

Leon said, "Oh, are you a firefighter too?"

"Uh, no. I was just in the wrong place when the Dixie fire decided to decimate Crest Lake."

Leon's mouth opened. "Oh my god, you're the guy. The one who got the Medal of Valor." He turned to his wife. "Remember I told you, honey. This guy helped Mike save a bunch of civilians." He shook my hand again. "What an honor."

"Thank you." I smiled and sat back down.

"I didn't mean to interfere with your dinner, but I sure would like to buy you two a drink. What heroes."

My heart sank farther.

About a million emotions flickered across Mike's face. Then his chest expanded and he said, "Could I take a raincheck on that, Leon? To tell you the truth, we're on a date, and this is a special occasion. Shane's my boyfriend."

A thrill started in my chest and spread out in a wave of bliss.

Leon blinked. "Oh, I, uh, I didn't know. I mean—"

"Yeah, but sure would like to make it another time." Mike smiled big, and I saw a mountain of tension drop from his face.

Marge took Leon's arm. "We totally understand. You're such a cute couple. Enjoy the rest of your evening." She led him away, and Leon only looked back once.

But I barely saw. All I could do was grin.

Mike sat down and heaved a breath. "Thanks for trying to

get me off the hook. But I'd like to not have to do that anymore. Get off the hook, I mean."

"My pleasure."

"As my dad would say—it's time to suit up. So…. Do you want dessert?"

I sighed. "Oh yes, and I know exactly what that is." I leaned closer. "In my bag, I have a bottle of lube the size of Delaware and enough condoms to protect all of the NFL."

"Oh my god."

I signaled for the waiter and presented our gift card to the restaurant that Pops had purchased.

He said, "Can't I tempt you with dessert? We have some lovely cannolis made today."

"Thanks, but I've got one of my own." I flashed my teeth, and Mike chuckled low enough that it could have been considered X-rated.

After leaving a nice tip and still having some cash left to put in my pocket, Mike and I hurried to the elevator. Just as the door was closing, a woman yelled, "Hold the elevator, please."

Damn. My plans for ravishment, compliments of the Otis elevator company, were curtailed.

A woman and her escort stepped on and, after a nod, turned toward the doors.

I inched in front of Mike, reached behind me, and extended a finger in the appropriate direction. After pushing aside his jacket, I discovered a slightly firm mound and started fiddling with it. Tickle, tickle, poke.

Mike cleared his throat, and the mound became a lump, getting harder and harder until my fingertip could make out the flare on the head. Oh yes. I ran my searching digit around the cap, played with the shaft a little, and—

The elevator stopped, doors parted, and I grabbed Mike's hand and pulled him so hard, he half-stumbled as he ran beside me toward our room.

My hands shook, and it took two tries to unlock the door, but finally, we fell inside, slammed the door after us, and started tearing at clothes. When we both got our pants to our knees but still had on our shoes and socks, I pulled back. "Hang on. I believe the principles of physics are against us. Let's get organized." I waddled to the nearest chair, sat, pulled off my shoes and socks, dragged my pants and boxer briefs off, and carefully folded them over the arm of the chair, took off my jacket, and gave it similar care. Even for sex, Christian Siriano was Christian Siriano. Wearing only my dress shirt, white with a high collar, I sprang to my feet, grabbed my bag, and extracted the supplies, and then leaped across the room where housekeeping had pulled off the bedspread, revealing crisp white sheets. I tossed the box and bottle on the bedside table, did a backward, high-jump leap onto the bed, and landed with my dick in my hand. "Shall I keep it warm for you?"

Mike still stood where I'd left him. He stared with glazed eyes and a bemused smile.

I hopped onto my knees, flipped my white shirt over my ass, and pointed. "Just so you know, this is your target area." I grabbed for the lube, popped the top, and squirted some into my hand. Then I started putting the slick where I needed it. "But I've gotten so tired of waiting I'm starting on my own."

Mike barked a little laugh and hopped on one foot as he dragged off the other shoe, then switched. With footwear off, his slacks fell to the floor, and he gave them a quick fold over the same chair, tossed his jacket and shirt in the same place, and stood there with his cock kissing his belly, looking uncertain. "I've, uh, I've never—"

I flipped on my back and pulled one leg up, revealing the goodies. "Remember that one girl you fucked?"

He nodded and swallowed so hard I could hear it.

"This will be much better."

"It doesn't hurt you?" His eyes were riveted on my ass.

"Only in the very best way."

"I've—I've watched porn, but I've never tried it in real life." He grinned mischievously. "I kind of wanted to get a dildo and experiment, but nothing ever comes into the Canali household that isn't discovered sooner or later, soooooo—I used a banana!"

I snorted a laugh. "A time-honored gay teen trick."

"Uhh, this was about three weeks ago."

My smile split my face. "Oh my god, I love you." I raised my eyebrows. "But despite the addition of extra potassium to your ass, we have all kinds of fun new stuff to try." I waggled a finger. "Now come here and let me suck you 'til you're rock hard."

"If I get much harder, you can rent me out for carpentry."

I pointed at my mouth. "Come to Mama."

I loved a man you didn't have to ask twice. He raced to the bed and had that dick in my mouth so fast I barely had time to swallow. Oh yes, the boy did love his oral.

I sucked and played the tip of my tongue into his slit until he was yelling. Then I popped my mouth off and rasped out, "I need you. Right the hell now." I pulled both my legs back to my ears.

"O-okay."

Looking a little shell-shocked, he knee-walked to the right position as he slid on a condom and then stared at the target with wide eyes. Despite his newbie status, his dick didn't lie, and it was not deflating even a little. He licked his lips as he poised his cock at my channel, panted for a moment, and then shoved.

Oh, yes, he was substantial. Not a damned thing happened except some lovely pressure. "Harder. Imagine there's a fire on the other side of that door, and you have to get in and put it out." Because, my oh my, there was a blaze, and having him inside me got more essential with each second.

He pushed again, and I yelled this time, "Harder. Much harder."

He leaned over me, arm propped on the bed, and shoved with gritted teeth. Pop.

Oh my god, he was inside. And not just inside, but the sheer force had pressed him in a few inches.

He stilled, gasping. "Oh shit. It's so tight."

"Stay still for just a second." I breathed through the exquisite burn.

"Jesus, it feels good." The last word came out on a breath.

"Pull out some. Not too far."

He did and his eyes widened in shock. "Holy shit."

"That what you've been waiting for, baby?"

"Oh man, yes."

"Then fuck me."

Still somewhat tentatively, he pushed in, then pulled out, then in. As my channel stretched and widened to accommodate him, his face settled into a mask of ecstasy, and he started to hump in earnest, building up to a hammering that had us both moaning, then gasping and finally screaming. The smell of raw sex filled my nostrils as waves of pleasure swamped my brain.

"Mike, oh god, Mike, it's so good."

"I never knew. Never. Oh man, just want to fuck forever. So good."

Too good to last, sadly. Mike's deprived cock couldn't take that kind of friction for long without exploding, and he reached for my dick and started pumping in time to his thrusts. No sex I'd ever had came close.

No more thoughts.

"Miiiiike." My head arched back, and I could feel the veins standing out in my neck as my balls gave up their load into Mike's hand.

At that moment, Mike stiffened, gasped, and pistoned his hips in hard, short thrusts until he gave a long, moaning,

"Ohhhhhhhhh." Then he dissolved into a heap on top of me.

For minutes, we shuddered in aftershocks and tried to breathe. Finally, we quieted.

He giggled. Yep, no other description. Too high to be called a chuckle. "How many times can we do that tonight?"

"You tell me, macho man. You're the one hammering nails."

Chuckling, he raised his head and kissed me, long and deep. "Thank you. I'm so glad I got to do that for the first time with you. I want to try it every which way. Bottom, top, sideways." He pecked my lips. "And how about if I never, ever do it with anyone else?"

I gazed into those dark, dark eyes. Was it possible that a gay man could have one relationship in his whole life? His steady love for his family and the dedication he showed to his job flowed into my mind. Yes, I honestly believed he could. "Sounds like an excellent plan."

He leaned his head on his hand and smiled. "Do you feel ready to come to Christmas at the Canalis?"

I raised up and kissed him again. "With you, I feel ready for anything."

TWENTY-TWO

MIKE

"So what if it's nine o'clock in the morning? It's Christmas Day." Donny poured a glug of rum into his glass of eggnog, despite Ma's comment and hairy eyeball. "Mike?" He held the bottle up in offering.

I moved my glass of eggnog farther away from him on the counter. "Nah, I'm good." Today would be tricky enough without adding alcohol to the mix.

"Okay, everyone! Breakfast is on the table," Ma announced at a supersonic decibel reserved for large family gatherings.

"But not everyone's here," I protested.

Ma gave me a look while loading up another platter with homemade cinnamon buns. "If we waited for *everyone* to be here in this household, we'd starve to death. There'll be plenty of food left when they arrive, Mimmo. Don't worry." She started to walk out of the kitchen with the plate, then paused, put it on the counter, and drew me into a hug.

Ma had been hugging me a lot lately. I think it was in part due to my close call in that warehouse fire and in part to make up for Pa's distancing. There'd have been a time when I would have slipped away from her with a "Ma!" But these days, I hugged her back, hard.

"Oh, is it still *hug Mike* month?" Tony asked, coming into the kitchen. He stopped and held out his arms to me with an exaggerated lovey-dovey expression.

"Stuff it," I said, laughing, as Ma let me go and hurried out with the cinnamon rolls.

"Want some kick in your eggnog?" Donny offered Tony, waggling the bottle like the family pusher.

"It's nine o'clock in the morning!" Tony made a face.

"So what? People drink at brunch, don't they? And it's Christmas!" Donny glanced at me. "I drink enough of this shit, I might wanna hug Mike too." He put down the bottle, grabbed me by the scruff of the neck, and gave me a noogie.

"Knock it off!" I yanked myself away, but I was laughing.

Donny had been weird since I came out. He was awkward, offering to get groceries or do shit at the house he'd never volunteered for before. It was as if he didn't know how to treat me anymore and was walking on eggshells, trying too hard. Around others he was super protective, like he was my own personal bodyguard.

I'd had a meeting with Chief Reiger and Pa after I got out of the hospital. I told them the truth—that I had been reckless that day, and I told Chief why, that I was gay and that keeping the secret had been putting a shit-ton of pressure on me. I thought I was fit for duty now, though, but Reiger took me off the roster until I got sign-off from a Cal Fire counselor. I'd had three sessions with her already, and I'd told her everything. I had hopes that she'd clear me for active duty early in the new year. I was damned lucky Cal Fire wanted to keep me on. But between being a Canali, and the Medal of Valor, Reiger said he really wanted to *make it work*.

Anyway, news about me being gay spread through Cal Fire like a gas leak. I was still going in for my shifts, even though I couldn't go out on calls, and so I'd had to deal with everyone's opinion on my orientation. Brian, Jordy, and a few others were cool with it. Surprised, but cool. A few others not so much. But one look at Donny's face as he hovered near me shut them up pretty fast. Taking on a lone Canali was one thing, but fighting two was not something any of those guys wanted to risk—especially since Donny had been at the station for three years and all the guys liked him.

The doorbell rang, and I shot away from Donny's attempt to drag me back for another noogie. "I'll get it!" I hollered.

I ran to the front door and threw it open. Shane and Pops stood there. It was a cold day in Resolute, with a trace dusting of snow. Shane wore a red sweater under a gold double-buttoned coat that looked old but high-quality—probably a thrift-store find. His cheeks were pink and his eyes bright. He held a shopping bag of gifts in one hand and a bouquet of flowers in the other. "Hey. I got these for your mom." He held them out.

"Not for me?" I teased. Then, fuck it, I leaned forward and kissed him briefly on the mouth in a hello.

A smile lit up his face like someone had turned on the Christmas tree. "Hi," he said again, softly.

"Hi." I stared at him, smiling.

"Merry Christmas. Can I push past you two lovebirds to get in the house? Freezing my balls off out here," Pops groused.

"Oh. Yeah, come in. And merry Christmas, Pops." I stepped back, letting him past me.

He shoved a foil-covered plate into my hands. "Shane made cookies. They're incredible. Funny how he'll make them for you, but not for me."

"They're for everyone," Shane said loudly. "It's Christmas."

"Thanks," I told him. "You didn't have to do that."

Shane made a face, biting his lip. And as Pops moved off

into the house, Shane and I stood in the foyer, looking at each other. I knew what the face meant. Shane was nervous. Me too. This was our first event at Ma and Pa's house as a couple. We'd gotten together as much as possible this past month, between my work schedule and his classes and work. I'd driven down to Sacramento, and he'd come up to Resolute a few times, but those times had been low-key visits, Shane walking around the side yard to get to my house. We'd wanted to give the family a little time to process. But Ma had firmly invited Shane for Christmas Day, and, God knew, if Pa and the other holdouts hadn't come to terms with it by now, they weren't ever going to if Shane stayed the invisible man.

"So cookies, gifts, and flowers were all you brought?" I teased, hoping to ease the tension.

He laughed. "I was going to kidnap Santa and bring him as a sign of my worthiness, but turns out he's mythological."

I made a shocked face. "He is?!"

"Dork." His smile faded quickly. "How's everything? Are you ready for this?"

"No. But let's do it anyway." I took his elbow since he didn't have a free hand and guided him farther into the house.

———

"Gee, thanks, Tony," I said, holding up the package of rainbow socks so everyone could see.

"The yellow matches your gear, don't you think?" Tony said. "You could wear 'em at work."

"So thoughtful." I gave him a phony smile.

"Tony thinks he's funny. Your real gift is in the pile." Viv picked up a wad of wrapping paper Lucy had just discarded, stuffing it in a large garbage bag.

"Uncle Mike, I have rainbow socks too!" Lucy enthused,

hugging her new doll. "Next time you come over, we can both wear them!"

I ignored Shane's snigger. He was sitting next to me on the couch. "We'll do that, Lucy. I think your dad and mom need a pair too."

"Yes!" Lucy whipped her head around to give her mother a pleading look. "Then we can be the rainbow sock family!"

"Life goals," said Shane.

"This one's for you," Tessa handed Shane a red-wrapped gift.

Shane looked at the tag. "From Tessa. Aw, thank you."

"Open it!" Tessa said. She was still in her PJs, red thermal leggings, huge socks, and an oversized black sweatshirt. She sat on the floor near the Christmas tree. As the youngest, it had been my job to play Santa and pass out presents for a lot of years, but Tessa took over the duty for me today since I wanted to sit with Shane. Soon, Matt would be old enough to read our family's crazy handwriting, and he'd take it over.

Shane opened the gift. His eyes lit up as he held up two fancy-looking notebooks and a fat teal pen.

"I figured you could always use notebooks, right?" Tessa said. "But you probably don't get yourself nice ones."

"I love them! Office products are my jam. Thank you." He gave her a smile.

"A man after my own heart," said Anita, who sat holding hands with Gabe on the other couch. She was cute and kind of brainy and probably better than Gabe deserved. We all liked her.

Shane smiled at her. "We can dish about office products later." I glanced at Pa. He'd been extra quiet today, sitting in his favorite chair. He was wearing jeans and a red chamois shirt that was so bright he only wore it on Christmas. He looked tired, and while he'd interacted with Matt and Lucy and others, he wasn't himself. I knew it was my fault—sitting here with my boyfriend. But, like Ma had told me, *It's your family too*. I'd spent my whole life not being myself to please Pa, and look where that had gotten me. Me and Shane was something Pa was just gonna have to get used to. Not that it didn't still twist my gut that he seemed to hate it.

We hadn't talked since I came out at the hospital. Oh, *hellos* here and there, and banal questions about work, but we hadn't *really* talked.

He caught me staring at him, and I looked away, frowning.

"Tessa," he said, "get that little one with the purple wrapper. No, not that one. Yeah. That's it."

Tessa read the card. "To Mike from Ma and Pa."

She passed it to me, and I sat up, holding it for a moment. Of course, all our gifts from our parents said *from Ma and Pa*, but Pa had specifically told Tessa to give me this one, so that meant he had a hand in it, right? It wasn't something Ma had picked up for me and just put his name on. I looked up at him questioningly.

"Open it." He took a sip from his coffee cup.

Shane leaned into my arm a little for emotional support as I unwrapped the gift, like he could tell I was tense about it. Inside was a rectangular white box. I took the lid off. It was a fireman ornament, a nice one in painted ceramic. It had our Cal Fire colors, and there was even a little Cal Fire patch on the sleeve. The fireman had dark hair and held an axe in an action pose.

"Read the back," Pa said gruffly.

I turned it over. On the back in gold was painted, "Our Hero. Mike Canali. 2022."

I looked up at Pa, questioning.

"You had a big year." He shrugged. "Started with Cal Fire. Saved a bunch of people and got the Medal of Valor. Stood up for yourself with the family…. Just thought you should have a keepsake to commemorate it."

"Tessa found an artist on Etsy who customizes these," Ma

put in eagerly. "We wanted you to know that we're proud of you, Mike."

Stood up for yourself with the family. If that's what he wanted to call my coming out, I'd take it. Pa was big on standing up for yourself. That was promising.

"Thank you," I said gruffly, swallowing the lump in my throat. I stood up, and Ma came over to give me a hug. I looked at Pa. He didn't stand up for a hug, but he did hold out a hand. Baby steps. I went over and shook it.

"Merry Christmas," he said, his eyes looking a little bright too.

"Thanks, Pa."

"One for Donny!" Tessa said. She shook it. "Oops. Sounds broken. Maybe it's his new girlfriend's chastity award."

"Ha ha," said Donny, grabbing it from Tessa.

"Hey, whatever happened with that chick who had a nose ring and she hung little swords and skulls and stuff from it? I always wondered how you managed to kiss her with those in the way," Tony mused.

"Got a cut on the lip from the sword once. Good times." Donny ripped open the gift wrap and held up his prize. "Peanut brittle from Disneyland! Thanks, Ma. My favorite."

"It's from Santa," Ma said, giving pointed glances toward Matt and Lucy.

"Yeah, thanks, Santa," said Donny. "So when do we eat?"

"You just had breakfast!" Ma cried.

"I know. But you made tiramisu for dessert, and I've been thinking about it for days. Can I have some now?" Donny gave her big eyes and a pout.

"No. You'll wait like the rest of us. Have some peanut brittle! Tessa, grab that big one that's under the Giants ornament."

I had a good haul—a new sweater in a ruby color I loved from Shane, a pair of new boots as my big present from Ma and Pa, candy, a book from Tessa, cologne from Tony and Viv, a bobblehead for my truck, and a Giants shirt from Donny and Gabe. Shane raked it in, too, since everyone had gotten him something. None of them were big gifts, but he seemed incredibly touched. There were presents for Pops, too, including a calendar of mountain towns I'd found for him, which he seemed to really like.

After we finished opening presents, Pa turned on a game, and Shane and Anita went out to help with the meal prep. I offered to go help, too, but Shane said I should stay and watch the game if I wanted. It was Browns at Packers, so I was happy to stay put and watch it.

Gabe plopped down next to me on the couch. "You're not gonna go fold napkin butterflies or something?" he asked dryly.

"Piss off. I'm watching the game."

He nodded. "See? What does that tell you?"

I gave him an incredulous look. "That you're clueless. Not all gay people hate football."

"Just sayin'," Gabe said in a singsong voice.

I rolled my eyes and turned back to the game, but a commercial had come on.

"Hey, you lot, heads up that we have some new guys starting in January," Pa said. "A couple of graduates and a couple of transfers, including a hotshot fire bomber pilot from Oregon."

I perked up. "Will we get any new grads at our station? Then I won't have to do the shittiest jobs anymore."

"Shht!" Pa glanced toward the kitchen in case Ma overheard.

"Sorry, the crappiest jobs," I amended.

"Dunno about that," said Pa. "I think there's only two newbies in all of NorCal. But that transferred pilot's goin' to McClellan, so he'll be in our territory."

"Yeah?" Donny's face lit up. "About time. We need more air support. What makes this guy a hotshot?"

Pa rubbed his jaw. "He was a pilot in the marines. Flew combat missions in Afghanistan. And he's flown in hundreds of fires in Oregon. Commander up there sings his praises. And he's got medals up the wazoo. I hear he'll even be teaching part-time at Ione." He looked straight at me. "Also, interesting fact, the guy's gay."

I smiled. I smiled so damn hard I thought my face might crack. I had to look back at the TV screen to try to hide my swell of pride. Oh fuck. A military vet and decorated fire-fighting pilot, and he's gay. Maybe hearing that had made my dad think a new thought or two. Whoever this pilot guy was, he had my sincere gratitude.

"Huh. I bet a gay guy like that would be really, really good at folding napkin swans," I said to Gabe, all innocently.

"Shove it," he grunted, giving me an elbow in the side.

We ate porchetta and manicotti, an amazing Shane salad with gorgonzola and pecans, and tiramisu. It was all so good I couldn't stop and thought I'd burst. Nonno sat at the table with us next to Pops, and he was more lucid than usual. He even seemed to understand who Shane was since he looked at Shane and then gave me a sly wink. I grinned back, so damned happy. Nonna smiled at him and petted his hair all through the meal. Ma declared it a Christmas blessing, and she wasn't wrong.

After dinner, Shane and I helped Nonno and Pops back to Nonno's cottage, where they were going to watch a movie. After we left there, Shane headed back for the main house, but I stopped him, grabbing his hand.

He turned to look at me. That gold coat did crazy magic to his blue eyes, turning them almost aqua. They were big and clear as always, and, standing outside in the crisp air, his pale skin and blue eyes contrasting with his dark curly hair and red and gold clothes, he was so beautiful he took my breath away.

Only now, I realized, it was different. At this moment, I

could look at him and feel everything that I felt for him, and it wasn't scary and it wasn't wrong. It didn't come with an anchor of questions—*how, when, if.* No, Shane was here today, Christmas Day, as my boyfriend, and the world hadn't collapsed.

Oh God. I was free.

The feeling was so overwhelming, it was almost too big for my body. Impulsively, I pulled him close to me, hugged him tight, and kissed him, right there on the sidewalk in front of Nonno's house—warm, sweet, and a little sexy, putting into it everything I felt.

When I finally let him go, we were both breathless.

"Wow. Merry Christmas to me," Shane said, giving a little shiver that I wanted to think was delight but might just have been the cold. "What was that for?"

"For today. For everything. For sticking with me while I worked through all this. Thank you for being patient with me. And for forgiving me when I fucked up."

Shane looked incredulous. "Are you kidding? I won the boyfriend lottery. A gorgeous guy who's sweet and loving and a hero firefighter to boot. And you even come with a big, crazy family. I needed one of those, it turns out."

"You're my family now, Shane," I said seriously, wishing I could show him my heart so he knew how much I meant it.

"Not sure how Lucille would feel about that," he tried to joke.

But I shook my head. "I mean it. Yes, I will always be a Canali, and I love my family. But you... you come first. I want you to know that."

He got a little misty-eyed and kissed me again. When he pulled away, he smiled. "Cool. Does this mean I'm a Hot Cannoli?"

"Absolutely. Honorary, but absolutely," I said gravely.

"I'll take it."

I gazed at him and tried to push all the love I felt into my eyes so he'd know. He'd always know. We'd talked about so many plans in the last weeks, like moving in together and maybe including Pops if he wanted to come. But one baby step at a time. We still had to scale the giant mountains called school and work. But that was for tomorrow. This moment, the sun shone, Christmas music drifted out from the main house, and Shane's hand felt warm, even through our gloves.

Together, we walked off toward the future.

HUNGRY FOR MORE?

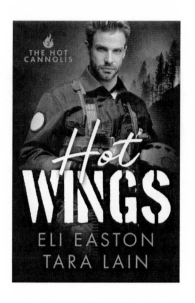

HOT WINGS

THE HOT CANNOLIS, BOOK TWO
AVAILABLE MARCH 29, 2022

The alpha meets his match.

Most macho of all the super-alpha Canali brothers and proud of it, Donny's famous for his gorgeous face, his firefighter prowess, and for going through girls his family doesn't approve of as fast as he changes jeans.

Donny's biggest hero is his fire captain dad, until his life gets saved from the skies by fire pilot Dell Murphy.

Dell's certain about most things. He's been proud to be gay since he was ten, handled a helicopter in Afghanistan like it was part of his body, and can fly a fire bomber in the worst conflagration. And he's absolutely certain that Donny Canali belongs to him.

Dell also knows how to show a lover he's in charge.

· · ·

Donny's shocked to discover how much he's turned on by dominant Dell, but Donny's not gay. He's not. He can't be. It would break his father's heart.

Leaving Dell will break Donny's.

HOT WINGS is a battle of the alphas, hot firefighters, two crazy families, dominant lover, HEA romance with a helping of laughter and even more feels.

Check out HOT WINGS on Amazon

ABOUT THE AUTHOR - ELI EASTON

As always, I very much appreciate my readers posting recommendations for my books on social media and reviewing on Amazon and Goodreads. Thank you! Your reviews truly make a difference in drawing other readers and that helps me continue writing full time.

It is awesome to hear from you and to know that I made someone smile or sigh. Feel free to email me: eli@elieaston.com.

You can also visit my website: www.elieaston.com. I have first chapters up for all my books and some free stories too. And you can sign up for my newsletter to get a monthly email about new releases and sales.

https://www.subscribepage.com/ElisNewsletterSignup

My Facebook group is a place to chat about Eli stories and get opportunity to read ARCs, excerpts from works-in-progress, and other goodies.

https://www.facebook.com/groups/164054884188096/

Follow me on Amazon to be alerted of my new books.

https://www.amazon.com/author/elieaston

I can promise you there will always be happy ending and that love is love.

Eli Easton
Olympic Peninsula, Washington, USA

———

ELI EASTON has been at various times and under different names a preacher's daughter, a computer programmer, a game designer, the author of paranormal mysteries, an organic farmer, and a profound sleeper. She has been writing m/m romance since 2013. As an avid reader of romance, she is tickled pink when an author manages to combine literary merit, vast stores of humor, melting hotness, and eye-dabbing sweetness into one story. She promises to strive to achieve most of that most of the time. She currently lives on Puget Sound with her husband, dogs, and lots of very large trees.

Her website is http://www.elieaston.com

You can e-mail her at eli@elieaston.com

twitter.com/EliEaston
goodreads.com/elieaston
bookbub.com/authors/eli-easton
amazon.com/author/Elieaston

BOOKS BY ELI EASTON

Stand Alone Titles

Before I Wake

Boy Shattered

Falling Down

Five Dares

Heaven Can't Wait

The Lion and the Crow

Puzzle Me This

Robby Riverton: Mail Order Bride

Snowblind

Superhero

Collections:

Gothika: Tales of Love & The Supernatural

Christmas Books:

Angels Sing (Daddy Dearest #2)

Blame it on the Mistletoe

Christmas Angel

Desperately Seeking Santa

Merry Christmas, Mr. Miggles

Midwinter Night's Dream

Unwrapping Hank

The Best Gift

Nerds Vs Jocks

Schooling the Jock

Coaching the Nerd

Head to Head

Betting on his BF

Sex in Seattle Series:

The Trouble With Tony (Sex in Seattle #1)

The Enlightenment of Daniel (Sex in Seattle #2)

The Mating of Michael (Sex in Seattle #3)

The Redemption of River (Sex in Seattle #4)

Men of Lancaster County Series:

A Second Harvest (Men of Lancaster County #1)

Tender Mercies (Men of Lancaster County #2)

Howl at the Moon Series:

How to Howl at the Moon (Howl at the Moon #1)

How to Walk like a Man (Howl at the Moon #2)

How to Wish Upon a Star (Howl at the Moon #3)

How to Save a Life (Howl at the Moon #4)

How to Run with the Wolves (Howl at the Moon #5)

Clyde's Corner Series:

A Prairie Dog's Love Song

The Stolen Suitor

One Trick Pony

Daddy Dearest Series:

Family Camp (Daddy Dearest #1)

Angels Sing (Daddy Dearest #2)

Ever After, New York Series:

Billy & The Beast

https://www.example.com

MEET TARA LAIN

Tara Lain believes in happy ever afters - and magic. Same thing. In fact, she says, she doesn't believe, she knows. Tara shares this passion in her stories that star her unique, charismatic heroes and adventurous heroines. Quarterbacks and cops, werewolves and witches, blue collar or billionaires, Tara's characters, readers say, love deeply, resolve seemingly insurmountable differences, and ultimately live their lives authentically. After many years living in southern California, Tara, her soulmate honey and her soulmate dog decided they wanted less cars and more trees, prompting a move to Ashland, Oregon where Tara's creating new stories and loving living in a small town with big culture. Tara loves animals of all kinds, diversity, open minds, coconut crunch ice cream from Zoeys, and her readers. She also loves to hear from you.

———

Come visit my website for a FREE download of my Sample Book. https://taralain.com/

If you like to stay up to date on books in general and mine in particular, come join my Reader Group, HEA, Magic, and Beautiful Boys

https://www.facebook.com/ groups/TaraLainsHEAMagicAndBeautifulBoys/

Subscribe to my Newsletter and get a drawing for fun prizes in every issue -- https://bit.ly/TaraLainNews

Follow me on Amazon for all the new releases, and on Bookbub for specials and to see the books that I love.

Of course, you'll find me on Facebook, Twitter, Pinterest, and Instagram

facebook.com/taralain

twitter.com/taralain

instagram.com/taralainauthor

bookbub.com/authors/tara-lain

amazon.com/author/tara-lain

goodreads.com/goodreadscomtara_lain

BOOKS BY TARA LAIN
AVAILABLE IN KINDLE UNLIMTED

THE HOT CANNOLI'S (with Eli Easton)

Hot Seat

Hot Wings

NERDS VS JOCKS (with Eli Easton)

Schooling the Jock

Coaching the Nerd

Head to Head

Betting on his BF

MOVIE MAGIC ROMANCES

Return of the Chauffeur's Son

Love and Linguistics

DANGEROUS DANCERS

Golden Dancer

Dangerous Dancer

COWBOYS DON'T

Cowboys Don't Come Out

Cowboys Don't Ride Unicorns

Cowboys Don't Samba

LOVE IN LAGUNA

Knight of Ocean Avenue

Knave of Broken Hearts

Prince of the Playhouse

Lord of a Thousand Steps

Fool of Main Beach

LOVE YOU SO

Love You So Hard

Love You So Madly

Love You So Special

Love You So Sweetly

THE MIDDLEMARK MYSTERIES

The Case of the Sexy Shakespearean

The Case of the Voracious Vintner

PENNYMAKER TALES SERIES

Sinders and Ash

Driven Snow

Beauty, Inc

Never

THE ALOYSIUS TALES SERIES

Spell Cat

Brush with Catastrophe

Cataclysmic Shift

EVER AFTER, NEW YORK STORIES

Better Red

Holding Hans

FUZZY LOVE

Passions of a Papillon

Prancing of a Papillon

Perils of a Papillon

BALLS TO THE WALL

Volley Balls

Fire Balls

Beach Balls

FAST Balls

High Balls

Snow Balls

Bleu Balls

Hair Balls

TALES OF THE HARKER PACK

The Pack or the Panther

Wolf in Gucci Loafers

Winter's Wolf

LONG PASS CHRONICLES

Outing the Quarterback

Canning the Center

Tackling the Tight End

GENETIC ATTRACTION SERIES

The Scientist and the Supermodel

Genetic Attraction

The Pretty Boy and the Tomboy

Genetic Celebrity

HOLIDAY NOVELLAS

Mistletowed

Be Bad, For Goodness Sake

STANDALONE TITLES

Home Improvement - A Love Story

Fairy Shop

Taylor Maid

Rome and Jules

Hearts and Flour

The Fairy Dance

SUPERORDINARY SOCIETY

Hidden Powers

Rising Magic

———

Audiobooks by Tara Lain available at Audible, Amazon, and Audiobooks.com

Made in United States
North Haven, CT
26 March 2022